STUART WOODS'

SMOLDER

BOOKS BY STUART WOODS

STONE BARRINGTON NOVELS

Stuart Woods' Smolder (by Brett Battles)

Near Miss (with Brett Battles)

Distant Thunder

Black Dog

A Safe House

Criminal Mischief

Foul Play

Class Act

Double Jeopardy

Hush-Hush

Shakeup

Choppy Water

Hit List

Treason

Stealth

Contraband

Wild Card

A Delicate Touch

Desperate Measures

Turbulence

Shoot First

Unbound

Quick & Dirty

Indecent Exposure

Fast & Loose

Below the Belt

Sex, Lies & Serious Money

Dishonorable Intentions

Family Jewels

Scandalous Behavior

Foreign Affairs

Naked Greed

Hot Pursuit

Insatiable Appetites

Paris Match

Cut and Thrust

Carnal Curiosity

Standup Guy

Doing Hard Time

Unintended Consequences

Collateral Damage

Severe Clear

Unnatural Acts

D.C. Dead

Son of Stone

Bel-Air Dead

Strategic Moves

Lucid Intervals

Kisser

Loitering with Intent

Hot Mahogany

Shoot Him If He Runs

Fresh Disasters

Dark Harbor

Two Dollar Bill

Reckless Abandon

Dirty Work

The Short Forever

Cold Paradise

L.A. Dead

Worst Fears Realized

Swimming to Catalina

Dead in the Water

Dirt

New York Dead

ED EAGLE NOVELS

Santa Fe Edge
Santa Fe Dead

Short Straw
Santa Fe Rules

HOLLY BARKER NOVELS

Hothouse Orchid
Iron Orchid
Blood Orchid

Orchid Blues
Orchid Beach

WILL LEE NOVELS

Mounting Fears
Capital Crimes
The Run
Grass Roots

Deep Lie
Run Before the Wind
Chiefs

TEDDY FAY NOVELS

Obsession (with Brett Battles)
Jackpot (with Bryon Quertermous)
Bombshell (with Parnell Hall)

Skin Game (with Parnell Hall)
The Money Shot (with Parnell Hall)
Smooth Operator (with Parnell Hall)

HERBIE FISHER NOVELS

Barely Legal (with Parnell Hall)

RICK BARRON NOVELS

Beverly Hills Dead

The Prince of Beverly Hills

STAND-ALONE NOVELS

Choke
Imperfect Strangers
Heat
Dead Eyes

L.A. Times
Palindrome
White Cargo
Under the Lake

AUTOBIOGRAPHY

An Extravagant Life:
   An Autobiography Incorporating
   Blue Water, Green Skipper

TRAVEL

A Romantic's Guide to the Country

Inns of Britain and Ireland (1979)

MEMOIR

Blue Water, Green Skipper

STUART WOODS'
SMOLDER

by **BRETT BATTLES**

G. P. PUTNAM'S SONS
NEW YORK

PUTNAM
— EST. 1838 —
G. P. PUTNAM'S SONS
Publishers Since 1838
An imprint of Penguin Random House LLC
penguinrandomhouse.com

Written by Brett Battles, carrying on the tradition of Stuart Woods.
Copyright © 2024 by SCW, Inc.

Library of Congress Cataloging-in-Publication Data

Names: Battles, Brett, author. | Woods, Stuart.
Title: Stuart Woods' Smolder / Brett Battles.
Other titles: Smolder
Description: New York : G. P. Putnam's Sons, 2024. | Series: Stone Barrington novel.
Identifiers: LCCN 2024000531 (print) | LCCN 2024000532 (ebook) |
ISBN 9780593540091 (hardcover) | ISBN 9780593540107 (e-pub)
Subjects: LCGFT: Thrillers (Fiction) | Action and adventure fiction. | Novels.
Classification: LCC PS3602.A923 S78 2024 (print) |
LCC PS3602.A923 (ebook) | DDC 813/.6—dc23/eng/20240119
LC record available at https://lccn.loc.gov/2024000531
LC ebook record available at https://lccn.loc.gov/2024000532
p.   cm.

Printed in the United States of America
1st Printing

Book design by Angie Boutin

STUART WOODS'
SMOLDER

CHAPTER 1

———◇———

Right on time," Herb Fisher said.

One of the Woodman & Weld associates carried an ice bucket with a bottle of Dom Pérignon into Herb's office, followed by another associate holding four champagne flutes.

"I take it you were confident about the outcome," Stone Barrington said. He was a partner at the law firm, and was standing with Herb in front of Herb's desk.

"Weren't you?"

"You've haven't failed me yet."

That afternoon, they'd won a suit for a client to the tune of thirty-two million dollars. Stone had asked Herb to handle the trial and his friend had done a masterful job.

After toasts were made and congratulations shared, the two associates returned to their desks, leaving Stone and Herb alone.

"Did you notice the way Winston Petry looked at you after the verdict?" Herb asked.

"It was hard to miss."

"For a second there, I thought he was going to charge across the courtroom and attack you."

"I wouldn't have been surprised. Petry and I have a history."

"You never mentioned that before."

"It wasn't relevant to the case."

"From his reaction, I'd say it was relevant to him."

Stone shrugged. "That's his problem, not ours."

"Can you tell me now?"

"Back when I was of counsel to Woodman & Weld, one of the firm's clients was sued by Petry for breach of contract. I turned up evidence that he'd falsified his financials to get our client's business, and thus proved the contract had been legally terminated."

"That's a long time to hold a grudge for losing one contract."

With a grin, Stone said, "Because of what I turned up, financial regulators swooped in. My understanding is that Petry barely escaped going to jail and had to close his business. It took him several years to rebound and build up his new company."

"Now I get it, though it doesn't seem to have hurt him too much. He's worth a few hundred million."

"Slippery as an eel, as they say."

"He's going to appeal," Herb said.

"And he'll fail again. Your case is airtight."

Carly Riggs poked her head into the office. "Hello, you two. I heard the good news."

Carly was a fast-rising star at Woodman & Weld. She and

Stone had had a passionate but short-lived relationship, ended by mutual consent, as working together and playing together was not a good idea, especially for a promising lawyer just starting her career.

"Herb did the heavy lifting," Stone said.

"Congratulations."

"Care to join us for a glass of champagne?" Herb asked.

"Can't. I'm heading out to an off-site meeting."

"Don't forget dinner at P. J. Clarke's tonight, seven-thirty," Stone said.

Carly grimaced. "Better make it eight-thirty."

"That's going to be one long meeting."

"Two meetings, back-to-back. Invite Dino. He can keep you company until I arrive. See you later." She hurried off.

"Why do I have the feeling she's going to be running this place someday?" Herb asked.

"By someday, I assume you mean next week."

"I wouldn't be surprised."

They clinked glasses.

That evening at P. J. Clarke's, Stone checked his watch, then signaled the waiter for another round.

"That's not going to make her show up any sooner," Dino said. Dino was Stone's best friend and the police commissioner for New York City.

"Carly's never late."

"She said she'd be here at eight-thirty, right?"

"Yeah."

"It's eight-twenty-six. She's not late yet."

Fresh drinks arrived, Knob Creek for Stone and Johnnie Walker for Dino. Stone took a hardy sip.

"Okay, spill it," Dino said.

"Spill what?"

"Whatever's bothering you."

"Nothing's bothering me."

"Says the man who keeps checking his watch."

"Fine. I just have this strange feeling something's up."

"Like what?"

"If I knew that I would tell you."

Dino started to respond, but then stopped, his gaze drawn to something beyond Stone. "Uh-oh."

"Uh-oh, what?"

"You can stop looking at your watch now."

Stone glanced over his shoulder and spotted Carly walking toward them in the company of Lance Cabot.

"I thought you told him to stay away from her," Dino whispered.

"I did."

"Try saying it loud enough for him to hear next time."

Lance had been eager to poach Carly for the CIA. Stone had disabused him of the idea. Or at least he thought he had.

As the pair reached the table, Dino checked his watch. "Look at that. Eight-thirty on the dot. You're right on time."

"Of course I am," Carly said as she took a seat next to Stone. "Why wouldn't I be?"

"No reason whatsoever."

"Good evening, Dino, Stone," Lance said. "I hope you don't mind if I join you."

"Would it matter if we did?" Stone asked.

"Probably not." Lance pulled out the remaining empty chair and sat.

Their waiter appeared, and Carly said, "Could you give us a few minutes?"

"Of course."

When the man left, Stone asked, "Why do I get the feeling you two didn't just run into each other outside?"

"Our meeting ran long, so I asked Lance to join us for dinner," Carly said.

"Your second meeting was with Lance?"

"It was," she said, as if the answer should have been obvious.

Stone narrowed his eyes at the head of the CIA. "I distinctly recall a discussion in which you promised not to approach Carly until a later date."

Lance held up his hands in mock surrender. "And I didn't. She called *me*."

Stone turned to Carly, surprised.

"Guilty," Carly said.

"Why would you do that?"

"Research."

"Research?"

"You're the one who told me that Lance was interested in recruiting me. I wanted to find out what that would entail."

"By calling him."

"We've already established that." Carly studied him. "Are you feeling all right?"

"I'm fine. I mean, I'm not *fine*, but I'm—"

Carly opened her purse. "I have Advil. Will that help?"

"I don't need Advil."

"Is it your stomach? I might have—"

"Carly, I'm not ill."

"You said you weren't fine."

"I didn't mean I was sick. You know what? Forget all that. You *called* Lance."

"Again, we've already established—"

Stone held up a hand, stopping her. "Let me guess. When he finished his spiel, he offered you a job."

"He did."

"And what did you tell him?"

"Per your instructions, I said no." Stone had made her promise she wouldn't join the Agency until after she'd gained more experience at the firm.

"Good," Stone said, relieved. "Sorry, Lance. You can't win them all."

Lance smirked. "Stone, we both know that's not true. Carly, you should probably tell him the rest."

"There's more?"

Carly nodded. "Lance has offered to let me go through training at the Farm with no obligation to join." The Farm was the CIA's training facility in Virginia.

"I thought it would be helpful to let her get a taste of what working for the Agency would be like," Lance said.

"How altruistic of you."

"Just doing my part to help Carly reach her full potential."

Stone stared at him for a beat, then shifted his attention back to Carly. "And you said yes to this?"

"I did," Carly replied.

"You do realize it's a trap, don't you? Once Lance pulls you in, he's going to do all he can to keep you there."

"Of course it's a trap. I'm smart, remember?"

"I thought you were, but now I'm beginning to wonder."

"You recall what I got on the bar exam, don't you?" Leave it to Carly to take what he said literally. "Perfect score. Did *you* get a perfect score when you took the bar?"

"I know the answer to that one," Dino said. "He did not."

"*Et tu, Brute?*"

"What? It's common knowledge."

Stone took a breath, then said to Carly, "When does training start?"

"A new session starts in the morning. Luckily, a slot happened to free up," Carly said.

"*Tomorrow* morning?"

"You seem to be having problems understanding what I'm saying. Are you sure you're okay?"

Ignoring her, Stone glanced at Lance. "And I bet if I asked, you'd say you had nothing to do with opening a spot."

"Do you really think so little of me?" Lance asked.

In unison, Stone and Dino said, "Yes."

Lance shrugged. "I might have made a call."

"What about the cases you're working on?" Stone asked Carly.

"I talked to Bill Eggers already, and he's agreed to let me take a two-month leave of absence. He said he thought it would be a good opportunity for me, and that you would handle reassigning everything."

Bill was the firm's managing partner. Stone made a mental note to have a word or two with him later.

Seeing that it was a fait accompli, he said, "Promise me one thing. When you finish, don't accept any job offer until you and I have talked through all the options."

She thought for a moment, then nodded. "I promise."

"Well, then," Lance said and stood. "If there are no more questions, we'll be off."

"*We?*" Stone asked, as Carly rose from her chair.

"Lance is heading back to Langley tonight and has offered me a seat in his helicopter."

"Of course he has."

"Now, now, Stone," Lance said. "No one likes a sore loser."

Stone ignored him. "What about dinner?"

"No time," Carly said. "Besides, I'm too excited to eat."

She waved goodbye and followed Lance out.

The waiter appeared and nodded at Stone's empty glass. "Another?"

"Bring him the bottle," Dino said.

CHAPTER 2

Benji Madigan eyed the Zurn estate through his binoculars. Decorative exterior lights spread throughout the property, illuminating pathways and entrances, while interior lights glowed from several of the mansion's windows.

On his right, Devin Barnes scanned the property while Lenny "Sticks" Martin, settled on the other side of him, picked at his teeth with the sharpened end of a match.

"Looks the same to me," Benji said. This was their fourth night in a row checking the place out. Like the other nights they'd cased the place, there was no sign of security guards.

Devin lowered his binoculars and nodded. "Good to go as far as I'm concerned."

The mansion was located outside Aspen, Colorado, and was the vacation home of financier Gordon Zurn and his family. The Zurns used it mainly for winter ski trips and the occasional summer getaway, usually around the Fourth of July. The latter had been more than a month ago, and from the info Benji had obtained from a reliable source, they weren't expected back for months.

When the family wasn't in residence, the lodge was occupied by a middle-aged married couple who acted as the caretakers.

As for security, the property was woefully underprotected. While their alarm system was top-notch, given what was inside the house, Zurn really should have sprung for several full-time guards.

Sometimes rich people could be so stupid about what they did and didn't spend their money on.

Benji glanced at the two other members of his crew. "Let's do this."

They returned to their Chevy Malibu. They'd stolen it in Denver and covered the outside in a preprinted vinyl wrap that made it look like it belonged to the local sheriff's department. They'd even mounted an emergency light bar on the roof. To complete the charade, they wore uniforms similar to those worn by actual local sheriff's deputies.

"Okay, Sticks, you're up," Benji said.

Grinning like a child on Christmas morning, Sticks put his phone on speaker and made a call. When it connected, three high-pitched tones sounded over the speaker. He tapped in a four-digit code, then the triple tone played again, triggering his devices to go off, and the line cut out.

Sticks looked up. "Done."

Devin fired up a remote control and flew their drone high into the sky. Benji and Sticks leaned in on either side of him, so they both could see the drone's camera feed on the screen.

The craft was high enough for the camera to take in the entirety of the Zurns' property and much of the dark slope behind it. Everyone's attention was on the latter.

After several seconds, Devin voiced what Benji was thinking, "They're not working."

"Relax," Sticks said. "Just needs a little time."

"It's usually faster than this."

"You saying I don't know what I'm doing?"

"Relax," Benji said. "That's not what he meant."

The last thing he wanted was to upset Sticks. The man was not right in the head even on the best of days.

Before anyone could say anything else, the yellow light of a flame flickered to life on the hillside. A beat later, two more appeared several feet away. Sticks's igniters had indeed worked.

"See," Sticks said. "What did I tell you?"

"Sorry," Devin muttered.

Sticks grunted but let it go.

They watched the fire spread through the underbrush. When it began climbing up a few trees, Benji said, "All right, that looks good enough. Let's get moving."

They hopped into their faux sheriff's car, with Benji behind the wheel. He waited until they reached the gate across the Zurns' driveway before turning on the emergency lights and bathing the area in flickering red and blue light. Leaning out the window, Benji pressed the button on the intercom box over and over until the speaker finally crackled to life.

"Can I help you?" The man sounded sleepy yet surprisingly calm for someone woken in the middle of the night.

"Pitkin County Sheriff's Department," Benji said, sounding

urgent. "There's a wildfire nearby. We need you to open the gate for emergency services, then you need to evacuate immediately."

"Fire? How close?"

"Too close to get into a conversation about it. Please open the gate, and then get everyone out of the house."

"Oh, of course, of course."

The gate swung open and Sticks laughed in delight.

"Quiet," Benji hissed, hoping the man on the intercom hadn't heard the outburst.

As soon as the gate was opened wide enough, Benji sped to the house.

"Radios on," he said.

He activated the one in his ear, then jumped out and ran to the front door.

It only took a few knocks with his fist before it flew open. Both caretakers were there, eyes wide and hair disheveled. The woman was loaded with several shopping bags stuffed with who knew what, while the man carried a soft leather briefcase and a half-zipped duffel bag.

Benji put an arm across the door like he was holding it open for them and motioned for them to move. "Get in your car and head into town. Go, go!"

They rushed outside, then stumbled to a stop when they caught sight of the blaze. It had grown to cover a large portion of the slope at the back of the property.

The wife grabbed her husband's arm. "Come on. We need to go!"

He blinked, then nodded. They raced toward the garage and, a few moments later, sped away in a Range Rover.

Once they were out of sight, Benji spoke into his radio, "Sticks, you know what to do. Devin, with me."

He and Devin hurried through the open door and into a large living room. Benji scanned the walls for their target, but it wasn't there.

"I'll take the first floor," he said, then nodded toward the stairs. "You take the second."

Devin nodded and took off.

Benji ran into the dining room and searched the walls. No dice. He made a quick pass through the kitchen, doubtful it would be there, but checking just in case. It wasn't.

As he rushed to the hallway that led to the other side of the house, he clicked on his mic. "Devin, anything?"

"Not yet."

"Sticks, how's it going?" He was outside, placing the devices that would set the house's exterior on fire.

"I'm busy. Don't bother me."

If Sticks wasn't so damn good at setting fires, Benji would have cut him from his crew a long time ago. "We've talked about this. Answer the question."

Sticks huffed, then said, "Everything's fine. Okay?"

"That's all I wanted to know."

The first room Benji reached was a bedroom. On its walls were several expensive-looking illustrations, but none was the piece he wanted.

The damn thing wasn't in the next bedroom, either.

Frustrated, he moved to the third room and shoved the door open so hard it bounced against the wall and closed again. Swearing under his breath, he opened it with a little less force and moved inside.

Instead of a bedroom, he found himself in a well-appointed home office. And there it was, the painting he was hunting, hanging on the wall behind the desk. The artist was Andrew something. Wyatt? Wayland?

Wyeth. That was it.

He compared it to a photo he had of it on his phone so that there was no mistake, then grinned.

"Found it," he said. "First floor. Office."

"On my way," Devin said.

Benji lifted the painting off the wall and set it on the floor, picture side down. A quick examination revealed how the frame was attached.

"Devin, I need the pliers!"

Feet pounded down the hallway. "Where are you?" Devin called.

"In here."

Devin rushed in huffing and puffing and set the small canvas bag that held their tools next to Benji. Benji set to work and soon removed the brackets holding the picture to the frame.

"Sticks, if you're done out there, we need you here now."

"Two minutes," Sticks said.

Benji lifted the painting out of the frame and placed it against the wall, out of the way. He then leaned the frame against the desk and held out a hand.

"Ashes."

Devin handed Benji a Ziploc bag filled with the ashes of a similarly sized canvas that had been created during the same era as the painting.

Benji spilled the contents on the floor, directly below where the painting had hung. He then moved the frame to the same area and laid it on the floor. The empty Ziploc went back into the duffel.

"Sticks, where are you?"

"Chill out. I'll be right there."

"How's the fire?"

"Gorgeous."

"I meant, how close is it to the house?"

"We have maybe five minutes."

Devin shot a wide-eyed look at Benji. Benji maintained his neutral expression, but he shared Devin's surprise. Five minutes away was cutting it a lot closer than they usually did.

By the time Sticks arrived, Benji was standing at the doorway, holding the painting. "Do what you need to do, and let's get out of here."

Sticks stepped over to the window and fingered the curtains. "These'll do."

Using a long-necked, barbecue lighter, he first set the empty picture frame ablaze, moved to the curtains next, then made his way around the room, lighting up whatever else would burn.

When he reached the door, he smiled at his creation. "So pretty."

"Back to the car," Benji said.

They hurried outside and stowed the painting inside the protective box in the trunk.

Once they were all in the car and the engine was running, Benji said to Sticks, "Set the rest off." Then he put the car in drive and whipped around toward the gate.

Using the same phone-call method as earlier, Sticks set off

the additional four igniters that he'd placed strategically around the house and garage while Benji and Devin had been searching for the painting.

If the brushfire that now dominated the slope didn't reach the mansion, the house would still burn down. And everyone would believe that the Andrew Wyeth painting had been lost in the fire.

The perfect crime.

CHAPTER 3

———◎———

The next morning, Stone's phone woke him from a deep sleep. He groaned and blindly grabbed for it.

"Hello," he croaked.

"So, you *are* still alive," his secretary, Joan, said.

He blinked, then sat up, and immediately regretted it. His head throbbed from one too many Knob Creeks the night before.

"Dino called and said you might need a little help getting started today," Joan said. "Don't worry. I shifted your schedule around. You have nothing pressing until this afternoon."

"Thank God for small favors."

"Small? Do you think I just snapped my fingers and your schedule rearranged itself?"

"Forgive me. For large favors."

"That's more like it. I hear Carly has flown the coop."

"Dino has a big mouth."

"That was from Fred. You told him on the ride home last night."

Flashes of the previous evening played in his head, including snippets of a diatribe about how Carly was making the biggest mistake in her life.

"Then Fred has the big mouth."

"You told him to tell me."

Stone didn't recall that, but if Fred said it happened, then it had to be true.

"Shall I have Helene send up your breakfast?"

"Just toast and coffee."

"Poor baby," she said and hung up.

Stone dragged himself into the bathroom, and after downing a couple of aspirin, took a hot shower. By the time he reentered his bedroom, he was feeling much better.

His light breakfast was waiting in the dumbwaiter. He ate a single piece of toast and drank a full cup of coffee before making his way to his office downstairs.

"You don't look nearly as bad as I thought you would," Joan said when he arrived.

"Your compliments need some work."

"That wasn't a compliment. It was an observation."

"Would it be too much to ask for some coffee?"

"I thought you already had one."

"*More* coffee."

"I'll bring it right in."

Stone spent the next few hours working through several e-mails and reviewing a contract for a client.

It was closing in on one in the afternoon when Joan buzzed him. "Herb Fisher on line one."

Stone picked up the phone. "Hello, Herb. What can I do for you?"

"Are you free today at four?"

"Let me check." Stone placed a hand over the phone and called out to Joan, "What's my afternoon look like?"

She appeared in his doorway. "Only a conference call with Steele Insurance in thirty minutes. I moved everything else to later in the week."

To Herb, Stone said, "I'm free. What's up?"

"Arrington Hotel business. I need to meet with you and Mike Freeman about the Phoenix property."

The property was the proposed location for a new Arrington Resort. Stone, his son, Peter, and Strategic Services, which Mike Freeman ran, controlled the majority of stock in Arrington's U.S. operations.

"I'll be there," Stone said. "But I'm not sure about Mike's schedule."

"I've already talked to him. He's free."

"I'll see you at four."

"I don't see that we have any other option but to pass. This location isn't suitable," Stone said, closing the folder Herb had given him at the start of the meeting.

Mike finished looking through an identical set of papers and nodded. "I agree."

"Sorry I wasn't the bearer of better news," Herb said.

"Your task was to perform due diligence on the proposed purchase and that's what you did," Stone said. "As always, a thorough job. Thank you, Herb."

Both Stone and Mike had been hopeful the site would prove to be a good location for the next Arrington Hotel. Unfortunately, Herb's analysis had revealed zoning issues and infrastructure problems that could delay the start of construction for three years or more. No one was interested in waiting that long.

"Should I have Raul restart the search?" Herb asked. Raul Staggs was a corporate real estate broker who did a lot of referral work for Woodman & Weld.

"Please," Stone said.

The meeting over, Stone made a stop by Bill Eggers's office before heading home.

Bill's door was closed, but a young woman Stone didn't know was at the assistant's desk. She had a serious, businesslike look about her.

"Good afternoon, is he in?"

"And you are?" she asked.

"Stone Barrington."

"Ah, *you're* Mr. Barrington. I'm Paulina, Mr. Eggers's new assistant."

"Pleasure to meet you."

"I'm supposed to tell you Mr. Eggers is out at a meeting."

"Just me or everyone?"

"Just you."

"Thank you, Paulina."

He opened the door and strode inside. Bill looked up from his computer and sighed.

"What the— I told Paulina not to let you in."

"Not true," Paulina said from the doorway. "You only said to tell him you were out. Which I did."

"I can attest to that," Stone said.

"It's the same thing," Bill said.

Paulina looked as if she did not agree. "Mr. Barrington, correct me if I'm wrong, but you would have gone in no matter what I told you."

"I would have."

"Mr. Eggers, physically restraining people from entering your office was not listed as one of the job requirements. If you need someone who will do that, that is not me. If you would like, I can contact HR and request that they begin a search for my replacement."

Bill grimaced. "That won't be necessary. Thank you, Paulina."

She smiled, then closed the door, leaving Stone and Bill alone.

"I like her," Stone said.

"Don't you even think about stealing her. She's only been here a week, and she's already the most organized assistant I've ever had."

"Hiring away someone who can so obviously put you in your place? I wouldn't think of it."

"I should probably talk to her about that."

"Good luck." Stone took a seat across from Bill. "As much as I enjoy talking about your new assistant, she's not the reason I'm here."

"I know exactly why you're here."

"I would hope so."

"Look, it's a good opportunity for Carly. How could I say no?"

"You gave her a *two-month* leave of absence."

"The training can only help to make her an even better attorney than she already is."

"Because weapons training and spy craft lessons are things every lawyer should know?"

"Maybe not every lawyer, but there's an argument to be made for the lawyers who work with you."

Though there was more than a little truth to that, Stone ignored the comment. "What are we going to do if she decides to join the Agency?"

Bill's brow furrowed. "She said it wasn't a job offer, just training."

"Do you think when she finishes the training, probably at the top of her class, they'll just let her walk away without trying to keep her?"

Bill stared at him, the idea obviously not having crossed his mind until then. "I might have made a mistake."

"You think?"

Bill seemed to come to a decision and his expression returned to his business normal. "I'll leave making sure Carly returns to the fold in your capable hands. Don't let the firm down."

"My hands? You're the one who let her go with Lance."

"And you're the one who knows her best. Plus, you and Lance are friends."

"We are most decidedly not friends."

"Business associates?"

Stone was a contracted adviser for the Agency. "There are days I wish you had never convinced me to take the bar."

"Funny, there are days when I wish I hadn't convinced you to do so, either." Bill smiled and motioned at the door. "Get out of here. You've wasted enough of my time."

Stone stewed all the way to the elevator, throughout the ride down to the lobby, and as he headed out to the street, where Fred waited with the Bentley. Which was why he didn't notice the man waiting just outside the building until he felt someone grab his arm and pull him to a stop.

Stone whirled around to find Winston Petry sneering at him.

"I have something to say to you," Petry said.

Stone jerked his arm free. "Anything you have to say can go through your lawyer." He started toward his car.

Fred had seen what happened and was already out of the Bentley, a hand slipping under his jacket for his fully licensed, concealed weapon. "Is everything okay, sir?"

"Fine, Fred."

Petry moved in front of Stone. "I was talking to you."

"Mr. Petry, before you say anything else, you should be aware of a few things. It's clear you were waiting for me to come out of the building. That is stalking. You grabbed me and physically impeded my progress. That's assault. Undoubtedly, you're here because you want to give me—one of the lawyers you lost to—a piece of your mind about the trial. That is harassment and possibly even intimidation. It would take very little effort to have you arrested and charged for any or all of these things. If I were you, I'd think hard about what I say next."

Petry took a step closer, putting them almost toe-to-toe. "Are you trying to intimidate *me*, Mr. Barrington? Because I don't get intimidated, especially not from a piece-of-trash ambulance chaser like you."

"If that's as creative as your put-downs can get, I pity you."

Petry's eyes narrowed. "What did you say?"

"I said I pity you."

"I should have taken care of you years ago," Petry snarled, then drew his arm back like he was going to throw a punch.

"I wouldn't do that if I were you," Fred said. He had moved up beside them and pulled back the flap of his jacket far enough for Petry to see Fred's other hand resting on the butt of his holstered gun.

Face reddening, Petry took half a step back but still looked ready to fight. "Stay out of this, if you know what's good for you."

To Stone, Fred said, "Just say the word, and I'll take care of the problem."

"Thank you, Fred. Mr. Petry, I think it's time for you to go."

Petry's gaze switched back and forth between Stone and Fred until it finally settled on Stone. "I have a message for your client."

"Any messages about your case should go through your—"

"Tell that little twerp he will *never* see a dime from me. The only people who will pay for that sham of a trial will be you, Barrington. You owe me, for this time and last!"

"And that sounds like a threat."

"Not a threat. A fact."

"Fred, you heard that, right?"

"I did, sir."

"Good. You'll be the first witness called at Mr. Petry's criminal trial."

"You son of a bitch!"

Petry cocked his arm back, but before he could swing, Fred grabbed Petry's arm and twisted it behind the man's back.

Petry yelped in pain. "Let go of me!"

Another twist of the arm forced Petry to his knees.

Stone looked down at the man. "If you had left when I told you to, or better yet, if you had been smart enough not to show up here in the first place, you wouldn't be in this position. I'm going to give you a pass this time, but if you ever do something like this again to me, to my client, or to anyone associated with Woodman & Weld, I will have you arrested and do everything in my power to make sure you are convicted and receive a maximum sentence. Have I made myself clear?"

Petry glared at Stone but said nothing.

"I'll take that for a yes. Fred, you can release him, but if he tries anything, feel free to shoot."

"Gladly, sir."

Fred released Petry's arm and took a step back.

Petry staggered to his feet and massaged his biceps. "This isn't over," he hissed and then stormed away.

Stone and Fred watched him until he disappeared around the corner.

"He seems like a nice fellow," Fred said.

"A real peach."

CHAPTER 4

———◎———

Petry stewed in the back seat of his Mercedes as he was driven to his apartment.

How dare Barrington humiliate him like that and make Petry lose his cool. And that Fred guy? He was lucky Petry had been focused on his boss. No way the tiny man would have gotten the drop on him otherwise.

Admittedly, it was probably a good thing the pip-squeak had stopped him from throwing the punch. If any of the federal investigators who'd taken Petry's first business down caught wind of yesterday's trial's outcome, they'd likely be all over him again, thinking he was up to his old tricks. Earning an assault charge would only make that outcome more likely.

Petry growled in frustration, startling his driver. "You all right, Mr. Petry?"

"Just drive," Petry said, then punched the button that raised the divider between them.

"Yes, sir. Sorry—" The driver's voice was cut off as the barrier closed.

Petry stared out the window, seeing nothing through his rage.

It was only Wednesday, and this was already the second worst week of his career. And wouldn't you know, both this and the first time had been caused by the same son of a bitch: Stone Barrington.

There was no way he would let the lawyer get a chance to do it a third time. There had to be a way to make Barrington suffer for his offenses without it being traced back to Petry. And the sooner that could happen, the better.

He pulled out his cell phone and called Nico Savage.

"Hey, boss," said Petry's personal lawyer and fixer.

"I got something that needs taking care of."

"That's what I'm here for. Lay it on me."

"Find out everything you can about a lawyer named Stone Barrington."

"The guy from the Baker case?"

"That's the one." Petry told him what had just happened, then said, "Find a weakness, something we can hit hard without it blowing back on us."

"On it. Give me twenty-four hours."

Nico started with a basic Internet search, expecting to find articles about other court cases but not much else. Instead, he learned Barrington was not only friends with New York City's police commissioner, Dino Bacchetti, but also with several other high-profile individuals, making him one very well-connected lawyer.

Nico would have to tread carefully.

Typically, the biggest weakness a person had was family.

Barrington had a married son who fit the bill. The problem was Peter Barrington and his wife, Hattie, were on the other side of the country. While it wasn't out of the question that Nico could use them to pressure Peter's father, the potential logistics nightmare made it less than desirable for a quick fix.

Nico wondered if there were any family members who lived closer. Parents, perhaps.

It didn't take long to discover that the lawyer was an only child and that both of his parents were deceased. Nico did turn up one interesting fact about Barrington's mother. Apparently, she'd been some kind of semi-famous artist. Nico had even found an article in which Barrington mentioned how important his mother's paintings and legacy were to him. What Nico could do with that, he had no idea, but he filed the info in the back of his mind.

Another half hour of digging turned up next to nothing. It was clear he needed information not available to the general public. Good thing he knew people who specialized in that. He made a few calls and gave his contacts until the morning to get back to him.

Nico got a late start the following day, thanks to Jamie, the beautiful blonde he'd brought home from the club he hit after work. She'd woken him in the most delicious way, and they'd gone for round three. Or was it four?

Whatever the case, it was the reason he didn't arrive at the office until eleven a.m. By then, he already had four messages from his boss wanting to know what he'd found out about Barrington.

Nico checked his e-mail and was happy to see all three of his contacts had responded. He started to read through the first file when Petry called his cell phone again.

"Hey, boss."

"Where the hell have you been?" Petry demanded.

"Gathering info on Barrington."

"And?"

"Give me fifteen minutes and I'll come down to your office."

"You have ten." Petry hung up.

Nico read through the reports and grinned. While he'd been sleeping, the beginnings of an idea, spurred by that article about Barrington's mother, had come to him. Now here, in the reports, was more info that made the idea even more attractive. Petry wasn't quite as imaginative, however, so Nico knew he had to finesse his presentation, give his boss something he'd be expecting, then tempt him with a more interesting—not to mention easier to manage—solution. Nico made a few quick notes and arrived at Petry's office two minutes early.

"Tell me you found a way we can hurt him."

"I have. He has family."

The corner of Petry's mouth arched into a sneer. "Yeah, that's good. What does he have? A wife or something?"

"No, he's a widower. But he does have a son and daughter-in-law in Los Angeles. Have you ever heard of Peter Barrington?"

"Should I have?"

"*Desperation at Dawn?*"

"Am I supposed to know what that means?"

"It's a movie. It won an Oscar for Best Picture not long ago."

"So?"

"So Peter Barrington directed it. He's a pretty big deal in Hollywood. His wife won an Oscar herself, for the music."

"Can we get to them?"

"Probably."

"Why do I sense a *but* there?"

"Being high profile means doing so wouldn't be easy, and we would risk opening ourselves up to possible exposure. Which you said you wanted to avoid."

Petry narrowed his eyes. "Then why are you even proposing this?"

"I'm not. I just wanted you to know I looked into the possibility. But I have a much better idea that will hurt just as much, be easier to implement quickly, and will keep our hands clean."

"I'm listening."

"Barrington's mother was Matilda Stone."

"Was? As in she's dead?"

"She is, but—"

"How does a dead woman help me break that son of a bitch?"

"Hear me out. She's a well-known artist, and even has a few paintings in prominent museums."

"Good for her. But again, how does this help?"

"Barrington reveres her work so much that he has several in his house and is apparently keen on getting his hands on as many others as possible. He's notified several galleries to be on the lookout for them. There was one article that called him the steward of her legacy."

Petry's patience began to slip again. "So the dead woman's a big shot. And? I mean, if there's a plan here, I'm not getting it."

"The *paintings*," Nico said, trying hard not to make it sound as obvious as it should have been. "All we need to do is have some people break into his house and destroy as many of them as they can. Each painting will be a piece of his mother he can never get back. Think of it as sticking multiple knives into his heart."

There was a brief moment when Nico thought his boss was going to read him the riot act for presenting such a stupid idea, but then a grin spread across Petry's face. "Look at you, Mr. Thinking-Outside-the-Box. You are one devious bastard. I don't know how you came up with that, but . . . I love it."

"I'm happy to hear that."

"It's a great first step."

"First step?"

"I'm not going to be happy until he's lying in a box, buried in the ground. But that can wait until things around me cool off. This idea of yours is good because no one will ever think I had anything to do with it."

"Thanks."

"One tweak. Wouldn't it be better if Barrington witnessed the destruction?"

Nico suppressed a frown. Ideally, the break-in would occur when the lawyer was away, as having him home could complicate things. "He might put up a fight."

Petry shrugged. "If he does, then rough him up a little. All I care about is that he's in good enough condition to watch his precious paintings get ripped apart."

Nico thought about pushing back, but he could tell his boss was in one of his don't-argue-with-me moods, which meant there was only one thing Nico could say. "I'll take care of it."

Nico got to work right away, hiring a guy he knew named Toby Hill to check out the security at Barrington's house.

That afternoon, Toby called back on one of Nico's throw-away phones.

"How did it go?" Nico asked.

"Not surprising, but the place definitely has an alarm system. I couldn't tell what kind it is from the street, or who Barrington's monitoring company is. I made a few calls, but none of my contacts know, either."

"Then how do we find out?"

"You said he works out of his house?"

"Yeah."

"Then my guess is that it's a commercial-grade system. Which means you should have at least thirty seconds after you enter to shut it off. That should be more than enough time for an alarm expert. However, you have a bigger problem. The locks."

"The locks? What's so special about them?"

"They're Israeli. Top of the line. Unless you have someone who knows what they're doing, it'd be easier to smash a window and climb in, because you'll never get them unlocked."

"Then we get someone who knows what he's doing."

"Do you know how many people in the city fit that description?"

"How many?"

"Two, and one is a retired cop who wouldn't touch this job."

"Who's the other?"

"There, you're in luck. It's me. But I ain't cheap."

"Name your price."

"Let's see. I assume you'll want me to deal with the alarm, too?"

"If you don't mind."

"Five grand should do it."

"Five? How about two?"

"What's my cut of the take?"

"No take. It's not a burglary. It's a trash job. We're sending a message."

"Then I'd say good luck finding someone else."

Sensing Toby was about to hang up, Nico said, "Okay, five grand. But I'm putting you in charge of the team."

Toby was silent for a few seconds. "Fine, as long as I can pick my own people. And that'll be an extra five to cover them."

Nico had budgeted twenty grand, so he'd be getting this for far cheaper than planned. Still, he hesitated a moment before answering so that Toby didn't think he was a pushover. "If that's the way it's got to be, then okay. You have a deal."

"Great. What's the job?"

Nico told him.

"Huh, that's different."

"Can you handle it?"

"Are you kidding me? Piece of cake."

"How long to set it up?"

"Seeing as it's Thursday, give me the weekend. We should be ready to go Monday night. If that works for you."

"That works just fine."

CHAPTER 5

On Monday, Stone sat in his office, feeling restless. Though it had been less than a week since Carly left, it felt closer to a month. He had come to count on her perspective and her keen legal mind.

It's just temporary, he told himself. *She'll be back.*

Probably.

"Are you still moping?" Joan said from his office doorway.

"I'm not moping."

"You are, and it's upsetting Tracy." Tracy West was Stone's new associate.

"I'm sure she's not upset."

"Let's ask." Before Stone could stop her, Joan called out, "Tracy, can you come here for a moment."

"Leave her alone," Stone said.

Still looking down the hall, Joan said, "Ah, there you are. Come, come."

A moment later, Tracy appeared beside her, holding a legal pad. She was a slip of a girl, with dark hair pulled back into a ponytail and wide round eyes that, at the moment, appeared nervous.

"Yes?" she said, her voice just above a whisper.

"Stone has a question for you."

Tracy looked into the office. "Yes, Mr. Barrington?"

"Don't pay attention to her, Tracy," Stone said. "You can go back to your office."

"Just a moment," Joan said. "Tracy, you know how Stone has been moping around all week?"

"Um, well, I guess."

"You did ask me about it, didn't you?"

Tracy looked mortified. "I—I—I didn't mean . . ."

Joan glanced at Stone. "She asked me if this is the way you always are."

Tracy covered her face with the pad. "Oh, God. I'm sorry. I, um . . ."

"It's okay, dear," Joan said. "You have excellent observation skills. And you are right to be upset. He *has* been moping."

Tracy stared at Joan, appalled. "You told him I was upset?"

"It's fine. He needs to hear those kinds of things now and then." To Stone, Joan said, "What you need is to get out of town. You have the Centurion Pictures board meeting coming up soon, you should head out now. Take in some sun."

"I can get plenty of sun here, thank you very much."

"Says the man who hasn't left the house since last Wednesday."

He smiled at Tracy. "I appreciate your concern. Thank you. You can return to your office." His gaze moved to Joan. "As for you, I'm sure there's something you can busy yourself with."

The phone began to ring.

"Like that," he said.

Joan disappeared and the ringing stopped.

"Dino on one," she yelled.

Stone picked up the line. "What do you want?"

"Just as I suspected," Dino said. "You're moping, aren't you?"

"Have you been talking to Joan?"

"Is this a trick question? She answered the phone."

"It's a coordinated attack."

"Now you're sounding paranoid. Maybe you should get out of town for a while."

Stone dropped his forehead into his hand.

"Are you still there?" Dino asked.

"I guess a trip might not be that bad of an idea," Stone admitted.

"When have I ever steered you wrong?"

"Do you want a complete list or just the highlights?"

"I'll pretend you didn't ask that."

"If I do go somewhere, do you want to join me?"

"Do you think I have unlimited vacation?"

"Based on past history, I'd say yes."

"That's where you're wrong. Plus, even if I did, I have too much going on here right now. And don't forget Viv and I are joining you in L.A. for the board meeting soon, so I'll be taking time off for that. Any travel before then, you'll have to do solo."

"Fine."

"Dinner tonight?"

"Patroon at seven?"

"Done."

Stone spent the next hour attempting to review the draft of a contract for a client, but he kept getting distracted by trying to figure out where he should go. He finally gave up and put his computer to sleep.

Maine was out. Memories of the last visit to his house on Islesboro when elements of the Russian mob had tried to kill him were still too fresh. Key West? Possibly. Though he didn't like the idea of going there alone.

Maybe Joan was right, and he should simply head to L.A. early. He could spend time with Peter and Hattie, and work remotely until the board meeting.

He was reaching for his desk phone to call Peter to make sure he'd be around when his cell phone rang. The caller ID read No Caller ID.

He scowled. It had to be Lance, calling to brag about how well Carly was doing. Stone almost let it go to voicemail, but ignoring Lance's calls, no matter how unwanted, was never a good idea.

He hit the accept button.

"Scramble," a voice said too quickly to be recognized.

"Scramble," Stone said, confirming his phone was using its CIA-installed encryption. "How can I help you, Lance?"

"I've been called many things in my life, but Lance is not one of them."

Stone instantly relaxed. "Holly. How are you?"

Holly Barker was the president of the United States, Stone's sometime paramour, and the only woman since Arrington with whom Stone would consider settling down.

"If you're expecting a call from Lance, we can talk later."

"Even if I was, he would be the one who would have to wait. Not you."

"How sweet."

"You haven't answered my question. How are you?"

"Feeling like I'm being pulled in a million directions at the same time."

"So, situation normal."

"Sadly, yes. I miss you."

"The feeling is mutual. Say, I've been thinking about getting out of the city. How about I come down to D.C. for a few days?"

"That would be lovely, but I won't be there."

"Oh."

"Don't tell anyone, but I'm sneaking away for some R & R myself, and I thought perhaps you'd like to join me."

"Very much. Where and when?"

"As far as the press and public will know, I'll be at Camp David, but really, I'll be staying at Kate and Will's in Santa Fe." Kate and Will Lee were her two immediate predecessors as president. "They'll be there tomorrow night, then they're leaving for Hawaii the following day. The place would be all ours. Well, ours and the Secret Service."

"When will you arrive?"

"I should be there in time for dinner."

"Then so will I."

Once they'd said their goodbyes, Stone buzzed Joan. "Call Faith. Tell her we'll be flying to Santa Fe tomorrow. I'd like wheels up at ten a.m."

"Taking my advice, I see."

"Accepting an offer I have no desire to refuse."

"You say potato."

"No. I believe I said, 'Call Faith.'"

"Wake up," Devin said, shaking Benji's arm.

Benji cracked his eyes open and looked around. They were driving down a street lined with dingy fast-food joints and old mixed-use buildings.

He stretched and sat up. From the angle of the sun, he guessed it was late afternoon.

"Welcome to Chicago," Devin said.

"How close are we?"

"Half mile."

"Anything from my brother?"

"Yeah. He texted about fifteen minutes ago. He's already there."

"Of course he is."

Benji smelled his armpits, then blew into his palm. He immediately cringed. "Please tell me you have gum?"

Devin pulled a pack from his pocket and tossed it to him.

After the heist in Aspen, they had gone to Denver. They dropped Sticks off at the airport, so he could fly to Vegas and wait until they needed him again. Next, they ditched the car they'd stolen, picked up a rental, and then spent a few days at the Lazy C Motor Lodge near downtown, keeping a low profile.

Confident no one was looking for them, they had set out that morning in the wee hours, and except for a few stops to fuel up and stretch, had been on the road ever since.

Devin turned onto a side road that was home to several unmarked buildings and nodded at a particularly ratty-looking one half a block away. "I think that's it."

Benji checked the address. "Yeah. Pull into the lot and go around back. There's supposed to be a roll-up door there."

Devin did as instructed.

The door was right where it was supposed to be, and as they neared, it began to churn upward.

Benji's half brother, Simon, stepped out and signaled for Devin to drive inside. Devin did so and parked next to a Mercedes S class. Behind them, the door rolled down again.

Benji climbed out first. "Hey."

"Any problems?" Simon had never been one for niceties, at least where Benji was concerned.

"The only cop I saw was going the other way." Benji glanced at Devin. "You see any?"

"A state trooper drove right past us without even looking at me. That's it."

"Good," Simon said. "Show it to me."

Benji popped the trunk and removed the two suitcases inside. Under them was the box that contained the painting. He pulled it out and set it on the ground.

He was about to undo one of the latches when his brother said, "Move."

Benji stepped back, then Simon opened the box and sucked in a breath. The painting was facing up, looking just like it had on the wall in Aspen, sans frame.

With great care, he removed it from the box and held it out so that he could take in every inch.

"Breathtaking."

Benji glanced over his shoulder. "It's not bad."

Simon gawked. "Not *bad*? This is an Andrew Wyeth. He is

one of America's greatest painters. And you say this is *not bad*? Don't speak of things you know nothing about."

"Sorry," Benji mumbled. "I just meant I liked it."

An alarm went off on Simon's watch. He placed the painting back in the box, then silenced the buzz.

"I need to go," he said. He pulled a fob from his pocket and pushed one of the buttons. The Mercedes's trunk swung up. "Put it in there."

While Benji and Devin transferred the box to the trunk, Simon climbed behind the wheel and started the engine.

Once the trunk was shut, Simon lowered the driver's window halfway. "The door."

"What about it?" Benji asked.

Anger flared in Simon's eyes. He pointed at the roll-up door. "Open it."

"Oh, right. Sorry."

Benji jogged over and pulled on the chain that controlled the door until there was enough room for the sedan to pass through.

Simon raced out of the building and drove off without another glance.

"Your brother's kind of a dick," Devin said.

"He was just in a hurry."

"If you say so."

CHAPTER 6

—————◎—————

That night, Stone was sound asleep when the alarm control panel on his bedroom wall began beeping.

His house was equipped with a state-of-the-art security system that included bulletproof windows, steel-reinforced doors, motion sensors, cameras, and the most advanced door locks available. Beeping in the night wasn't common, but with such an advanced system, small glitches weren't unheard of.

He went to the panel. On the screen was the message INPUT CODE, and below this a countdown that had just changed from 17 to 16. This particular message only appeared when the security system was armed and an exterior door had been opened, giving a person thirty seconds to turn it off after entering the house.

Stone switched on the camera feed that covered the area around the downstairs control panel.

A dark shape huddled in front of the panel, with three other figures standing a few feet away, shining flashlights on the keypad.

Stone jammed the button that would immediately set off the alarm, then retrieved his pistol from the nightstand and rushed out of the room to the top of the stairs.

The *whoop-whoop-whoop* of the alarm filled the house, and from below he heard someone swear.

He hurried down until he was on the landing above the floor the intruders were on.

"We should split," one of them said.

"If we do, none of us makes a dime," another argued.

"Look," a more authoritative voice said. "We have at least three minutes until the police show up. Let's do as much as we can before we go."

"You go ahead," the first voice said. "I'm out."

"Me, too," a new voice said.

Stone heard the front door fly open and then slam shut again, and for a beat thought all four men had left.

But then the authoritative voice said, "Come on. What we're looking for is upstairs."

Stone pointed his gun at the lower landing, hoping the sight of it would be enough to scare the remaining intruders into giving up.

The beam of a flashlight hit the bottom step, then one of the remaining black-clad men stepped into view, followed immediately by the other.

"Freeze," Stone barked, channeling his NYPD days.

Both men's heads snapped up. One of their flashlights mirrored the motion, and its beam hit Stone in the eyes.

"Gun!" one of them yelled.

"Oh, shit," the other said.

Nearly half blind, Stone almost missed the guy closest to him starting to raise his own weapon. Stone pulled his trigger.

The shot thundered down the stairs, and the light jerked sideways. Stone couldn't see much, but he could hear steps running, followed by the front door opening again, and then more steps that soon faded to nothing.

He slapped the wall until he found the switch and flipped on the light.

A body lay on the floor at the bottom of the stairs, a gun on the floor nearby.

Stone crept down to him, alert for anything that would signal that the other intruder was still around, but the house was silent.

There was another light switch near the bottom of the stairs. He flipped it on and lit up the area beyond. Carefully, he peeked around the corner.

He could see all the way to the open front door, and there wasn't a soul in sight.

He crouched next to the body. The man's shirt was drenched in blood. Though he was sure it was too late, Stone checked the man for a pulse. There was none.

Stepping lightly, he moved toward the entrance, clearing each space he passed to ensure no one was lying in wait. When he reached the door, he peered outside and confirmed that the immediate area was clear.

From a few blocks away, he could hear a siren heading in his direction. He ducked back inside, shut the door, and went to the nearest phone.

"Why are you calling me in the middle of the night?" Dino answered. "Did someone die?"

"So says the corpse in my hallway."

"No joke?"

"No joke."

"How did he die?"

"Painfully, I would think." As briefly as possible, Stone told him what happened.

"You actually hit him?"

Stone was deadly with a rifle, not so much with handguns.

"I've been practicing."

"Have you called nine-one-one?"

"There's a siren pulling up out front, so I'd say the NYPD has responded to my alarm."

"Try not to kill anyone else before I get there."

CHAPTER 7

———◎———

You're sure there were four of them?" Detective Morris asked.

They were in Stone's kitchen, out of the way of the crime scene techs. This was the third time Stone was going through what happened.

"I only saw four. There could have been more."

Morris frowned, unconvinced. He was young and, based on his aggressive questioning, newly promoted.

"And you're still saying the dead guy intended to shoot you, so you shot first?"

"I can't tell you what was going on in his head, but when someone points a weapon at *you*, Detective, what do you do?"

"This isn't about me, Mr. Barrington. This is about—"

"He would have done exactly what you did," Detective Brennan said calmly. He was Morris's partner and a veteran detective Stone knew. "I think we've heard enough, don't you, Jimmy?"

"I think he's hiding something," Morris said.

Brennan snorted. "You think everyone's hiding something."

Dino walked into the room. "Who's hiding something?"

"Morning, Commissioner," Brennan said.

Morris's eyes widened in surprise. "Commissioner Bacchetti."

"I was beginning to wonder if you fell back asleep," Stone said. It had been more than thirty minutes since Stone had called him.

"Trust me. I thought about it. What's going on here?"

"I've been explaining what happened to Detectives Brennan and Morris."

Dino jutted his chin toward Morris. "How many times has he made you go through it?"

"Two and a half so far."

"Not too bad. I remember you making suspects go through their story five or six times, when you were still green."

"Yes, but they were all guilty."

"And you're not? Correct me if I'm wrong, but you did shoot that guy I saw the coroner wheeling out."

"True. But as I was explaining—"

"For the third time," Dino clarified.

"For the third time, I shot him in self-defense."

"I buy it." Dino looked at the two detectives. "Any reason to think otherwise?"

"Nope," Brennan said.

"Sir, I would like to question Mr. Barrington further," Morris said.

"You mean retired NYPD Detective Barrington?" Dino said.

"Detective?" Morris shot a look at Brennan. "You didn't tell me that."

Brennan put a hand on his partner's back and said, "That'll be all, Stone. Thank you for your cooperation."

He guided Morris out of the kitchen.

"What does a guy have to do to get some coffee around here?" Dino asked.

"Allow me, Commissioner." Stone made Dino a coffee, then asked, "I don't suppose there's any news on the ones who got away?"

"I put out an APB after I talked to you, but you didn't give me much to go on."

"So that's a no."

"Perceptive as always."

Stone motioned toward the hallway where the techs were working. "You're not going to need me to stay in town because of all this, are you?"

"I don't know. Could be fun to let Detective Morris spend a little more time with you."

"I'm supposed to meet Holly in Santa Fe tomorrow night." Stone checked his watch. It was almost three a.m. "Make that tonight."

"Far be it from me to stand in the way of the president and her boy toy."

"Promise me you'll never say that again."

"I don't know. I kind of like it. Hey, maybe the Secret Service can use it as your code name."

"Don't even think about suggesting it."

"Would I do you dirty like that?"

"In a heartbeat."

"If going to Santa Fe will keep you from being so cranky, go with my blessing. I'll let you know if we need you back here."

"Thanks, Dino."

"Dinner's on you when Viv and I see you in Los Angeles."

"It will be my pleasure."

Twenty minutes earlier, Nico paced his office, wondering what was going on. Toby had sent him a text, telling Nico he and his crew were going in, and then nothing.

How long did it take to rip up a few paintings?

"Screw this," he said, and headed to his car.

Driving by Barrington's place was probably not the best idea in the world, but what could it hurt? It wasn't like Nico was going to stop and get out. He'd just cruise by and make sure everything was quiet.

The moment he turned onto Barrington's street, the bottom dropped out of his stomach.

In front of the lawyer's home were a half dozen police cars, lights flashing, and what looked like an ambulance.

It's okay, he told himself. Barrington contacting the police after Toby and his team finished the job was to be expected.

As Nico neared the house, two men carried a stretcher out the front door. The sheet covering the person on the stretcher from head to toe could only mean one thing. Someone had died.

Barrington?

Maybe that was why Toby hadn't called in yet. Killing the lawyer hadn't been part of the plan, not that Nico's boss would be too upset.

Nico turned at the next intersection, then found a place to double park. He returned to the corner on foot and found a spot in the shadows from where he could watch the action at Barrington's house.

Not much happened for the next quarter hour, and then a man in street clothes stepped outside. He looked back toward the door and seemed to be talking to someone inside.

Stone Barrington moved into the doorway.

Nico swore under his breath.

The lawyer smiled at something the other guy said. He then gave him a wave and reentered the house. He did not look like a person whose most prized possessions had just been destroyed.

"Oh, shit."

Toby had failed.

Nico's boss was *not* going to happy.

CHAPTER 8

———◎———

The last of the police left as Joan arrived in the morning.

"What did I miss?" she asked Stone.

"A few unexpected visitors. I'm surprised they didn't wake you."

Stone owned the house next door, which had been divided into apartments, one of which Joan called home.

"I didn't hear a thing," she said.

"What is the name of that service that specializes in cleaning up crime scenes?"

"JN Associates?"

"That's the one. See if they can come this morning and take care of the blood at the bottom of the stairs. I'd rather Helene didn't have to deal with it."

Joan arched an eyebrow.

"One of the intruders took a bullet to the chest," he explained.

"You shot someone without me?"

"Sorry. There wasn't time to call you first."

"Likely story."

"Get ahold of Mike Freeman, too. I doubt whoever they were will be back, but it wouldn't hurt to have Strategic Services watch the place for a few days."

"What about your trip?"

"What about it?"

"Are you still going?"

"I've been given permission to leave by the commissioner himself. You'll have to carry on without me."

"Thank God."

Stone had been hoping to sit left seat when his G-500 took off from Teterboro so that he could log some flight time, but having been up a good part of the night, he opted for a reclined seat in the back and let Faith handle the duties.

This turned out to be a sound decision, as he was out before they reached cruising altitude and didn't wake again until they began their descent into Santa Fe.

By the time he drove up to the Lees' front gates in his rental car, it was early afternoon.

Two Secret Service agents searched his vehicle while a third looked on from the other side of the fence. After he'd been given the okay, the gate slid open, and he headed up to the house that had once been his. He had swapped it several years ago with the Lees for their townhome in D.C., which Stone had then let Holly use when she was secretary of state.

Will Lee was out front waiting for him when he climbed out of the car. Stone grabbed his luggage and headed over.

"So glad you could fly out," the former president said. "It's been too long."

Will pulled him into a bear hug.

"You're looking well," Stone said.

"That is a damn lie, and you know it. But thank you."

A Secret Service agent appeared from seemingly nowhere. "Let me take that for you, sir," he said, reaching for Stone's suitcase.

"Thanks, but I've got it."

"I must insist."

Will leaned toward Stone and whispered, "He needs to run it through their X-ray machine. That's the downside of being friends with us."

"If that's the only downside, then I'd say it's worth it."

Stone handed over his luggage, then followed Will inside.

"I guess we can forgo the tour," Will said. "We're putting you in the larger guest room. I assume you remember where it is."

"I do."

"How about something to drink? Just whipped up a pitcher of margaritas."

"I will not say no to that."

Will led him into the kitchen, where a woman was cutting fruit into bite-size pieces. A wide smile appeared on her face when she saw Stone.

"Hello, Martha," Stone said. "How have you been?" Martha had occasionally worked for Stone when the place had been his, and had been brought on full-time by the Lees.

"I am good, Mr. Barrington. But you . . ." She looked him up and down, then tsked. "Too skinny. You need to eat more."

Stone had neither lost nor gained a pound since the last time he'd seen her. "I only accepted the invitation to come here because I missed your cooking."

"Don't try to sweet-talk me," she said, blushing.

"Martha, what happened to the margaritas?" Will asked.

Pointing with her knife, she said, "I put them in the refrigerator so the ice would not melt." Then she started chopping again.

Will retrieved the pitcher and pulled three margarita glasses from a cupboard.

"You carry these," he said, handing the glasses to Stone. "Kate's at the pool, and Billy is down for a nap." Billy was their son.

They headed outside and joined Kate at the poolside patio table.

Once the margaritas had been handed out and tasted, Kate asked how the flight was.

"You'd have to ask Faith," Stone said. "I slept the whole way."

They caught each other up with their lives while enjoying a platter of fresh fruit, delivered by Martha. After they'd been talking for twenty minutes, one of the Secret Service agents approached Kate quietly, whispering something in her ear.

"Holly should be here by five," Kate said, after he left. "How does dinner at seven sound?"

"Okay by me," Stone said.

"Me, too," Will said.

Kate smiled. "Stone, don't get me wrong, while we're always happy to see you, we were especially pleased when Holly told us you were coming today. There's something Will and I would like to discuss with you before she arrives."

"You can't breathe a word of this to anyone," Will said, "but Sam Meriwether is going to resign next week." Sam was Holly's vice president.

Before Stone could ask why, Kate said, "He has a heart condition and will be undergoing surgery in a few weeks."

"I had no idea."

"Only a handful do."

"The problem is the election," Will said.

Stone's brow furrowed. "What about it?"

"Holly's told us that she's unsure if she wants to run again," Kate said. "She said she's mentioned as much to you, too."

"She has." That had been some time ago, and neither had brought it up since.

The primaries wouldn't start until early next year. While a half dozen politicians had announced their intentions to run for the nomination of the opposing party, no one had yet done so in Holly's. Everyone was assuming she was going to run again.

Will picked up the pitcher and began refilling glasses. "If she decides not to run, Sam would be our next best candidate, but he won't be in any shape to do so now."

"Does Holly know about his condition?"

"He told her this morning before she left."

"You both knew before she did?"

"Only because he wanted our advice."

"So, you're going to ambush Holly, and you want me to be a part of it?"

"We would never do that to you," Will says.

"After we make our pitch, she'll need someone she trusts to talk to," Kate said. "And she trusts *you* more than anyone."

CHAPTER 9

—————◎—————

Nico arrived at work around the same time Stone's jet left Teterboro that morning.

Angry and wound up about the failed mission at Barrington's house, he'd managed only a couple of hours of sleep. His mood was not improved when he woke up to several missed calls from Petry. Nico hadn't called back. As much as he wasn't looking forward to it, informing his boss what had happened would best be done in person, where he might be able to direct his boss's ire somewhere other than at Nico himself.

Petry's assistant was waiting for him when he stepped off the elevator on the fourteenth floor.

"I know," he said. "He wants to see me."

The assistant nodded. "He said you are to go straight to his office."

Nico motioned toward the hallway. "After you."

Petry Innovations occupied the entire floor, and Petry's office was in a corner, far from the elevators. When they arrived, the assistant pulled the door open and said, "Mr. Savage is here."

Petry grunted from somewhere inside, and the woman stepped out of the way so that Nico could enter.

Petry was standing at the floor-to-ceiling window behind his desk, looking out at the city. As soon as the door closed, he whipped around.

"Why didn't you answer my calls?"

"I was gathering information." This was true to a point. Nico had talked to a contact at the police station to get details of what had gone down, but that had happened before Petry had tried to reach him.

"I didn't see anything on the news. Did it happen or not?"

"There was a . . . complication."

"What the hell does that mean?"

"Barrington's security system was better than expected." This Nico'd learned from his friend with the NYPD, something he wished he'd known prior to the job.

"And?"

"And the people we sent must have set off an alarm that woke up Barrington."

Petry's face began to flush. "Are you saying they didn't do anything?"

"Barrington was waiting for them with a gun. He killed one of them, and the others got away."

Petry stared at him, slack-jawed. "Are you shitting me?"

"I wish I were."

Petry grabbed a tablet computer off his desk and hurled it at the wall. "It was a simple job and you fucked it up!"

It was *not* a simple job, nor did Nico fuck it up, but he wasn't going to say that.

"There'd better be no way my name gets dragged into this!" Petry said, his tone harsh and threatening.

"The only person on the team I had direct contact with is the man who was killed."

"Well, that's a small miracle. You're sure none of the others knew about us?"

"I'm sure. I set it up that way on purpose."

"Can the police find us through your contact?"

Nico shook his head. "I never met him in person, and for all calls, I used a burner that's already been destroyed."

Petry turned back to the window. "When are you going to try again?"

"Again? I don't think that's a good idea. Getting through his security isn't going to get any easier. I'm told even the officers on scene were impressed by it. And I wouldn't be surprised if, after this, Barrington beefs up what he already has."

"Do you think I care about any of that? Figure out a way to get this done or start praying you can find a new job after I nuke your reputation. Or worse."

"Yes, sir."

Nico made a hasty exit and hoofed it to his own office at the opposite end of the floor.

His assistant, who always introduced herself as "Karol with a K," shot out of her seat the second she saw him, a look of worry on her face. "M-M-Mr. Petry has been looking for you all morning."

"I just saw him."

"Oh." She glanced past Nico, as if expecting to see Petry heading this way. "Is everything okay?"

"Couldn't be better. Get me some coffee."

"Coffee. Sure."

He entered his office and shut the door behind him.

Petry was out of his mind. There was no way Nico would send anyone back to Barrington's house. Doing so would only end in another disaster, making connecting the job back to them even more likely.

The very definition of a fixer's job was to never let who he was working for get caught. But Nico was sure Petry would not let this go. There was more to his boss's desire to hurt Barrington than mere retaliation for the trial's outcome. Nico didn't know what it was, nor did he want to. What he needed to concentrate on was finding a compromise that would sate his boss, or he could kiss his highly paid career goodbye. Or, as Petry had so eloquently put it, worse.

Karol brought him his coffee and left again as quickly as she came. He sipped it as he went back through the reports about Barrington that his contacts had given him, trying to come up with a solution that would satisfy Petry.

The paintings were such an obvious answer. Damn Toby for messing that up!

A page near the back of one of the reports caught his eye. It was a photo of a document found at a gallery that Barrington had asked to be on the lookout for more of his mother's work.

While Barrington had apparently made it clear he was interested in any of her pieces, he had also provided a list of the paintings he was most keen on acquiring.

Nico had only glanced at it before as it had no relevance to his plan to break into the lawyer's house. Now, however, he realized the paintings were the answer, and a new plan formed in his mind.

Implementing it would require a resource he didn't have direct access to, but he knew someone who could point him to the right people.

Grinning, he called Eddie Benitez, the man who'd gotten Nico into the fixer business.

CHAPTER 10

———◎———

Holly's plane landed right on time. Unlike the imposing 747 bearing the presidential seal that usually shepherded her around, this aircraft was an unadorned Gulfstream G-800.

The aircraft taxied to an open hangar, where it was then towed inside. Everyone remained on board until the hangar doors were closed.

Stone had tagged along with the Secret Service detail assigned to pick her up. When Holly deplaned, she walked right into his open arms.

"Welcome to Santa Fe," he said and gave her a long kiss.

"I didn't expect to see you until I reached the house."

"And why would I waste a minute of valuable time?"

"I've always liked the way you think." She kissed him again.

They left the hangar in a black Suburban with tinted windows, flanked by identical vehicles, and were at the Lees' in no time.

The front door swung open as they walked up. Kate stood just inside, holding a margarita in each hand.

"Thirsty?"

Holly smiled. "It's like you were reading my mind."

Kate handed one to her and the other to Stone, then leaned in and hugged Holly.

"Where's Will?" Holly asked.

"Giving Billy a bath. We won't be eating until seven, so why don't you settle in. I'm sure Stone wouldn't mind showing you where you're staying."

He smiled. "It would be my pleasure."

Less than a minute after they were alone, Stone and Holly were under the sheets, their clothes scattered across the floor.

Having been lovers for years, they instinctively knew what the other wanted. Their kisses and caresses and nibbles building each other's pleasure to a shared crescendo, leaving them both gasping.

"God, I miss that," Holly said as she rolled onto her back. "Maybe we should reconsider you moving into the White House. You wouldn't mind being confined to the bedroom, would you? I could probably trot you out for a state dinner now and then."

"You make it sound so attractive."

"It would mean unlimited sex."

"Sold!"

Holly nuzzled his shoulder. "Or we could just stay here."

"Something tells me your absence would be noticed."

She nudged his chest. "I have enough devil's advocates in Washington. Your job is to agree with whatever I say."

"My mistake. Let's stay here."

"That's more like it." She tilted her head so she could see him. "I have another idea, too."

"You do?"

"This one I know you'll like."

She pulled him on top of her.

She was right. He did like it.

Dinner was carne asada, sautéed asparagus, frijoles de la olla, and homemade tortillas, served at the table by the pool. To complement this, Will uncorked a bottle of Catena Zapata Malbec Argentino.

It wasn't until they'd finished, and Will had split the last of a second bottle among them, that Kate said, "I heard Sam talked to you."

Holly smirked. "I was wondering when you were going to bring that up."

"I take it that he also told you he'd already talked to us."

"He did."

"Don't be upset with him for that," Will said. "He just wanted advice."

"I'm not upset. If I were him, I would have done the same."

Kate picked up her glass. "Is he still planning to announce his departure next week?"

Holly nodded.

"Any thoughts on who you might replace him with?"

"Do you think your son would be interested?"

"I can say with confidence, he would be open to the idea." Kate's elder son was the junior senator from New York.

"I actually meant Billy."

"There might be an age requirement problem," Stone said.

Will nodded regretfully. "Plus, you'd have to work around his nap time."

"And don't forget about the attention span problem," Kate said. "Seriously, though, I think Peter would do a marvelous job."

"I'll be honest. He *is* the first person I thought of."

"Would you like me to discuss it with him? Off the record, of course."

"Do that. But don't make any promises yet."

"Understood."

Will leaned forward. "Sam's situation does bring up another issue."

Holly sighed. "I know what you're going to say. The election."

"That I was."

Stone took Holly's hand and gave it a squeeze. She acknowledged the support with a wan smile, then said, "I'm listening."

Will and Kate made their case for Holly running again.

When they finished, Will said, "We're not saying you need to make a decision tonight."

"Good," Holly said. "Because that's not happening."

"But you *do* need to decide soon."

"I realize that."

Kate pushed her chair back. "We've badgered you enough for one evening. And we have an early flight in the morning."

She and Will stood.

"Enjoy your stay. And even though we might be half a world away, we'll make ourselves available anytime you'd like to talk."

"You didn't seem surprised by the conversation," Holly said after she and Stone were back in their room.

"They gave me the heads-up this afternoon."

"I suppose you're now going to tell me all the reasons I should run again."

"Not at all. I'm a neutral observer."

"You have no opinion?"

"My opinion isn't the important one. The only thing you need to know is that I'll be waiting for you whenever you leave office." He pulled her into his arms. "You remember what I told you in Los Angeles, when you first talked about possibly not running again?"

"You mean when you bought that Malibu house I liked."

He smiled. He had purchased the house and told her that if she decided not to run again, he would give it to her once she left office. And that if she did run, he'd donate the purchase price to a PAC supporting her reelection.

"My offer still stands."

"But I only get the house if I don't run again?"

"Are you trying to negotiate with me?"

"A question has been asked, Counselor. Your response?"

He kissed her cheek. "What would I do with a house in Malibu? I have too many houses as it is."

"You could sell it."

"Get rid of your dream home? I don't think so."

"Then it's mine either way?"

"It is."

"That's what I wanted to hear." She pulled his face to hers. "Enough talking."

Later, as they lay in the afterglow, sleep tugging at them, Holly whispered, "If I do run again and win, that'll mean another four years of this. Do you promise you'll still be there for me at the end?"

"Since it would be illegal for you to serve a third term, I could probably manage it."

"Probably?" she teased, then tweaked his nipple.

He pulled her close so she couldn't do it again. "Do you really think it would be that easy to get rid of me?"

"You think another four years of this would be easy?"

"Compared to what we've been through until now, it'll be a walk in the park."

She snuggled into him.

"Besides, I have a feeling you've already made up your mind." He brushed a strand of hair from her face. When she didn't respond, he asked, "Am I right?"

But Holly was already asleep.

CHAPTER 11

In New York City, earlier that day, Winston Petry's intercom beeped. "Yeah?"

"Mr. Savage to see you," his assistant said.

"Send him in."

Nico entered and approached Petry's desk.

Without looking up, Petry said, "So, what's it to be? Did you bring me your resignation letter, or do you have a new plan?"

"A plan."

Petry leaned back in his chair and looked at Nico for the first time. "Let's hear it."

"We go after his mother's artwork."

Petry cocked his head. "Excuse me if I'm wrong, but I distinctly remember you saying that getting back into the house was not an option?"

"I'm not talking about the paintings at his house."

"Then what the hell *are* you talking about?"

"Barrington has several art dealers on the lookout for any Matilda Stone paintings that might come up for sale. Apparently, he's dead set on acquiring most of them."

"Yeah, you told me that, too. How does that help us?"

"What if we get our hands on some of them before he can?"

"What? Like outbid him? Why would I waste money doing that? And even if I did, who knows when any of her stuff might come up for sale? It could take years. I'm not waiting that long."

"Not a bidding war. And not years. There are alternative ways of obtaining art besides through legitimate dealers."

Petry stared at him for a moment, then leaned back. "Go on."

"I've made some inquiries and have identified someone who specializes in obtaining art from private sources for a fraction of the cost compared to the open market."

"By obtaining, you mean . . ."

"Stealing."

The corner of Petry's mouth ticked upward. "And your plan?"

"We hire this guy to steal a few Matilda Stones, then record them being ripped apart, and send the video to Barrington. Not only would his mother's work be destroyed, her legacy will be tarnished. Any time her work is brought up in print, online, or is shown at an exhibit, what was done to her paintings will come up, keeping the wound fresh. And the cherry on top: Stone will have to live with the knowledge that these were paintings of hers that can never be his. You want to demoralize Barrington? That should do the trick."

Petry thought for a moment and nodded. "Okay. This is good. Really good." He chuckled. "I'm not going to lie, you've surprised me. I was convinced you were going to crawl in here and tell me there was nothing we could do. But this? This is the kind of creative thinking I hired you for."

"I'm glad you like it. It *will* require more cash than we'd originally allocated."

"How much more?"

"I'm guessing it could be up to a few hundred grand."

Petry thought about it for a second. It was more than he originally planned, but if he could humiliate Stone, *break* him, it would be worth every penny. "I'll okay you up to half a million but try to keep it under that."

"That should be plenty."

"No mistakes this time. I'm not putting up that much cash for you to blow it again."

"No mistakes. I promise."

Petry held Nico's gaze for a moment, then said, "Get moving. I don't want to wait forever."

Simon Duchamp was in the American Airlines business class lounge at O'Hare International Airport when his cell phone pinged with an e-mail notification.

It was from Reed Langston, a New York City investment banker, and one of his special clients. The last time Simon had spoken to him was last year, at an exhibit at Simon's New York gallery.

He assumed the banker was in the market for something new, but that was not the case. Langston was passing on contact info for a potential client named Nico Savage. And since it was coming from Langston, Simon knew this Savage guy would not be the kind of client interested in anything hanging in one of the legitimate art galleries Simon owned throughout North America.

Simon checked the time. He was headed to Santa Fe, New Mexico, to attend one of his gallery's exhibition openings happening in a couple of days. His flight wouldn't start boarding for another twenty minutes.

He found a quiet corner and called Langston.

"Reed, it's Simon Duchamp. How are you?"

"What do you want?" Like many of Simon's clients, Langston was a busy man with no tolerance for wasting time.

"I just got your e-mail."

"Yeah? And?"

"I was hoping you could tell me a little more about Nico Savage."

"Like what?"

"How long you've known him. Where he's based. Things like that."

"I don't know him."

"I'm confused. If you don't know him, why would you pass his name on to me?"

"He's an acquaintance of a guy who's done work for me. I did it as a favor."

"Wait, how many people have you told about *me*?"

"Relax. Neither of them knows who you are. Just that I use unconventional means to expand my collection. Eddie said this guy's interested in the same. That's all I know. Now, if you'll excuse me . . ."

The line went dead.

Simon wasn't sure whether he should contact this Nico

person or not. He searched for the man on the Internet. Unfortunately, there were several people with that name, most appear-
ing unable to afford his services.

He sent an e-mail to a PI friend, who was better at this kind
of research, then headed to his gate.

CHAPTER 12

———◎———

F ive minutes."

Stone stirred at the sound of Holly's voice and mumbled, "Five minutes until what?"

When she didn't answer, he reached over to pull her close, but he couldn't find her. He cracked open an eye. Her side of the bed was empty.

"Holly?"

He turned to find her exiting the bathroom, dressed in one of her trademark presidential business suits and with a phone to her ear.

"Yes. That will be fine." She hung up and gave Stone an apologetic smile. "Sorry, I didn't mean to wake you. Go back to sleep."

Stone pushed up on his elbows. "What time is it?"

"Six."

"You look awfully formal for breakfast."

She sat beside him and took his hand. "An hour ago, North Korea performed an unannounced missile test. The missile came down within fifty kilometers of a joint naval exercise we're participating in with South Korea and Japan. No one was hurt, and it *should* all blow over, but . . ."

"But you're the president of the United States."

She nodded. "And it wouldn't look good if I suddenly started making statements from somewhere I'm not supposed to be." She leaned down and kissed him. "I'll make it up to you. I'm just not sure when."

"When are you leaving?"

"Now, I'm afraid. I'm catching a ride with Kate and Will to the airport."

"Let me see you out, at least."

He pulled on some clothes and walked her to the front door.

A half dozen suitcases were lined up in the entryway.

"I didn't realize you'd brought so much."

"Those would be ours," Kate said, walking up behind them.

Will was with her, carrying their still sleeping son.

The front door opened, and a Secret Service agent stepped in. "Madame President, Madame President, Mr. President, whenever you're ready."

Stone walked them to the Suburban while several agents carried the Lees' luggage to another vehicle.

"We'll be gone the rest of the month," Will said to Stone, following Kate into the SUV. "Stay as long as you want."

"Thanks and have a great trip," Stone said.

Holly wrapped her arms around him. "I was so looking forward to this."

"Me, too."

They kissed until Will rolled down his window and said, "I don't mean to be an asshole, but there's a beach in the Pacific calling my name."

Stone and Holly reluctantly parted.

"Don't have too much fun without me," she said.

"Me? Never."

She snorted. "Right." She entered the car, and the motorcade departed.

While Stone ate breakfast, he considered flying on to L.A. that day, but that would mean arriving more than a week before the Centurion board meeting. As much as he enjoyed Los Angeles, it couldn't compete with the peace and calm of Santa Fe. And after everything he'd been through in the last few months, a little bit of peace was welcomed.

Besides, Will and Kate weren't his only friends in town.

He picked up his phone and called Ed Eagle, a lawyer who worked out of an office in town.

"Stone, this is a nice surprise. How are you doing?"

"I'm good, Ed. And you and Susannah?"

"Happy and healthy."

"Glad to hear it."

"When are you going to come out and visit us again?"

"How about today?"

"Don't tell me you're already in town?"

"Guilty as charged."

"And you're not staying with us?"

"You *do* realize you're not the only ones I know here, right?"

"Ah, I get it. You'd rather stay with a couple of has-been ex-presidents than with your good old friends."

"I'll be sure to tell Will and Kate what you think of them when I see them."

"It's nothing I haven't said to them in person. Wait a second. Didn't Will tell me they were off on vacation this week?"

"Hawaii. They left this morning."

"And you're in that big house by yourself?"

"Yep. Just me and a half dozen Secret Service agents. Holly was here, but she ended up having to leave, too."

"That stuff with North Korea?"

"You are well informed."

"If you get lonely, our guest room's waiting for you."

"Thanks, Ed. I'm settled in here, so I should be fine. But I was thinking that we could grab a meal."

"How long are you here for?"

"A few days, maybe a week."

"I'd say more than one meal, then. How about we start with lunch today?"

"That sounds great."

"Come to my office around one, and we can go from here."

In a luxury townhouse on the other side of Santa Fe, Simon Duchamp had just finished breakfast and was about to head to the local Duchamp Gallery when his phone pinged. His PI friend had responded to his request.

Nico Savage worked for someone named Winston Petry, in

New York City, as a lawyer and fixer who handled Petry's dirty work.

According to the PI, Savage made a good salary, but didn't have the kind of money to afford Simon's services. Which meant he had to be fronting for his boss, who was loaded. Apparently, Petry was the kind of guy who felt the law didn't apply to him.

Simon grinned. Loaded and not worried about being an upright citizen were two of his favorite traits in a client.

He called Savage on a burner phone.

"Nico Savage."

"Good morning, Mr. Savage. Reed Langston tells me that you'd like to talk."

"You're his art guy?"

Simon bristled at the description but kept it out of his voice. "I understand you might be interested in acquiring a particular piece?"

"Not one. Several."

"By several, you mean . . . ?"

"Three should be enough."

Simon frowned at how arbitrary that sounded. "Okay. Which artists?"

"Matilda Stone."

"And?"

"Just her."

"I see. Are there particular pieces of hers you're interested in?"

"I'll send you a list."

"I just want to make sure you're aware, there is the possibility I might not be able to acquire three from your list. Are you okay with that?"

"If would be a shame, but if unavoidable, any Stone paintings will do."

"I'm sorry?"

"We want three. As many of those as you can from the list would be appreciated."

"I'll . . . see what I can do."

CHAPTER 13

S tone was waiting on a couch outside Ed's office when the door opened. Ed stepped out in the company of a man and two women, all in their forties or fifties.

From the trio's similar facial features, Stone guessed they were related, and from their grim expressions, he was sure the topic they'd been discussing had not been a happy one.

The older of the women shook Ed's hand. "Thank you, Ed. We know you're doing what you can. We'll discuss everything and decide how we want to proceed."

The other two also shook hands with Ed, then Ed's secretary escorted them out.

Once they were alone, Ed clapped Stone on the back. "I don't know about you, but I'm starved."

They walked to an Italian restaurant called Cavano's, a couple of blocks from Ed's office.

Before Stone had a chance to crack open his menu, a white-haired man sporting an impressive mustache approached their table.

"Ed, it's been too long."

"Danny, I'm starting to worry about your memory," Ed said. "I had lunch here three days ago."

"I know. Three days is too long."

"If I ate here every day, I'd be as big as a house."

"You're as big as a house now, so what would it matter?"

Danny wasn't wrong. While Stone considered himself tall in most circumstances, at nearly six foot eight, Ed towered over him by several inches, and was sturdily built.

"Let me introduce you to my friend Stone Barrington. Stone, this is Danny Cavano, the owner."

"A pleasure to meet you," Danny said, shaking Stone's hand.

"The pleasure's all mine." Stone opened his menu. "What do you recommend?"

Danny snatched it from him, then grabbed Ed's. "Do me the honor of ordering for you."

"My stomach is in your hands."

"What would you like to drink?"

"Do you have Knob Creek?"

"Do I look uncivilized? Of course we do. Ed?"

Ed grimaced. "I have a meeting later this afternoon, so I'm afraid I'll have to stick to iced tea."

"Very good." Danny gave them a small bow and left.

"I helped Danny out of a difficult situation with his former landlord, so now I get the royal treatment. I would come more, but he doesn't let me pay. Feels wrong to take advantage of that, but it's the best Italian food in town."

"How long has he been here?"

"About two years."

"I take it he has a better landlord now."

"I might be biased, but I'd say so." Ed smirked. "Susannah and I own the building."

A waitress arrived with their drinks and a caprese salad for each of them.

After she left, Ed said, "I hear the Russian mob's been keeping you busy."

"Don't believe all you read."

There had been several articles about the incident at the New York State Bar Association dinner in which Stone played one of the starring roles. And though he had pulled as many strings as possible to keep his name out of it, stories in a few of the less reputable papers had implied his participation, to a surprisingly accurate degree.

"And on a completely unrelated note," Stone added, "I've been reliably informed their unsavory attention has moved elsewhere."

"I'm glad to hear that."

"You and me both."

"And how are things going with the Arrington?"

Stone grimaced.

"Trouble?"

"We're starting to expand in the U.S. like Marcel's been doing in Europe, with the International Arrington Group. We were looking at a property in Phoenix, but it fell through last week."

"Sorry to hear that."

"As both you and I know, that's business."

Their conversation turned to other things and soon Danny returned with their waitress, carrying their lunch.

As she set the plates in front of Stone and Ed, Danny said, "This is a personal favorite. Lobster ravioli in creamy white wine sauce. Lobster flown in this morning, and pasta made fresh today. Please enjoy." He and the waitress retreated.

Stone took a bite and his eyes lit up.

"Not bad, right?" Ed said.

"Ed, not bad doesn't even come close to how good this is."

When they were finished, Ed requested the check, but Danny was having none of it. When he wasn't looking, Ed slipped some cash under his plate, and Stone and Ed headed out.

"Do you have plans this afternoon?" Ed asked.

"I'm a free man."

"Take a drive with me?"

"Don't you have a meeting?"

"I'll be back in plenty of time."

"Then sure."

Ed drove Stone to the outskirts of town and parked on a quiet side road in what appeared to be the middle of nowhere. From there, they walked through a grove of pines to the top of a small ridge.

Ed nodded at the view. "Not bad, huh?"

Below, the land was a mix of trees and clearings, with not a building in sight. And beyond, the mountains cut a jagged line against the sky.

"Gorgeous," Stone said.

"I was thinking that this would be a wonderful spot for an Arrington Resort."

Stone looked at Ed, then back at the land, and assessed it anew.

"I take it this land is available."

Ed nodded. "You remember the people who left my office before lunch?"

"I do."

"They're Alfonso Otero's children. Alfonso was a fixture here in Santa Fe for decades."

"I've met him a couple of times," Stone said. "But did you say was?"

"He passed away two weeks ago."

Ed explained that while Alfonso had once been one of the city's most successful businessmen, he had racked up considerable debt by the time he'd died.

"As executor of his will, I had to deliver the bad news. None of his kids were involved in the business and had thought everything was okay."

"They were expecting a big inheritance?"

"No, but I'm sure they wouldn't have turned it down. What they *weren't* expecting was to inherit a company that owed more than it was worth." Ed motioned to the area below the ridge. "What you're looking at is the estate's most valuable asset."

"Why didn't he sell it before he died?"

"He tried, but there were no takers."

"Is there something wrong with it?"

"Not a thing. Just didn't find the right buyer."

"Zoning restrictions?"

"Nothing that can't easily be dealt with."

Stone studied the land for several moments. "If the Oteros are able to sell it . . ."

"They'd be able to cover their debts, maybe even have a little extra to split between themselves."

Stone scanned the land again, liking what he saw. "I'll discuss it with Mike Freeman. No promises, though."

"I wouldn't expect any."

Once they were back in the car, Ed said, "If you're free tomorrow night, Susannah and I are going to an exhibition opening at a gallery in town, and we'd love to have you join us."

"Count me in."

"Dinner first?"

"A man has to eat."

"I'll call you with the details."

Stone sent Mike photos of the property as soon as he returned to the Lees' house and had no sooner set his phone down when it rang.

"A potential location for the new Arrington?" Mike asked.

"Right in one."

"It's breathtaking. Where is this?"

"Santa Fe."

"Ah, I should have recognized the mountains. You're there now?"

"I am. Ed Eagle represents the estate that owns the property. He's the one who showed it to me."

"Your thoughts?"

"It's definitely worth looking into."

"I agree. I'm flying to San Diego the day after tomorrow. I can make a stop there and drop off an assessment team."

"That's a great idea. And bring Herb Fisher, if he's free. He can coordinate everything and handle an offer if we decide to make one."

"Will do."

CHAPTER 14

L ater that afternoon, Simon Duchamp locked himself inside the small office at the back of Duchamp Gallery Santa Fe and used a new burner phone to call Dalton Conroy.

Conroy was his inside man at Vitale Insurance. The company offered a wide variety of specialized plans, including policies for valuable works of art. Conroy oversaw fraud investigations, had access to who had what art pieces, where the pieces were kept, and any security that was used to protect said pieces.

It took four rings before the insurance exec picked up. "Yes?"

"Is this a bad time?"

"Oh, it's you. Call you back in five."

The line went dead.

Simon looked at his phone, eyebrow raised.

Conroy had a higher opinion of his status than was warranted, both in his importance to Simon and at his day job. Simon knew for a fact the man often took credit for work done by subordinates.

For a long time, Simon had been able to overlook the man's arrogance thanks to the quality of information passed on, but recently, Conroy had begun acting as if Simon couldn't operate without him.

While it was true that the information he sourced was useful to each job, Conroy was not irreplaceable. There were plenty of other well-placed people who could do what he did. All it took was identifying a person's weakness, applying pressure where needed, and then offering a suitable amount of money to "solve the problem." The classic stick and carrot.

It was almost ten minutes before Conroy called back.

"What do you want?" Conroy said.

"If I'm troubling you, I'll find what I need elsewhere."

Conroy laughed. "Like you could do that."

"I could. Easily."

The line went quiet for a moment.

"Sorry," Conroy mumbled. "Things are a little busy here. I've been looking for a replacement for that person I had to fire last week, while making sure the cases she'd been working on are covered."

"Finding the right people for a job is always difficult." Simon could care less about Conroy's personnel problems, but as the saying went, you catch more flies with honey.

"You can say that again. Anyway, what are you looking for?"

"The artist's name is Matilda Stone, active second half of the last century."

"Title of the picture?"

"I just need to know the location of as many of her paintings as you can find. And I need the info asap." While Simon had the list from Nico, there was no need to share it with Dalton.

"Sounds like a big job."

"The size of the job is not your concern."

"All right, all right. I didn't mean anything by it. I should have something for you in three or four days."

"Two days tops. One would be better."

"I can't promise you that."

"Then your services are no longer needed. Goodbye, Mr.—"

"Hold on. I didn't say I *couldn't* do it."

"It sounded that way to me."

"I'll have it for you in two days."

"That's better."

"But I want . . ."

"You want what?"

"I—I want double my usual fee."

Simon narrowed his eyes. "Standard fee, per our agreement."

"I'm updating our agreement."

Simon didn't respond.

"Or I guess I *could* let the authorities know about your operation."

"You seem to forget that if I go down, you go down with me."

"Mutually assured destruction. But then again, you're the bigger fish, which means it should be easy to get immunity in exchange for my testimony."

Simon definitely needed to start looking for a new source. This wasn't just boring, it was getting on his nerves.

"All right, Mr. Conroy. Double fee on this job. But this is a onetime thing. Do not expect it to happen again in the future."

"Whatever you say."

Simon stabbed the disconnect button and then called Phillip, his bodyguard.

"Yes, Mr. Duchamp?"

"I'm in the back office."

"I'll be right there."

Phillip entered a few moments later. He was a big, bald slab of muscle shoved into a black suit and tie. Because of this, he was often assumed to be lacking intelligence. That was far from the case.

"I'm growing concerned about Dalton Conroy," Simon said.

"I see."

"I don't want you to do anything yet, but I have a feeling our relationship with him will soon need to be terminated."

"I'll await your word."

"Thank you, Phillip. How are we doing on the other matter?"

"I should have the problem dealt with soon."

"Have you figured out who it is?"

"I'll know by tomorrow evening."

There was a leak somewhere in Simon's operation. Ironically, he would not have known about it if not for Dalton. The leaker had apparently contacted an investigator who worked under him. Unfortunately, Dalton didn't know the leaker's identity.

"Very good. The sooner we can put this behind us, the better."

"Understood."

CHAPTER 15

———————◎———————

The following evening, Stone and the Eagles enjoyed an excellent steak dinner, then headed to the exhibit at Duchamp Gallery.

The place was packed with people dressed in everything from Prada dresses and Armani suits to ripped Levi's and Black-Pink T-shirts. Stone spotted three well-known actors who had vacation homes in the area, and an aging pop star now famous for judging TV singing shows.

"The artist is local," Susannah said. "Ivonne Cervantes. Have you heard of her?"

"I haven't," Stone admitted.

"Then you're in for a treat."

There were more than thirty paintings on display, most of them mounted to the walls, with a few scattered throughout the space, hanging from the ceiling on wires.

Susannah guided them to the nearest piece, a stunning

photo-realistic portrait of an older Hispanic woman defiantly staring forward, over an abstract background of multicolored rays.

Susannah was right. Cervantes's work was stunning.

A woman approached, smiling broadly. She had long salt-and-pepper hair that fell well below her shoulders and looked like a younger version of the woman in the painting.

"Ed, Susannah, I'm so glad you could make it."

She gave them each a kiss on the cheek.

"Wouldn't have missed it for the world," Susannah said. "Stone, I'd like to introduce you to Ivonne Cervantes. Ivonne, this is our friend Stone Barrington."

"A pleasure to meet you, Mr. Barrington."

"Please, call me Stone. And the pleasure is all mine, Ms. Cervantes. Your work is exquisite."

"You are too kind. And if I'm to call you Stone, then you must call me Ivonne."

"Ivonne, then." He gestured to the painting "I take it she's a relative."

She smiled. "My mother."

"Speaking of mothers," Susannah said. "You may be familiar with Stone's."

"Oh? And who is she?"

"Matilda Stone," Stone said.

"My God. I love her work."

"As do I."

"I attended an exhibit in New York that included several pieces of hers. They drew me in instantly."

"She would have appreciated that. For me, each is more than just the painting itself. They're memories of her and my father and our lives together. Which makes them priceless as far as I'm concerned."

"Do you own many yourself?"

"Not nearly as many as I'd like." He looked back at the painting on the wall near them. "I must say, your work shares the same qualities as hers."

Ivonne tucked her arm through his. "For that, you get a guided tour. And, please, don't feel the need to hold back on compliments."

She took Stone and the Eagles around the gallery, giving insights into each painting they passed.

They were about halfway through the exhibit when a man approached, smiling broadly. "And who do we have here?"

He couldn't have been more than five and a half feet tall, and was dressed in a vibrant blue suit, matching blue tie, and black shirt. His thick-framed glasses were also blue, and his spiked graying hair seemed glued in place.

"These are my good friends Susannah and Ed Eagle, and their friend Stone Barrington," Ivonne said. She motioned to the man. "This is Simon Duchamp, owner of the gallery."

Simon flashed a set of bright white teeth. "Isn't Ivonne's work marvelous?" Without waiting for an answer, he leaned forward and stage-whispered, "We've already sold six. So, if there's one you're interested in, I wouldn't wait too long."

"Oh, Simon, stop with the hard sell," Ivonne said, though the news clearly pleased her.

"Are you collectors?" Simon asked.

"We have several works by local artists in our home," Ed said. "Including two by Ivonne."

"I love hearing that. And you, Mr. Barrington?"

"I am."

"His mother was Matilda Stone," Ivonne says.

Simon's expression seemed to momentarily freeze, then his eyes brightened as if he were impressed. "My, my. That's wonderful. Such a talent. Do you have any of her paintings?"

"Over a dozen."

"How remarkable. Would you ever consider selling any? If so, I know I wouldn't have any problem finding a buyer."

"Not even if I was down to my last penny. But if you ever hear of one coming on the market, I would be very interested. I take pleasure in finding them and adding to my collection." Stone pulled out a business card and handed it to Simon.

"If that happens, you'll be my first call." Simon slipped the card into his pocket. "Now, if you'll excuse us. Ivonne, there's someone you should meet."

"Do you mind continuing on your own?" Ivonne asked.

"We've already monopolized you more than we should have," Stone said.

"Nonsense. I enjoyed every second."

"Lunch next week?" Susannah asked her.

"Absolutely." Ivonne gave them a quick wave and followed Simon into the crowd.

Ed excused himself to use the restroom, and Stone and Susannah moved to the next painting, joining two women who were already admiring it. Both had dark hair, one with hers cut just above her shoulders, and the other with hers falling halfway down her back. The former looked familiar to Stone, but he couldn't place where he'd seen her.

"Donna?" Susannah said.

The woman with shorter hair looked over. "Susannah."

They hugged.

"It's good to see you out," Susannah said.

She introduced her to Stone as Donna Otero, and upon hearing the name, he realized she was one of the people who'd left Ed's office the day before.

Donna introduced the other woman with her as her cousin, Monica Reyes.

Monica's dark eyes lingered on Stone's as she said, "Nice to meet you."

"And I you," he said, his gaze lingering in the same way.

"Do you live in Santa Fe, Stone?" Donna asked.

"I used to have a house here, but my home has always been in New York."

"What do you do there?"

"He's a partner at one of the most prestigious law firms in the city," Susannah said.

"We like to think *the* most," Stone said.

Donna's face brightened. "You're the one interested in my father's property, aren't you?"

"Well . . ."

"Sorry. I didn't mean to blindside you. Ed told my brother that he'd shown the property to someone he knew from New York who might be interested in buying it. He never mentioned a name."

"Interested, yes, but no promises an offer will be forthcoming."

"I understand. But you should know we are . . . What's the term?"

"Motivated sellers?" Monica offered.

"That's it."

"Don't let Ed know you told me that, or he'll give you a stern talking to," Stone said.

"Don't let Ed know what?" Ed said, rejoining them.

Donna mimed sealing her lips, then whispered to Stone, "Remember, motivated."

CHAPTER 16

———◎———

"Tell me a little bit about you," Stone said to Monica, handing her a glass of champagne.

They'd become separated from the others and had been making their way through the gallery at their own pace.

"Me?" Monica said. "Well, let's see. I'm from a little town in—"

"Don't tell me. Georgia, and the town's name is Delano."

"That's oddly specific."

"Let's just say I've met a few people from there."

"Sorry to disappoint, but I've never been to Georgia in my life."

"Oh."

"I'm from a little town called Fillmore in California. Have you heard of it?"

"I don't think so."

"It's in Ventura County, north of Los Angeles. Farm country."

"And were you a farmer?"

"My father was a supervisor at an avocado farm, but we lived in town. No farm work for me, I'm afraid. I *was* a barista on weekends and can still make a mean latte."

"Is that so? I might have to test you."

"Careful. You'll never want one from anyone else."

After they'd seen everything, Stone led her back to a painting of a young woman riding a horse over a similar background as the one in the portrait of Ivonne's mother. The rider looked a lot like Arrington. On the info card beside the painting was written the title *Escape*.

"I take it this one's caught your eye," Monica said.

"It has."

"It's stunning."

Stone motioned for a gallery employee to come over.

"How may I help you?" the man asked.

"Has this one been sold yet?"

"One moment, I'll check." The man disappeared into the crowd.

"Are you thinking of buying that for yourself?" Monica asked.

"For my son."

Peter often mentioned having loved watching his mother ride when they lived in Virginia.

"How old is your son?"

"Old enough to have won an Academy Award."

Monica looked confused, then her eyebrows shot upward. "*Peter* Barrington? The director?"

"That's him."

"I've seen all of his films. I love his work."

"I'll tell him you said so."

The employee returned. "Good news. It's still available."

"Not anymore."

The paperwork was quickly dealt with and arrangements were made to have the painting shipped to Peter in L.A. after the exhibit closed.

"You're very decisive," Monica said.

"In most things."

"Is that so?"

"Would you like to come back to my place for a nightcap?"

"I see what you mean."

He offered her his arm. "Shall we, then?"

She took it. "Lead the way."

Monica's phone vibrated as Stone drove her to the Lees' house.

She looked at the screen, frowned, and hit reject.

Moments later the cell began ringing again, and once more she declined the call.

"Someone you don't want to talk to?" Stone said.

"You could say that."

The phone rang for a third time.

"Whoever it is seems persistent."

She sighed. "Do you mind?"

"Not at all."

She accepted the call. "What do you want? I don't care what you said. You have *nothing* to do with me anymore, remember. What I do is my business." She listened again and then snorted. "Also not your business . . . Deal with it . . . Okay, I've heard enough. I'm blocking your number, so don't waste your time calling again."

She hung up without another word and promptly did what she'd promised.

"Boyfriend?" Stone asked.

"Ha. I haven't had one of those in . . . God, longer than I can remember."

"Husband, then?"

"That, I've never had."

"Glad to hear it."

She remained silent for a few seconds, then said, "A former employer."

"I don't think you've mentioned what you do."

"Finance related. Boring stuff."

A few minutes later, they arrived at the Lees' gate and a Secret Service agent appeared at Stone's window.

"Where did he come from?" Monica asked.

Stone rolled down the window.

"Good evening, Mr. Barrington," the agent said. He looked across at Monica. "Good evening, miss. Could I see an ID, please?"

She glanced at Stone, confused.

"He's just doing his job," Stone assured her.

"Um, okay." She retrieved her driver's license and handed it to Stone, who passed it to the agent.

"One moment." The man disappeared into the dark

"You have a security staff?" Monica asked.

"It's a friend's house."

"That's right. You don't live here. I didn't realize anyone in Santa Fe had this kind of security."

"My friends are a special case."

The agent reappeared and returned the license to Stone. "Everything checks out. Have a good evening."

The gates rolled open and Stone drove in.

As they got out of the car, another agent greeted them.

"Miss Reyes, I'll need to check your bag."

"What do you think I could possibly hide in here?" she asked, touching her small clutch.

"I wouldn't know, miss. That's why I need to check it."

She handed it over, and he jogged around the side of the house, out of sight.

"Where's he going?"

"To run it through the X-ray machine."

She stared at Stone. "X-ray machine? Where the hell have you taken me?"

"Not hell, I assure you." Stone opened the front door. "After you."

She peered into the house without taking a step. "Who lives here? The president?"

"Two of them, actually."

She laughed and stepped inside, then halted a few feet in when her gaze landed on a picture of both Presidents Lee with their son.

"Oh, my God. You weren't joking." She turned to Stone. "This is . . . this is Kate Lee's house."

"Will might be offended you left him out."

She twirled around, as if expecting to see them.

"They're in Hawaii."

"You're . . . housesitting?"

"I'm just using their place while I'm in town."

"Wait, the guards. Are they Secret Service?"

"Now you're getting it."

"You actually *know* Kate and Will Lee."

"More than know. They are dear friends."

She looked at him for a moment longer, then walked deeper into the house.

"Wow. This place is beautiful."

"Thank you."

"Why are you thanking me? You said it wasn't your place."

"It was once. I traded it with Will and Kate for their town-house in D.C."

"Traded houses. With the Lees." She shook her head, as if she couldn't fully comprehend the words. "Next you're going to tell me you know Holly Barker, too."

Deciding it best not to completely overwhelm her, he said, "I may have met her a few times."

"I could use that nightcap now."

"How does a nice port sound?"

"At this point, peppermint schnapps would be fine."

Stone poured two glasses of Taylor Fladgate Vintage Port, gave one to Monica, then sat with her on one of the couches.

She took a fortifying sip, then cocked her head. "Who *are* you?"

"Exactly who I said I was."

"A New York lawyer who happens to know two presidents."

Stone held up three fingers.

"Right. Three presidents."

He shrugged, conceding the point.

"My friends back home will never believe this."

"In Fillmore?"

"Them, too. But I was thinking of the ones in New York. I

live there, too, almost two years now. How long have you been there?"

"My entire life."

"And how long has that been?"

"I still have a few good years left in me, if that's what you're asking."

She looked him up and down. "You definitely do."

He nodded at her empty glass. "Another?"

"Please."

As he refilled their glasses, she said, "I've been wondering something."

"How I know three presidents?"

"That, too, but we can get to that later. In the car earlier, what would you have said if I had told you the person who called me was a boyfriend or husband?"

"It's not so much what I would have said, as what I would have done."

"Which would have been . . . ?"

"To politely escort you home and tell you I had a wonderful evening."

She considered this for a moment, then said, "And now that we've almost finished our nightcap? Are you still planning on escorting me home?"

"I am. But not until after breakfast."

CHAPTER 17

S tone woke to the brush of Monica's lips traveling down his chest.

"Good morning," he said.

She moved her lips several inches south. "Only good?"

"Is that what I said? I meant great."

He drifted into a half-dream state as she worked him to the edge of endurance, then backed off to prolong his agony. Finally, she rolled onto her back and pulled him on top of her, then gently guided him home.

She held him close as his rhythm rocked her into the mattress. With one hand, she guided his pace, sometimes urging him faster and other times slower, teasing the most out of every moment.

Sensing he could hold out no longer, she clutched him even tighter, and as he finished, she shuddered below him. When the world finally came back into focus, they kissed soft and deep and long.

Stone had been with more physical lovers, but seldom had there been one so sensuous. She was, in a word, intoxicating.

While Monica showered, Stone found Martha in the kitchen and discussed breakfast. After he was clean and dressed, they ate eggs, chorizo, and skillet-fried potatoes poolside.

"I could get used to this," Monica said.

"Then what do you say to breakfast again tomorrow?"

"Just breakfast?"

"Naturally, we'll have dinner together this evening first. Unless you have other plans."

"I do have some work to do today, but I could make myself available later."

"Pick you up at seven?"

"You haven't even dropped me off yet."

"Technicalities."

She smirked. "Seven is perfect."

After they finished, Stone drove her to her cousin's house, then headed to the airport.

Having arrived a bit early, he stopped by to check on his G-500 and found Faith there.

"Morning. Didn't expect to see you here. Everything all right?"

"One of the tires needed changing. Had the FBO do it this morning. Just checking their work." FBO was short for fixed-base operator, companies that provide aviation services to private and chartered aircraft, among others.

"All good now?"

"Aces," she said. "I was thinking about taking a road trip to

Roswell. My boyfriend's son is into UFOs lately, and I'd like to get him a few souvenirs."

"Boyfriend?"

This was news to Stone. He and Faith had had a short-lived relationship before she had started working for him, which was when he learned about her rule of never sleeping with anyone more than three times. Not wanting to be controlled by what he considered a random number, he had ended things after two.

"I know, I know," she said. "I'm just as surprised as you."

"Is he good to you?"

"Very."

"Then I'm happy for you."

"Thanks. And my side trip?"

"Go. I'll call you if I need you to come back."

The rumble of an approaching jet drew their attention to the sky.

"Another G-500," Faith said. She squinted. "Is that the Strategic Services jet?"

Stone checked his watch. "I believe it is."

The plane landed without issue and taxied to the area in front of the hanger Stone's plane was using.

"Try not to get abducted by aliens," Stone said to Faith, then walked over to the newly arrived jet.

Mike exited first, followed by Herb Fisher, and three people Stone didn't know.

"Good flight?" Stone asked.

"Textbook," Mike said.

He introduced the rest of the team. Architect Eliza Dinh and project manager Cory Aldridge were representing the architectural firm Athey & Li, and engineer Ellen Herlin, Black/Ross Engineering.

Mike and Herb rode with Stone, while the others took a rental van.

As they neared the site Herb said, "This place is gorgeous."

"I second that," Mike said.

"Hold your reviews until you see the actual site," Stone told them.

They soon arrived and made their way to the same vista point Ed had taken Stone.

"The property goes to just beyond those trees," Stone said, pointing across the shallow valley. "And spreads in both directions about the same distance."

The others took in the view, no one saying a word.

Finally, Mike asked, "Is this ridge part of the property?"

"It is. The property line abuts the road we came in on."

"And is that the only access?" Eliza asked.

"Yes, but Ed Eagle said there's a good place on the west side for a road that could connect to the main highway."

She made a note on her tablet computer. After a few more questions were asked and answered, the three experts hiked farther along the ridge, leaving Stone, Mike, and Herb behind.

"What do you think?" Stone asked.

"I think I'm glad Phoenix fell through. Barring technical issues, this place is perfect."

"I agree." Stone turned to Herb. "Meet with Ed Eagle and work up a purchase agreement. Make sure he understands it's contingent on our final decision."

"You got it," Herb said.

Mike checked his watch. "I need to get back to the plane. Herb, you have your hotel information?"

"All set."

"I feel good about this," Mike said.

"So do I," Stone said.

He dropped Mike back at the airport and was heading back to the Lees' when Monica called.

"Are you free for lunch?" she asked.

"I thought you had work to do."

"I thought I did, too, but the person I'm supposed to meet with isn't getting back to me."

"In that case, I would love to have lunch with you. Shall I pick you up?"

Dalton Conroy had big ambitions. Ones, he'd come to realize, he'd never achieve at Vitale Insurance, his current employer.

He'd joined the company confident he'd quickly rise to the top. He'd even had delusions of being the company's youngest ever CEO. Instead, he was one of a couple dozen vice presidents, and least senior of the bunch—a status that the others seemed to enjoy reminding him.

There would be no meteoric rise for him. At best, it would take decades before he'd have a shot at the top job. And waiting that long was out of the question.

He could barely tolerate the idea of remaining a minor VP at a company that insured the property of the elite for another day, as it was. What he wanted was to *be* one of the elite.

Which was why he hadn't even given it a second thought

when Simon Duchamp approached him with the offer to pay him for inside information.

But while the money was good, he wasn't earning it fast enough to build the fortune he craved. Nor, he'd come to believe, was the amount Simon paid him commensurate with the value of the information he was providing. After all, without the information he passed Simon's way, Simon's illegal activities would come to a crashing halt.

The only fair deal would be one in which Dalton received a percentage of the take from each job. And not some piddling amount, either.

Fifty percent seemed fair, but Dalton was not an unreasonable man. He would settle for a third.

He had intended to make the case when Simon last called but decided it was not a conversation to have over the phone, and ended up settling for double his fee.

Which was why, instead of messaging Simon the info on the Matilda Stone paintings, Dalton had taken a flight that morning from New York to Santa Fe, arriving just before lunch.

While he waited in line for his rental car, he checked his phone and saw that he had a text from Simon.

Call me

No doubt it was about the Matilda Stones.

Dalton sneered and shoved the phone back into his pocket. Simon would get the info after they renegotiated their deal.

Dalton's stomach growled.

Make that after Dalton grabbed a bite to eat, and then renegotiated their deal.

One of the clerks at the rental desk waved Dalton forward. "How can I help you, sir?"

Nico was just about to bite into a sandwich when his office door flew open and Petry strode inside.

"Well?"

"I'm sorry?"

"The paintings."

Nico quickly rose from his desk and closed the door, then turned to his boss. "What about them?"

"Have we got them yet?"

Choosing his words carefully, Nico said, "Not as far as I know. Remember, I told you it would take—"

"Yeah, yeah. You said it would take time. We've given them time. What's it been? A week now?"

Nico had said it could take up to a month, but best not to remind Petry of that. "It's been two days."

"Two? That's all?" Petry had never been a patient man.

As calmly as possible, Nico said, "Yes, sir."

Petry huffed. "When was the last time you talked to what's-his-name? Seymour? The painting guy."

"Simon."

"Whatever. When?"

"An hour ago," Nico lied.

His last conversation with Simon had actually been yesterday, to confirm Simon had received the preferred list. But Nico didn't want to tell Petry about the list until Simon had at least one in hand, because if Nico let it slip now and none of Barrington's most wanted paintings could be obtained, Petry would go ballistic. Best to control the man's expectations.

"Oh," Petry said, some of the wind knocked from his sails. "And?"

"And everything's on track."

"I see. Have you figured out the plan for what we do once we have them?"

"I have several ideas I'm working on. I'll have choices for you next week."

Petry nodded to himself, mulling it over, then said, "Next time you hear from Seymour, let me know right away."

He spun around and marched out.

"It's Simon," Nico muttered to himself.

CHAPTER 18

S tone ordered the broiled salmon, while Monica opted for the southwest chicken salad. For drinks, Stone chose the Kellerei Cantina Terlano Pinot Grigio.

"I have to admit, I'm pleasantly surprised," Monica said, after they'd each taken a drink.

"By the wine?"

"By you."

"Me? What did I do?"

"It's more what you didn't do."

"Which is?"

"Disappear on me. In my experience, men have the habit of making themselves scarce after a night together."

"Has this happened often?"

"Often enough to be a pattern."

"The thought never crossed my mind."

"I'm glad for that." She put a hand over his and gave it a squeeze. "You never told me what part of New York you live in."

"Turtle Bay."

"I'm not sure where that is."

"You know where the UN is?"

"Yes."

"Turtle Bay."

"That's a nice neighborhood. You have an apartment?"

"A full townhouse."

"Lucky you," she said.

"You don't know how right you are. I inherited it from my great-aunt when I was still on the police force."

"You were a cop?"

"A homicide detective."

"How does a homicide detective with an inherited house from a great-aunt become a high-powered attorney who is friends with presidents?"

"By means of a bullet to the knee, police department politics, and a lawyer friend who lent me a hand when I needed it most. The rest is just details."

"I'm not sure where to start unpacking all of that."

"How about you? Where do you live?"

"I should probably lie and say I live on the Upper East Side, but the truth is I missed out on the rich great-aunts. The biggest place I was shown in Manhattan that I could afford was barely larger than the closets in my parents' house back in Fillmore. Which is why I live in a one-bedroom in Brooklyn." She smirked. "I'm sorry. Does that mean you *are* going to disappear on me now?"

"Hardly. Besides, I've known people who lived in Brooklyn."

"Name two. And I don't count."

"Ah, here comes our lunch."

The waiter arrived and set plates in front of each of them. "Is there anything else I can help you with?"

"I think we're good for now," Stone said, shooting a glance at Monica for confirmation.

She nodded, and the waiter left.

"If you're interested in moving across the river," Stone said, "I have an empty apartment you are welcome to use. It's in the house next door to mine. It's been divided into several flats."

"Is this a serious offer?"

"It could be."

"Thank you. I'll think about it."

The salmon was as good as Stone had hoped, and from Monica's look of satisfaction, her salad was equally delicious.

While they waited for their check, Stone said, "I know we have plans for dinner already, but if you don't need to work this afternoon, can I entice you into a little outing?"

"I'm intrigued. What kind of outing?"

"Oh, no. You need to choose first."

"One second." She pulled out her phone, studied the screen, then set the device down. "Still no word from the person I'm supposed to meet, so it appears that I'm free. Now can you tell me?"

"Absolutely not. But I would suggest putting on something more comfortable."

"You don't like what I'm wearing?"

She had on a pale yellow sleeveless dress that looked stunning against her golden skin. "I like it very much, but trust me, you'll be happier if you change."

"Into what?"

"Pants and a comfortable shirt. Jeans would probably be best if you have them."

"You're not going to be putting me to work, are you?"

"You'll find out soon enough."

After Stone paid the bill, Monica nodded toward the restrooms. "I need to make a stop."

"I'll meet you in front."

When Stone reached the lobby, the only other people present were the hostess and a man looking at his phone, waiting for a table.

Monica soon reappeared in the dining room, walking toward the front. She was almost abreast of the hostess when the waiting diner looked up.

She stopped short when she saw him, both of them staring at each other in surprise.

"What the hell are you doing here?" the man said.

Monica quickly regained her composure and started to walk past him without answering. But he grabbed her arm and stopped her.

"I asked you a question."

One step, and Stone was standing beside him, his hand clamping down on the man's shoulder.

"Hey!" the man said.

"Let her go."

"Stay out of this, buddy. It isn't any of your concern."

As he said this, Monica twisted her arm out of the man's grasp and took a step back.

"I'm not finished with you!" he yelled.

"You damn well are," she said. "I don't work for you anymore, Dalton. Remember?"

His eyes narrowed. "Wait. You're not still trying to prove that ridiculous hunch of yours, are you?"

"We have *nothing* to talk about. Come on, Stone."

She headed out the door with Stone.

Dalton followed after them. "This is so typical of you. You were always going off rogue and never listened to me. *That's* why you lost your job, you know. If you'd shown even a little respect, I might have kept you around."

She kept walking without looking back.

"See! I'm right. Still not listening."

Stone had had enough. He turned and stepped in front of the man. "Dalton, is it?"

"I said this is none of your business."

He tried to go around Stone, but Stone shifted so he was still in the man's path.

"Actually, it is." He pulled out a business card and held it out. "Allow me to introduce myself. I'm Miss Reyes's attorney. If you continue harassing her, I'll have a restraining order slapped on you before the day's out, and I will inform your employer about your behavior."

Dalton looked at the card. "This has a New York address. I doubt you're even licensed to practice in New Mexico."

"You don't think that I have contacts here who would be more than happy to do it for me?"

Dalton grimaced in frustration, then balled up Stone's card and tossed it on the ground. Glaring past Stone at Monica, he shouted, "I don't ever want to see you again!"

"I can assure you the feeling's mutual," Stone said.

Dalton's eyes settled on Stone for a second before he headed back into the restaurant.

CHAPTER 19

———◎———

D alton contemplated ordering a third martini but forced himself to refrain. He needed to stay sharp.

That damn Monica Reyes.

Two months ago, she'd come to him with a theory about several recent insurance claims for high-end art that had been destroyed in various incidents. She believed they weren't destroyed at all, but had been stolen by the same group of people. The little evidence she had was circumstantial at best, but she'd been convinced she was right. Which, of course, she was.

His first instinct had been to shut her down completely, but he worried that doing so would only strengthen her suspicions. So, instead, he'd given her a little rope, in the hope she'd hit a dead end and lose interest.

What he hadn't counted on was Monica's tenacity. Though unaware of it, she'd come close to foiling jobs more than once. Dalton had been forced to take a more active role in deflecting her interests, even going so far as to plant false evidence that should have derailed her investigation.

But she just kept pushing and pushing. Two weeks ago, she'd told him she'd been contacted by someone claiming to have first-hand knowledge of the thefts. He'd pressed her for the person's name, but she said all contact was via a generic e-mail account, so she didn't know. As proof of the source's credibility, the e-mailer had provided several bits of info that aligned with Monica's theories, so Monica was sure the person was on the up-and-up.

That was troubling enough, but when she asked for funds to cover a trip to Santa Fe to meet her source in person, the alarm bells in Dalton's head really started clanging. Simon had a gallery in Santa Fe. Though Monica hadn't mentioned the art dealer's name, Dalton couldn't take the chance that her source wasn't connected in some way.

Dalton's first act was to inform Simon of a possible leak within his organization. He said an anonymous tip had come into Vitale Insurance about the thefts, which was true, and warned Simon it must have been someone in his inner circle. He purposely didn't mention Monica's involvement. He didn't want to give Simon reason to think that he couldn't control his own staff and therefore was a liability.

Dalton ultimately altered reports that Monica had filed on several past cases, intentionally introducing errors, then used them as reasons to terminate her. He'd assumed that had stopped her meddling, but given that she was here in Santa Fe, he was clearly wrong.

Whether he should have told Simon about Monica when she'd first started sniffing around the thefts or not, he had no idea. What he *did* know was that if he told him now, Dalton could kiss away any chances of getting a bigger piece of the pie.

He wasn't about to let that happen, which meant he would have to deal with Monica himself. Exactly how he'd have to figure out. But right now, it was time to see Simon to change their arrangement.

Dalton straightened his tie, cleared his throat, and rang the doorbell of Simon's townhouse. Moments later, the door was opened by a huge man with a hard face and a shaved head.

"Yeah?"

"I'm looking for Simon Duchamp."

"So?"

"Is he home?"

"Who are you?"

"A friend."

"I know all his friends. You ain't one of them."

"We work together."

"Listen, bud. You either give me a name or I shut this door in your face."

"Dalton. Dalton Conroy."

"Wait here."

The door slammed closed. A minute went by, then two. Dalton was beginning to wonder if he should ring the doorbell again when the door opened. This time, instead of the brute, Simon stood in front of him.

"What are you doing here, Dalton?"

"Bringing you the information you asked for."

Simon considered him for several seconds, then frowned and said, "Come in."

He led Dalton into a spacious living room and motioned him to sit.

"Something to drink?"

"I'm fine."

"Do you mind if I have something?"

"Not at all."

Simon took the chair across from Dalton. "Phillip, could you bring me a glass of chardonnay?"

"Yes, sir."

Dalton jumped at the sound of the big man's voice. He hadn't realized the guy had been standing in a back corner.

"Are you all right?" Simon asked.

"I'm fine."

"You said you have the information?"

Dalton removed a thumb drive from his pocket. "Right here."

"So kind of you to deliver it personally. Thank you."

Simon held out a hand, but Dalton kept hold of the drive.

"Something we need to talk about first."

Simon leaned back. "Anything you want to talk about could have been done over the phone."

"Some subjects are better discussed in person."

Phillip reentered the room and handed Simon a glass of wine.

"Thank you."

Instead of leaving, Phillip took a few steps back and stood quietly, hands clasped behind his back.

Dalton eyed him for a second, then looked back at Simon. "I think this is a conversation we should have alone."

"We are alone," Simon said.

"What about him?"

"Think of Phillip as an extension of me."

Dalton fought to keep the annoyance from his face. "Fine."

"What is it you want to discuss?"

"My share."

"You are already getting double your fee for this."

"I didn't say fee. I said share."

"That's not how our arrangement works."

"It is now."

"And what makes you think that?"

"The way I see it, I'm an integral part of your business, and it is only fair you pay me what my information is really worth."

"And how much do you think that is?"

"Forty percent."

"Of what?"

"Every job it plays a part in."

Simon laughed.

"Look," Dalton said. "My ass is on the line every time I dig something up for you. I deserve at least that much." He waved the thumb drive in the air. "Or I could just take this and leave right now."

"Relax, Dalton. I didn't say no, did I?"

"No, you laughed."

"I did, didn't I?"

Dalton stood up. "I've told you what I want. Call me when you're ready to take me seriously."

Simon held up a hand to stop him from leaving. "I might be able to swing twenty percent, but only if you increase the amount of information that you provide."

"Increase how?"

"On top of my regular requests, you'll proactively send me anything you think I will be interested in. And you'll develop sources at other companies who will supply you with similar intelligence on their clients."

"I'll need money to pay them."

"Anything you pay them will come out of your cut, just like operation expenses come out of mine."

"Thirty-five percent."

"Twenty-five."

"Make it a straight third and you have a deal."

Simon shrugged and nodded. "A third it is."

Dalton could barely contain his excitement. Even with the cost of a few lackies at other companies, he should be able to hold on to more money than he'd realistically hoped to get.

He took a step closer to Simon and held out his hand. "Deal."

While Phillip escorted Dalton out, Simon plugged the thumb drive into his laptop and quickly scanned through the files.

Vitale insured seven clients who owned Matilda Stones. There was one painting each in Boston, Chicago, and Dallas, and four in California.

Or there soon would be four.

One of the paintings had recently been purchased by someone in Los Angeles. The buyer was not insured by Vitale, but the auction house that sold it was. On the thumb drive was information on how and when it was being delivered. And best of all, it was one of the paintings on the list from Nico. Sadly, none of the others were.

Phillip entered the room.

"He's gone?" Simon asked.

"Yeah. Do you want me to deal with him now?"

"Not yet. If what he's given me doesn't work out, I may need him to find alternatives."

"Just say the word." Phillip dipped his head and left.

Simon called his brother.

"What's up?" Benji answered.

"I need you and your crew in Los Angeles before the day's out."

CHAPTER 20

———◇———

While Dalton was at lunch, stewing over his encounter with Monica, she and Stone were headed across town in silence.

Monica, who was still rattled by seeing her former boss, had been staring out the window and didn't rouse from her stupor until she realized the vehicle had stopped in front of her cousin's house. "What are we doing here?"

"A change of clothes. Remember?"

"Oh, right." She sighed. "Maybe I should take a rain check."

"Not a cloud in the sky."

"You know what I mean."

"Because of Dalton?"

"I can't begin to tell you how sorry I am about all that. He's the last person I expected to run into."

"I got that impression, but I don't see why you have anything to be sorry about. Nor do I think you should let him ruin your day."

She took in his words, then smiled for the first time since lunch. "You're right. To hell with him."

"Seconded!"

She opened her door. "Something comfortable, you said? Like for a hike?"

"That'll work."

"I won't be long."

Ten minutes later, she was back in the car, wearing a pair of sturdy boots, blue jeans, and a green button-up shirt. "How's this?"

"It couldn't be more perfect."

"What about your clothes?"

"I'll change when we get there."

"Ooh, do I get to watch?"

"If you do, we may not get to do the other thing I have planned."

"I'm willing to take that chance if you are."

He drove her to the ranch of a friend he'd made while he'd still owned the Lees' house. After retrieving a change of clothes from the trunk, he led Monica into the stables, where a ranch hand had two horses saddled and waiting.

"We're going riding?" Monica asked, excited.

"I take it this isn't your first time."

"In years, yes, but not my first. My high school boyfriend was president of the FFA club." She was referring to the Future Farmers of America. "It was one of our favorite things to do."

"Then you *won't* be joining me while I change?"

She looked torn.

"Too many good choices?"

"Something like that." She took a breath. "Go change. We'll have time for taking advantage of each other tonight."

"I'll hold you to that." He grinned.

Once Stone changed outfits, they set off on a trail that took them into the mountains.

"I'm glad you didn't let me back out of this. It's exactly what I needed. And thank you for helping at the restaurant, too. I should have said that before."

"Even if I wasn't there, you would have held your own."

"It's nice to know there's someone who would back me up like that."

"Dalton used to be your boss?"

"Yes."

"The same boss you talked to on the phone last night?"

She nodded.

"I can understand why you left for another job."

Grimacing, she said, "I haven't been completely open about my situation. Technically, I'm unemployed."

"Left or fired?"

"The latter. And unjustly."

"When?"

"Twelve days ago."

Smirking, Stone said, "If his demeanor at work was anything like his behavior at the restaurant, he must have been a delight to work for."

"Yeah, he's quite the prick."

"I think you're being too kind."

She laughed. "Probably."

The path narrowed for a bit, forcing them to ride single file. When it widened again, Stone moved his horse to the side to make room for Monica.

"You mentioned working in finance, but you never said exactly what you did," he said.

"Insurance, actually. I'm a fraud investigator at Vitale Insurance. *Was* a fraud investigator, I mean."

"And the prick?"

"My VP."

"Ah, a prime example of the dregs rising to the top."

"Why does that always seem to happen?"

"Trickle-down stupidity," Stone said. "Let me guess, all the execs there are like him."

"It *is* a boys' club, so kind of. But he's developed his special brand of assholery."

"Why did Dalton think you're working on something?"

"Because I am."

"And that would be?"

"The same case I was working on at Vitale when he let me go. He thinks it's a waste of time, but I know it isn't. And once I crack it, I'll present my report to his bosses and get *him* fired."

"That's what he meant by the going rogue comment?"

She nodded.

"What's the case?"

"I specialize in art theft, and it's my belief that there's an organized ring operating in the States right now."

"You have evidence of this?"

"It's admittedly thin, but I trust my instincts, and my instincts say something's going on."

The path forked, and Stone guided them onto the trail on the left. "I would think that kind of theft would be easy to prove. I mean, a piece of art is either there or it's not."

"You would think so, but it's not quite as clear-cut as that."

"How so?"

"One client kept a pair of Picasso drawings on a yacht that, just over a year ago, sank in water deep enough to discourage salvage attempts. Authorities determined it to be an accident, and Vitale forked over a nice check."

"But you don't think the drawings went down with the boat."

"I did at first. But then a few months later, a Matisse, worth millions, was lost in a house fire on Martha's Vineyard. The only thing left was the corner of a frame.

"Before that a cargo truck that had been transporting a Frida Kahlo went up in flames. Then there was another boat that burned and sank on Lake Michigan with several expensive pieces on board. And I've found at least two other cases where insured artworks were destroyed in ways that made identification impossible. But while I saw a pattern, Dalton thought I was making something out of nothing."

"Then Dalton's an idiot, though I guess we've already established that. Do you have anything concrete that connects the cases together?"

"Not yet, but I'm close. That's why I'm in Santa Fe actually. I was contacted by someone who claimed to have information about a couple of the destroyed paintings. Before I could set up an official meeting with him, Dalton fired me. I wasn't going to give up, though. I kept pressing the source. Three days ago, he agreed to meet me at the Ivonne Cervantes opening last night. But right before Donna and I arrived, he texted saying that he needed to postpone until today. I haven't heard a peep from him since."

"Cold feet?"

"I'm hoping not."

"What's his name?"

"Honestly, I don't even know if he's a man. All our communication has been either by e-mail or text."

"Has he given you anything you can use?"

She shook her head. "He was going to do that when we met in person. What do you think? Am I wasting my time on nothing?"

"Even with the little you've told me I can see it's worth looking into."

"Thank you, Stone. You don't know how much I needed to hear that."

"You know, if things don't work out with Vitale or even if they do and you'd like to take your talents elsewhere, I can be of some assistance."

"Does your firm employ fraud investigators?"

"Not my firm, but Steele Insurance does."

"Steele Insurance? Do you know someone there?"

"Yes. Me. I'm on their board."

She stared at him, wide-eyed. "You are a handy man to know."

"Feel free to show your appreciation later tonight."

"Why wait for tonight?" She turned her horse back the way they'd come and looked over her shoulder. "Coming?"

He brought his gelding around. "After you."

Stone came out of the bathroom the next morning to find Monica sitting on the end of the bed, frowning at her phone.

"Something wrong?"

"I think my contact is officially ghosting me."

"Have you tried calling?"

"I don't have his number."

"I thought you said you texted with him."

"He texts me from a blocked number. I can contact him via e-mail. He said he wanted it that way to protect himself."

"Then it sounds like you've done all you can. How about some breakfast?"

They dressed and relocated to the kitchen. Since Martha had the day off, Stone rooted around in the refrigerator to see what was available. "How does a mushroom and spinach omelet sound?"

"Divine. Anything I can help with?"

"Coffee?"

Stone was plating the second omelet when Monica's phone began ringing.

Her face brightened.

"Is it him?" Stone asked.

"Maybe. The number isn't blocked, but I don't recognize it."

She accepted the call.

"Hello? . . . Yes, this is she." Her eyebrows pinched as she listened. "Good morning, Detective." She listened for a moment and then turned on the speaker function so Stone could listen in. "I'm sorry, could you say that again?"

A woman's voice came through the speaker. "Do you know a man named Joshua Paskota?"

"I've never heard that name before."

"You're sure?"

"I am. What's this about?"

"There was an accident the night before last. A single car crash, one fatality."

"Joshua Paskota?"

"Yes, but that information is still withheld from the public until we contact his next of kin. We were hoping you could help us with that."

"Me? Why would you think that?"

"We found a cell phone in Mr. Paskota's suitcase that had only one number in its contacts. Yours."

"Mine?"

"Yes. In fact, it's the only piece of information on the phone. The call logs are empty and there are no text messages."

Monica shared a look with Stone. It was clear they were thinking the same thing. Joshua Paskota had to be her contact.

"You're sure you don't know him?" the detective asked.

Stone shook his head.

"Until you said his name, I'd never heard it before," Monica said.

"Sorry to have bothered you. Thank you for your time."

As soon as the call ended, Monica said, "Why would my info be the only thing on the phone?"

"If I had to guess, I'd say it's a throwaway that he only used to contact you."

"That makes sense. Why did you not want me to tell her he was my source?"

"Because it wouldn't have helped anything. The detective said it was an accident, not murder. They're not looking for suspects or motivation. They're looking for family."

She sighed. "I guess this means I made the trip here for nothing."

Stone raised an eyebrow. "Nothing?"

She leaned over and kissed his cheek. "Well, maybe not for nothing."

"That's better."

Monica said little as they ate. Stone could empathize. He'd had cases both as a cop and as a lawyer where a promising lead hadn't panned out. What had often helped him figure out how to move forward was taking a step back.

"Why don't we swing by your cousin's place? You can pack a bag and we'll drive up to Taos. Spend a night or two. Forget about work for the weekend."

"Where do I sign up?"

Forty minutes later, they arrived at Donna Otero's house.

"I was beginning to wonder if you'd gone back to New York," Donna said to Monica, as she walked through the door.

"My fault, I'm afraid," Stone said. "I've been monopolizing her time."

"Well, I guess I can forgive you. She's in a much better mood than when she arrived."

"How so?"

"Let's just say that she was ready to pick a fight with anyone who looked at her wrong."

"I wasn't that bad," Monica said.

Donna patted her arm. "Whatever you want to believe." To Stone, she mouthed, *Thank you.*

"I'll just be a few minutes," Monica said.

She headed into the back and soon returned with a small suitcase.

Donna walked them to the door. "Any idea when you'll be back?"

"Sometime on Monday," Stone said. He glanced at Monica. "If that works for you."

"Works fine."

"Oh, I almost forgot," Donna said. "Something came for you."

She went into the kitchen and came back with a legal-size envelope, which she handed to Monica. Handwritten on the front was Monica's name.

"It arrived while we were at the exhibit the other night," Donna told her, then grinned. "But you've been a little tied up since then."

Monica thanked her, then she and Stone returned to their car. Once they were back on the road, she opened the envelope and pulled out a piece of paper.

She looked up, surprised. "It's from Joshua Paskota."

"How did he know where you were staying?"

"I have no idea."

"Did he know when you were arriving?"

She nodded. "We hadn't set up our meet yet, and I told him what flight I was on, so he could suggest a time and place. You don't think . . . You don't think he followed me, do you?"

"I would have if I were him, to make sure you were who you said you were. What's the note say?"

Reading, she said, "'I apologize for you coming all this way, but I'm not going to be able to meet with you. I think they're suspicious of me. I'm leaving town, so don't bother trying to find me. There is someone else who might help you. His name is Tristan Williams. He lives in L.A.'" She looked up. "That's it except for a phone number that I guess is Tristan's. Stone, I think maybe the crash wasn't an accident."

"I think you're right. I'll ask a friend to nudge the police into taking a closer look into it."

"I'll try Tristan." She punched in his number, waited several seconds, then said, "Voicemail." She waited for the beep. "Hi, Tristan. My name is Monica Reyes. Please call me at your earliest convenience." She left her number, then hung up. "I guess all we can do now is wait."

"Oh, I think we can figure out a few things to do to fill the time."

CHAPTER 21

On Monday morning at the Centurion Pictures lot in Los Angeles, a preproduction meeting was just wrapping up for Peter Barrington's next feature. In addition to Peter, the participants included Ben Bacchetti, head of Centurion and one of the film's main producers; Billy Barnett, the film's other main producer; the line producer; various department heads for such things as costumes, sets, lighting, locations, and transportation; and a handful of assistants.

Billy Barnett's real name was Teddy Fay, but only a handful of trusted people knew that. As far as most of the world knew, Teddy—a former member of the CIA—had died in a plane crash several years ago. A master of disguise, he had created his Billy Barnett identity so that he could operate freely in Hollywood.

"When do you think you can have a revised schedule?" Billy asked the line producer.

She looked over her notes. "Lunchtime tomorrow okay?"

"Good by me. Ben?"

"Me, too," Ben said. "Anyone else have something we need to discuss?"

There were head shakes all around.

"Great. We'll meet again next week same time."

As everyone stood and began gathering their things, Stacy Lange—Billy's personal assistant—leaned toward him and whispered, "Party."

"Right." He raised his voice and said, "Those of you who are helping with the party on Saturday following the board of directors meeting, make sure you let Stacy know if you need anything. No last-minute hitches, please." He glanced at Stacy. "That was it, right?"

She gave him a thumbs-up and joined the line heading out the door.

"Billy, Peter and I are going to grab lunch," Ben said. "You want to join us?"

Billy checked his watch. "No time. I need to be at my house by two."

"That's right," Peter said. "Today's the day."

"It is, indeed."

"The day for what?" Ben asked.

"The surprise for my dad," Peter said.

"Oh, right. Hey, Billy, are we going to get a sneak peek?"

"Don't even bother asking," Peter said. "I've already tried. Billy says no one sees it until Dad does."

"One hundred percent correct," Billy said.

"You're no fun," Ben said.

"I'm a producer. I'm not supposed to be fun." Billy pulled the strap of his leather briefcase over his shoulder. "Now, if you gentlemen are done wasting my time, I'll be off."

Benji grabbed his phone the moment it started to vibrate. "Yeah?"

"Just turned into the canyon." Devin's voice was almost lost in the growl of the motorcycle he was riding.

"You sure they haven't seen you?"

"They have no clue I'm here."

"Keep it that way. ETA?"

"Fifteen minutes, give or take."

"Let me know when you're about to turn onto Mulholland Drive." Reaching Mulholland would put Devin less than ten minutes out.

Benji reached over and gave Sticks a shake.

The wiry man groaned and yawned, slowly parting his eyelids. "Is it time?"

"They're on their way up. Get into position."

Sticks stretched like he had all the time in the world.

"Now, if you don't mind," Benji said.

"All right, all right. I'm going. Chill out."

"And put your earpiece in."

Sticks grumbled and shoved his Bluetooth earpiece in place as he climbed out of the car.

The Ford Taurus they'd stolen had been dressed up to look like a security company patrol car. There were at least a dozen such companies serving the homes in the Hollywood Hills, so even though the logo on the vehicle's door was for a company that didn't exist, no one would question their validity. To complete the look, Benji and Sticks wore matching security guard uniforms.

The road they were on had been chosen because it was on their target's route, was little used, and had a convenient bend twenty yards from the closest intersection, that took vehicles into a blind spot perfect for Benji and his crew's needs.

As soon as Sticks disappeared around the bend, Benji turned on his walkie-talkie.

"Sticks, come in." Nothing. "Sticks, you hearing me?"

Something clicked on the line, then, "For God's sake, I hear you."

"Is everything still set?"

"Yeah. Why wouldn't it be?"

Benji took a breath, and reminded himself that anyone who had a passion for arson was bound to have more than a few screws loose.

His phone vibrated with another call from Devin.

"About to turn onto Mulholland."

"Excellent. We're ready and waiting. Turn on your walkie. You should be in range."

A moment later, Devin's voice came over the radio. "Check. Check."

"I read you," Benji said. "Sticks, they're almost here."

Around the bend, Sticks grinned. *Finally*, he thought.

He began moving dry tree branches into the middle of the road from where he and Benji had piled them on the shoulder. The road was narrow, with bushes and trees lining both sides, so by the time he finished, there was no way to drive around the low barrier he'd created.

"Two minutes," Devin announced.

Sticks doused the wood with lighter fluid, then started counting in his head. When he reached sixty, he flicked on his lighter, set a handful of twigs ablaze, and threw them on the pile.

The wood burst into flames with a low *whoosh*.

He grinned like a schoolboy at the sound, then beamed as the inferno filled the road.

Back around the bend, Benji had already repositioned to the T-bone intersection from where their prey would be coming. Their scheduled route would have taken them straight through, but now a delineator blocked the way.

Benji turned on his mic. "Status?"

"We're almost there," Devin said.

"Anyone else around?"

"No one."

Benji donned a face mask and sunglasses, then strode out to the barrier. He heard the auction house's delivery van a few seconds before he saw it. He began signaling for the van to turn down the less-used road.

It slowed as it approached, then instead of turning, it stopped. The driver rolled down his window. "Is there a problem?"

"Brushfire ahead," Benji said. He pointed again toward the other road. "This route will get you down the hill."

As hoped, the mention of a fire sparked fear in the driver's eyes.

"Sir, we need to keep traffic moving." Benji motioned again toward the other road.

The driver nodded, then turned down the road, all according to plan.

Following right behind him was Devin. Once both vehicles made the turn, Benji moved the delineator onto the road behind them, blocking the route to any other traffic.

CHAPTER 22

———◇———

The delivery van driver slammed on the brakes and stared at the sight ahead.

"Oh, shit," his coworker said from the passenger seat.

A wall of fire filled the road, a few dozen feet in front of them. "Back up, back up!"

That snapped the driver out of his daze. He reached for the shifter, but before he could put it into reverse, someone knocked on his window.

Standing outside was a man in a uniform and face mask, just like the guy who had sent them down this road.

The man motioned for the driver to roll down his window. He did so.

"You can't come this way," the man said.

"I see that. I'm going to turn around."

"Can't go that way, either."

"What do you mean?"

"Exactly what I said."

Without any other warning, the man brought up a small canister and sprayed its contents into the cab.

Within seconds, both deliverymen were unconscious.

By the time Benji reached the van, Devin and Sticks had subdued the men inside, and Devin searched the driver for keys.

Benji glanced at the still burning barrier, then said to Sticks, "You want to take care of that before it becomes a problem?"

"I don't see why. It'll probably burn itself out."

That is *not* what it looked like to Benji. In fact, it appeared to him that it was just moments away from jumping to the dry vegetation beside the road.

"Take care of it," Benji snapped. Starting a major blaze was not part of the plan.

"Fine. Waste of a good fire, if you ask me."

Sticks walked off with one of their fire extinguishers.

Devin backed out of the cab, holding a set of keys. "Found 'em."

"Give them to me, then go help Sticks. I'll take care of this."

Devin tossed him the keys, then grabbed the other extinguisher and jogged toward the fire.

Benji opened the back of the van and grinned. A picture-shaped item covered in protective wrapping was strapped against the side of the van.

He cut through the restraints, slit open the Bubble Wrap, then peeled back the plastic and confirmed it was the correct painting. He took a photo of it and sent it to Simon with the message: Bingo.

After transferring the painting to the trunk of the sedan, he keyed the walkie. "You guys done yet?"

"I think so," Devin replied.

"Sticks?"

"Yeah, good enough."

"Then let's get out of here while our luck's holding."

The delivery van was overdue, and Teddy didn't like it.

He called June Marnell, his contact at the auction house.

"Good, Mr. Barnett. I was just going to call and check how the delivery went."

"Exactly the reason I'm calling you. It has not happened at all."

"I'm sorry?"

"The van has yet to arrive."

"That's odd. I should have been notified if they were running late. Can you hold for a moment? I'll check on their status."

"I can."

She was away for longer than he had expected. When she came back on, her earlier cheery disposition had vanished. "It appears something has happened."

"What kind of something?"

"Unfortunately, I can't tell you because we don't know. GPS tracking puts the van three-quarters of a mile from your home, and it's not moving."

"You've tried calling them?"

"Yes, but no one answers. Our delivery manager thinks they might have a mechanical problem and are in an area with spotty cell coverage. Someone has been sent up to check on them, and I'm told they should be there in twenty minutes. I do apologize for the delay. I'll let you know the revised delivery time as soon as I—"

"Where exactly are they? If they're that close, I can be there in a couple minutes."

"There's no need for you to do that."

"It would ease my mind to confirm your delivery manager's theory."

"Oh, well . . . Hold for a moment. Let me get that."

Teddy was already heading toward the front door. On the way, he stopped at his vintage stereo console cabinet, flipped open the record player compartment, and pressed down on the speed control selector for three seconds. A panel covering one of the speakers swung out like a door. Inside was a speaker a quarter the size of the original 1950s era version, and a Smith & Wesson 9mm pistol, two extra magazines, and an attachable silencer. He grabbed everything but the speaker and raced to his Porsche.

As he was slipping into the driver's seat, June came back on the line. "I can give you an approximate address."

"If it's not too much trouble, could you text that to me?"

"Of course. Right away."

"Thank you, June."

The Porsche rumbled to life, and he swung it around the driveway to the street. A check of his phone confirmed the text had arrived.

It took seven minutes to reach the turn onto the road the van was supposedly on. While he didn't immediately see it because of a bend in the road ahead, thanks to the top being down on his roadster, he did smell the one thing that no one who lived in the hills ever wanted to smell.

Smoke.

He slowed as he took the bend, then screeched to a stop, barely keeping from ramming into the back of the delivery van.

The van was sitting in the middle of the lane, its back doors wide open and its cargo area empty.

But Teddy had no time to even think about that, because approximately thirty feet on the other side of the van, at least three trees and several bushes were on fire.

He dialed 911 as he hopped out of his car and ran up to the van's cab. Two men were inside, both either unconscious or dead.

"Nine-one-one, what is your emergency?"

"There's a brushfire," he said. "Hollywood Hills, not far off Mulholland." He relayed his exact location.

"And your name?"

"Billy Barnett. There are also two men unconscious in a van nearby. I need to get them away before the flames reach them. I'll take them to my house."

"You live nearby?"

"Yes." He gave her his address. "Please hurry. There are a lot of homes up here."

He hung up without giving her a chance to ask another question.

His first thought was to take the van, as his Porsche did not have a back seat, but he couldn't find the key. While it would be a squeeze, the roadster would have to do.

He manhandled the driver out of his seat and was relieved to find that the guy was still breathing. He placed him as carefully as possible in the Porsche's front passenger seat.

He retrieved the second man—who was thankfully also still

alive—and laid him half on top of his partner, and half leaning on the door.

Teddy jumped behind the wheel, made a U-turn, and sped away from the fire. He was halfway home when several fire engines raced past him in the other direction. Given that the fire was relatively small, he thought their chances of containing it were good.

He hit the remote for his gate as he neared it, drove through as soon as it was wide enough, then tapped a second button on the remote that would keep the gate open.

As soon as he parked, he laid both men on his driveway, then checked them for injuries. Neither had anything obvious.

His phone vibrated.

"Mr. Barnett, it's June Marnell. Were you able to locate the van?"

He gave her a quick explanation of what he'd found.

"Is the delivery team okay?" she asked.

"I'll leave that determination to the doctors. But they seem to be breathing normally and are not in distress."

"Oh, thank God."

What she said next was drowned out by three rapid trills coming from the phone. A message appeared on the screen:

Brushfire in your vicinity.
You are urged to evacuate the area.

"Sorry," Teddy said. "I need to go."

"I'll contact you again later."

A news helicopter flew over his house toward the fire. As the sound of the rotors faded, a wail of sirens took its place. The whooping grew louder and louder until two ambulances turned into his driveway, with a police car following them.

While EMTs assessed the unconscious men, Teddy gave his account of what he'd found to a pair of police officers.

The officers' radios crackled to life. "Be advised, evacuation order lifted. Fire has been contained."

Teddy felt the tension he'd been holding on to ebb. If he hadn't discovered the fire and reported it when he had, it would have been a completely different story.

CHAPTER 23

————⟡————

Simon arrived in Los Angeles mid-afternoon. Dalton had insisted on tagging along. That was fine by Simon. He wanted to keep Dalton close so there would be no delay in dealing with him when the time came.

Phillip had taken an earlier flight and was waiting for them at the curb outside baggage claim when they exited the terminal.

Without a word, Phillip took their bags and placed them in the trunk of the town car.

Dalton had started to get into the back with Simon, but Simon blocked his way. "You're in front."

"Why?"

"I have business to conduct that is of no concern to you."

Dalton's expression turned suspicious. "How do I know that?"

"Because I just told you."

"We're partners now, remember?"

"We are not partners in all of my business dealings. And in the part that we are, my decisions will be made without your input. Now, get in the front."

Dalton grumbled but did as he was told, and soon the town car joined the mass of vehicles making the slow trek out of LAX.

Simon raised the privacy barrier and called his brother. "Well?"

"All done."

"You got it?"

"Yeah."

"Any issues?"

"Um, not really."

Simon's eyes narrowed. "What happened?"

"Nothing big. We got the painting. Everything's fine."

"What happened?"

"The fire we used as a distraction flared up again after we left. It's no big deal. The fire department put it out before it could damage any homes."

"I told you not to cause a scene." It had been an impossible task, given the nature of what they had been doing, but drawing more attention to the theft was not something Simon wanted.

"It's fine. The only casualties are a few trees."

"That's not the point! I need you to do what I tell you, no matter what."

"I know. I'm sorry. We thought we'd put it out. I should have double-checked. Won't happen again."

Benji had always been a thorn in Simon's side. They were fifteen years apart and shared the same father. Simon would have broken off all contact with him years ago if it weren't for the fact that Benji was willing to do whatever Simon asked of him. Having someone like that in his pocket had been very handy.

"Where are you now?" Simon asked.

"A motel in the Valley. North Hollywood, I think."

"Text me the address. I'll come to you."

As expected, the motel in which Benji had chosen to hold up was a dingy place. Simon was loath to set foot in it, but he supposed it was better than meeting someplace like the Hotel Bel-Air, where his brother would stand out like the proverbial sore thumb.

"Stay here until I call you," Simon told Phillip and Dalton.

"What are we doing here?" Dalton asked.

"*We* are not doing anything. *I* am."

Simon exited the car and slammed the door shut.

He found Benji's room at the far end of the first floor, and his knock was quickly answered by Benji's partner Devin.

"Hey, Simon."

Simon pushed past him without responding. The fire guy with the stupid nickname was on a bed, eyes on his phone. There was no sign of Benji.

"Where's my brother?"

From the back of the room came the sound of a flushing toilet and then a door opening.

"I'm here," Benji said. He walked into the room, still zipping up his pants.

Simon glared and said, "The painting?"

"In the trunk of our car."

"You *left* it in your *car?*"

"I didn't think you'd want anyone to see us bring it inside."

Benji had a point, not that Simon was going to acknowledge it. "Show me."

"Sure." Benji headed for the door, and Simon followed.

The car was backed into the spot directly outside of Benji's room. After his brother opened the trunk, Simon leaned in, peeled back a portion of the plastic covering the package, and gazed excitedly at the canvas.

"Absolutely lovely."

"Yeah, it's nice, isn't it?" Benji said.

A retort leaped onto Simon's tongue, but he bit it back and said, "Bring it to the gallery at midnight. Phillip will meet you at the back entrance."

"Cool."

After Benji closed the trunk, Simon handed him a piece of paper. "Your next job. It's in a town just north of San Francisco."

"Okay. What's the piece?"

"I'll send you the information along with the security specs and blueprints of the location. It's a quick turnaround."

"How quick?"

"The sooner the better. Be on the first flight out tomorrow. If you see an opportunity tomorrow night, take it."

"Tomorrow night? That's kinda fast. We won't have enough time to . . ."

Simon's glare cut Benji off.

"Just do it."

"Sure. Whatever you want."

Nico Savage sat on the couch in his boss's office, listening to Petry apply the hard sell to a potential client over the phone.

"I don't understand your reluctance," Petry was saying. "You won't find a better company to partner with than us. With our help, you are all but guaranteed to succeed."

Through the speaker, the CEO of the start-up Petry was courting said, "I've heard some disturbing news about a lawsuit brought against you that you lost."

The muscles in Petry's jaw flexed. "Oh, that. It's not what you think. Sadly, the judge had it out for us right from the start and excluded vital information that would have exposed the other party as an opportunist trying to take advantage of me. We've appealed and are reliably told the judgment will be overturned."

"You're appealing?"

"You bet I am. In any sane courtroom, the suit would have been dismissed on the first day."

Nico's phone vibrated. He looked at the screen: No Caller ID. It could be any number of people, most of whom he would have no trouble ignoring. Unfortunately, there was at least one person he could not.

He accepted the call and whispered, "Yes?" into the receiver.

Petry shot him an annoyed glare, then continued on with whatever nonsense he'd been spewing.

"Nico? It's Simon. Is this a bad time?"

"Depends on the reason you're calling."

"I have very good news."

"Hold on." Good news was something Petry should hear.

Nico walked over to his boss and whispered in his ear, "It's about the paintings."

Petry's eyes lit up. "Mr. Greer. Unfortunately, I have a meeting about to start. I'll call you back and we can continue this discussion then."

Greer said, "I don't think that will be—"

"Bye now." Petry hung up before Greer could say anything else. He pointed at Nico's phone and mouthed, *Put it on speaker.*

Nico did so, then said, "Sorry about that, Simon. What's this good news you wanted to share?"

"We are now in possession of our first Matilda Stone painting. It's even on the list."

Nico cringed.

"What's that mean? On the list?" Petry whispered.

"I'll tell you later," Nico whispered back.

"Fine, but why only one?" Petry asked, his tone turning annoyed. "What's the holdup?"

"I told you this would take time," Nico whispered back. He raised his voice again, "Thank you, Simon. That is good—"

"Give that to me," Petry said, no longer hiding his presence. He grabbed the phone out of Nico's hand. "This is Winston Petry, Nico's boss."

"Mr. Petry, I didn't realize you were there. A pleasure to meet you."

"Yeah, yeah. How long is it going to be before you have any more?"

"I should have a second painting within a week, and a third a week after that."

"That's unacceptable," he snapped.

"I'm sorry?"

"How many can you get by Friday?"

"*This* Friday? Are you joking?"

"Answer the question."

"I don't think we can get any others in that time frame."

"Then the deal's off. Keep the painting you have. I'll keep my money. Oh, I'll make sure anyone who wants to use your service knows how unaccommodating you can be."

"Hold on," Simon said. "Let's not be hasty. What if I could deliver two?"

"Three, or I'm walking."

"Why the rush? Is this for an event?"

"A private showing."

"And you don't care which ones we get?"

"As long as they were painted by Matilda Stone, I couldn't give a shit. Can you do it or not?"

"I'll need to check a few things, but—"

"See, I knew you could make it happen."

"*But* not for the five hundred grand we agreed on."

"A deal's a deal."

"Our deal gave me a month-long window, not four days."

"Hang on for a moment," Petry said, then muted the call. He shot Nico a look. "A *month?*"

"You and I discussed that, remember? You never said anything about wanting them by—"

Petry waved him off and unmuted the call. "What would you need to meet my deadline?"

"Double," Simon said.

"A million? Are the pictures even worth that much?"

"This isn't about worth. This is about the risks I will be taking to meet your deadline."

Petry locked eyes with Nico as if this was all his fault. "Fine. One million."

"Half now," Simon said. "The rest on delivery."

"And you'll have them by Friday."

"I'll have obtained them by then, but the earliest I could get them to you in New York would be Saturday."

"I don't need them in New York. I need them in Los Angeles. Can you do that?"

"I might be able to arrange that. I would need to verify a few things first."

"Then why are you still talking to me?" Petry snarled and disconnected the call.

"We never talked about Los Angeles," Nico said. "Why there?"

Petry snorted. "I guess I'm better at digging up information than you."

He plucked a thin folder from his desk and shoved it into Nico's hands. Inside was a printout of a column from the *Hollywood Reporter*, covering upcoming industry events.

"The second item," Petry said.

Nico skimmed down until he found it.

The board of directors for Centurion Pictures will conduct
their quarterly meeting at the Studio on the twenty-third and
twenty-fourth of this month. Rumor has it that Academy Award–
winning producer Billy Barnett will host a dinner party at his
house that Saturday evening for the attendees and invited guests.

"You told me yourself, Stone's on the board, right?" Petry said.

Nico nodded.

"What better way to humiliate him than to destroy his mother's precious paintings in front of all his business associates and friends?"

"About that."

Petry tensed. "Is there a problem?"

"Quite the opposite." Nico explained what Simon had meant about the list, while covering up how long Nico had known about it.

Petry let out a laugh. "That's fucking fantastic. So, the paintings we're going to rip apart are extra special to him?"

"At least one of them will be. The other two will depend on what they can get their hands on with the new timeline." Nico could see his boss's mood start to sour. "But they'll all be by his mother and will still matter to him."

"You damn well better be right."

Instead of being elated at getting an additional half million from Petry, Simon felt uneasy.

He'd hedged about the delivery of the second painting. Barring a disaster, Benji should be handing it over to Simon on Wednesday. A third Stone would be tricky but doable. And an L.A. delivery wasn't a problem, obviously.

What bothered Simon was Petry's insistence on an accelerated timeline and the man's total disregard of the art itself.

Whatever Petry's intentions were, Simon knew they couldn't be good. And while Simon might not have been a scrupulous art dealer, he had nothing but respect for the art itself. Which meant he very much wanted to know what Petry's intentions were.

He called his PI friend, to see if he could find anything out, thinking that would ease the knot in his stomach. It didn't.

There was one other thing he could do, a just-in-case measure. It would mean spending a bit of the cash Petry was paying him, but with the man paying him double now, the hit wouldn't be as painful.

It took five rings before Rudy Morgan answered Simon's call with a distracted, "Yeah?"

"Rudy? Simon Duchamp."

"Simon, long time no talk. I was beginning to think you didn't need me anymore." Rudy was the best forger on the West Coast, possibly on the entire continent.

"Not true. I just haven't had any jobs requiring your services, that's all."

"I take it that's changed."

"It has."

"I'm listening."

"Are you familiar with the American painter Matilda Stone?"

"Sure. Great eye. Beautiful work. New York City settings."

"That's the one. I'm in need of a few of her pieces."

"How many is a few?"

"Three. Can you do them?"

"I can do her style, but it'll depend on when you need them."

"Friday, ten a.m."

Rudy laughed.

"I'm not kidding."

"Simon, you've always been a good customer, but I'm going to have to pass on this one."

"I'll pay a premium."

"Good for you. That doesn't change the fact that I couldn't even get one done in that time."

"Here's the thing. They don't have to be perfect. They just have to be good enough to pass a quick look from someone who knows nothing about art."

There was a beat of silence before Rudy said, "What are you playing at?"

"You know I can't go into details about a client. But suffice it to say this one won't even notice they aren't original."

"He might not figure it out right away, but at some point he would, wouldn't he?"

"I don't think so. But even if he does, he'll never know you had anything to do with it."

"What kind of a premium are we talking about?"

Simon smiled. "Twenty thousand."

"All together? Or each?"

"Each."

The line went quiet for several seconds as Rudy thought it through.

Finally, the forger said, "Drying's going to be an issue."

"You can use whatever method it takes to have them ready in time. As long as they look close enough to the originals, it doesn't matter."

If Simon determined he needed to use the forgeries, then on top of the million Petry was going to pay him, he could also sell the originals for more than he'd pay Rudy. He even had a buyer in mind. Thinking that way, sixty thousand for a few forgeries would be a good investment.

"You send me the info on the originals right away, and you got yourself a deal."

"What would you say to having the originals to work from?"

"I would say that would be the most helpful thing you could do."

"I'll bring the first one to you tomorrow."

"Someday, I want you to tell me what this is all about."

"I will, and thank you, Rudy. I knew I could count on you."

CHAPTER 24

———⊙———

Stone and Monica returned from a relaxing weekend in Taos to the Lees' place at lunchtime. The only hiccups in their time away were Monica not yet hearing back from Tristan Williams, and Dino reporting that the Santa Fe police still considered Joshua Paskota's death an accident.

Stone had several messages from Joan and spent the rest of the afternoon catching up with work.

When he finally finished, the sun was setting. He could hear Monica swimming laps outside, so he donned his swimsuit and went out to join her.

"I was beginning to think you'd never show up," she said, after he dove in.

"Won't happen again."

"Promise?" she asked impishly.

He turned his attention to the sky. "My, what a lovely sunset."

She splashed him. "I thought as much."

In retaliation, he dove under, grabbed one of her feet, and pulled her down with him. They tussled playfully before resurfacing, their bodies tight to each other.

"This would be a lot more fun without bathing suits," she said.

"I'm game if you are. As long as you don't mind giving the Secret Service a show."

"Tempting, but I'll pass."

They kissed with the passion of lovers who truly enjoyed each other's company, then leaned their foreheads against each other.

Nearly out of breath, she whispered, "Maybe we *should* put on a show."

"If you insist."

As he moved to kiss her again, Martha appeared poolside. "Mr. Barrington, Miss Reyes, dinner is almost ready. Would you like it inside or out here?"

"Here?" Stone said to Monica.

"Please."

"Outside," he told Martha.

"Very good." She retreated into the house.

Monica sighed. "It looks like we don't have any time for—"

Stone slipped a hand under the back side of her bikini bottom. "Are you sure about that?"

As if it took every ounce of strength, she pushed him away and swam for the stairs.

They dined on a meal of chicken mole and grilled peppers paired with a bottle of Marian's Vineyard Old Vine Zinfandel from California.

When they finished, Martha asked if they would like dessert.

"I don't think I could eat another bite," Monica said. "I haven't had mole that good in years. It was just like my *abuela's*."

Martha smiled in pleasure.

"I agree with Monica," Stone said. "Though I can't comment on her grandmother's version."

Martha's grin doubled. "May I take your plates?"

"Please."

As she began gathering the dishes, a phone buzzed on one of the deck chairs.

"That's me," Monica said. She retrieved her phone and looked at the screen. "It's Tristan Williams." She accepted the call. "Hello? . . . Yes, this is she . . . Hi, Tristan. Thank you for calling me back." She turned on the speaker and retook her seat.

The voice that came out of the phone was male and guarded. "What can I help you with?"

"I was given your number by someone who thought you could help me."

"Who's that?"

"Joshua Paskota."

Silence on the other end, then, "He's dead."

"I'm aware. He was helping me with an investigation."

"What kind of investigation?"

Monica eyed Stone before she responded, "I work for an insurance company, and am looking into several potential art thefts."

They heard movement on the line and then three beeps.

"He hung up," Monica said.

"Try him again."

She did, but instead of ringing, she was sent straight to voicemail.

After the beep, she said, "This is Monica Reyes again. Please call me back. I really need to talk to you." She hung up. "He must have turned off his phone. If he doesn't return my call . . ."

"Wait here." Stone went into the house and retrieved his phone. After retaking his seat, he said, "What's Tristan's number?"

Monica brought Tristan's info up on her phone.

Stone called his friend Bob Cantor. Bob was a former NYPD officer who'd made a lucrative post-force career as a security technology expert and private investigator.

"Hello?"

"Bob, it's Stone."

"Hi, Stone. Long time no talk."

"Sorry about that. I've been a little busy lately."

"I heard about the mess with the Russians. Glad you came out of it okay."

"You and me both. Listen, I need your help with a phone number. I don't know if it's a cell or a landline, but I'd like to know where it's located."

"Sure. Give it to me."

Stone did so.

"L.A. area code," Bob said. "Of course, that doesn't mean that's where he is."

"Is this something you can look into right away?"

"I was just about to settle in with the new season of *Only Murders in the Building*, but that can wait."

"I appreciate it. How long do you think this will take?"

"Depends. Could be a few minutes, could be a few hours. Also, if it's a burner, chances are whoever you're trying to find will have already dumped it."

"Do what you can, Bob, and call me when you have something. Don't worry about the time."

"Consider me on the job."

Stone hung up and lifted the wine bottle. "Another glass?"

"How about a shower and change of clothes first. It's getting a little chilly."

They relocated to the guest suite, where they did more than merely soap each other's backs.

After toweling off, Stone checked his phone. He had a missed call and a text from Bob, the latter reading: Call me.

Stone did so.

"The number is for a cell phone that belongs to someone named Tristan Williams," Bob said. "I have an address for him in Echo Park. That's near downtown, next to Dodger Stadium."

"Were you able to get a location on the actual phone?"

"The most recent location I could get was from an hour ago, on Melrose Avenue in the Fairfax District."

Stone knew the area. It was near West Hollywood and was a fifteen-minute drive from the Arrington, depending on traffic.

"I'll text his home address and where I got the hit," Bob said. "The latter won't be exact, mind you, but should be close."

"Thanks, Bob. Please send an invoice to Joan."

"I already have."

Stone hung up and told Monica what he'd learned.

"Well, I guess I know where I'm heading next," she said.

"When would you leave?"

"Too late to get a plane out tonight, so tomorrow." She opened her phone and began scrolling for flights.

"May I make a suggestion?"

"Sure."

"I need to be in Los Angeles in a few days, but I can just as easily leave tomorrow. Why don't you fly with me?"

"You have a plane?"

"I do."

"It's not one of those little prop planes, is it? If so, thank you very much for the offer, but I'm afraid I'll have to pass."

"You have an issue with prop planes?"

"My first and last experience in one involved a thunderstorm and a very hard landing."

"That sounds more like your pilot was unprepared than a problem with the plane itself."

"True. The pilot was my boyfriend when we took off and my ex the moment my feet were back on the ground."

"Then I understand your reluctance, but to ease your mind, my plane is a Gulfstream G-500 jet."

She crossed her arms and reappraised him. "Have I told you how handy you are to have around?"

They arrived at the Santa Fe airport at nine a.m. and found Faith performing her preflight inspection.

"How was Roswell?" Stone asked.

"Paradise, if you believe in aliens."

Stone introduced her to Monica, and the two women shook hands.

"Will you be wanting the left seat for takeoff?" Faith asked Stone.

"If you don't mind."

"Why don't you two get on board. I'll have Dean take care of your luggage."

"Dean?" Stone asked.

"He's our flight attendant today."

Faith oversaw the hiring of whatever crew was needed.

Once Stone and Monica were inside the aircraft, Monica said, "What was all that about the left seat?"

"The pilot sits in the left seat, and the copilot sits in the right."

"You're going to be piloting the flight?"

"Just the takeoff and landing. Faith will handle the in-between. And before you ask, I have been flying for many years, and have more than the required hours doing so in this very aircraft."

"All the same, I'm beginning to wonder if I made a mistake accepting your offer."

Just then, a trim young man in a blue suit entered.

"You must be Dean," Stone said.

"I am."

Stone gestured to Monica. "This is my friend, Monica Reyes. She'll probably want a glass of champagne before we take off."

"Make that two," Monica said.

Stone rejoined Monica in the cabin shortly after takeoff.

"That was very smooth," she said. "I should never have doubted you."

"I'll forgive you this once, on the grounds of your previous experience."

"You have my gratitude."

Dean brought them an array of cheeses and fruits, and two glasses of champagne.

"Do you know where I'll find the Hertz counter at LAX? I've arranged for a rental."

"That's going to be a problem. We're not going to LAX."

She sat up. "I thought you said we were."

"I said we were going to Los Angeles, and we are. Just not LAX."

"Then where?"

"Van Nuys Airport. It caters to private jets. I used to use Santa Monica Airport, but they've shortened the runway and are planning on closing the airport entirely in a few years."

"Doesn't LAX allow jets like yours?"

"They do, but they are also one of the busiest airports in the world. We could find ourselves endlessly circling the city as we wait for clearance to land."

"I wonder if I can transfer my reservation to Van Nuys. Does Hertz even have an office there?"

"Whether they do or not is of no matter. A driver will pick us up."

"That's very kind, but I don't want to put you out."

"Where do you want to go?"

"I have a friend who lives in Altadena. I was going to stay with her."

"You know, you're welcome to stay at the Arrington with me."

"You're not tired of me yet?"

"Not even close." He leaned over and kissed her.

"Good. Keep it that way." She returned his affection.

CHAPTER 25

———◎———

They deplaned in Van Nuys, and Dean transferred their luggage to a waiting Porsche Cayenne SUV. The Arrington had a fleet of them for VIP guest use.

"Good to see you again, Mr. Barrington," the driver said as Stone and Monica climbed in. "Straight to the Arrington?"

"Please."

Monica was in for yet another surprise when, instead of being dropped off at the front of the hotel, the Porsche stopped at the entrance to a large house behind the main building.

"What is this?" she asked.

"My L.A. home," Stone said.

"Your home is in the middle of a hotel?"

"This property was inherited by my late wife when her first husband, Vance Calder, died."

"The actor?"

"The very same. When Arrington passed, Peter and I decided

to turn the land into a hotel, with a home built specifically for me."

"You *own* the Arrington."

"Along with Peter and a company run by my friend Mike Freeman."

Before Stone could grab the door handle, it swung open from the inside.

Dino smiled out at them. "I thought I heard voices."

Monica looked at Stone. "Your butler?"

"Fortunately, no. This is my friend Dino Bacchetti. Dino, this is Monica Reyes. Dino would make a lousy butler."

"I concur," Dino said.

"Dino Bacchetti?" Monica asked. "Why do I know that name?"

"Probably because he's the New York City commissioner of police."

"That right! I've seen you on the news. You look better in person."

"Thank you, I think."

Stone put a hand to the side of his mouth and stage-whispered, "We try not to compliment him too much. Goes straight to his head."

"Are you coming in or not?" Dino asked.

"I thought you weren't arriving until the day before the board meeting," Stone said, walking in and proceeding into the living room.

"You can thank the king of Sweden," Dino said.

"I don't actually know the king of Sweden."

"Neither do I. He was supposed to visit the city this week. Tour around, see a few shows, shake hands with the mayor, things like that. There was talk that Holly might show up, too, until that nonsense with North Korea. But the king caught the flu and canceled his plans. Suddenly, my calendar was free."

"His misfortune was our gain."

"Something like that."

Stone said, "Is Viv here, too?"

"Not yet. She's in Luxembourg, or Brussels. I can't keep her schedule straight. She's flies in late tonight." He moved to the bar. "Can I get either of you a drink?"

"Thanks, but nothing for me," Monica said. "I have somewhere I need to go."

"Leaving already?" Stone said.

"I want to go by Tristan Williams's place and see if he's home. Oh, wait. I still need a car. I suppose the hotel can help with that?"

"I'll arrange for you to use one of the hotel's vehicles."

"That would be wonderful. Thank you. I'd like to freshen up first. Which way is our room?"

"Follow me."

He led her to the master suite. "Your bathroom is on that side." He pointed at the door.

"My bathroom?"

"Mine is over there," he said, pointing at the door on the opposite wall.

"Two bathrooms. How convenient."

"I think so."

He left her to do what she needed and returned to Dino, who handed him a glass of Knob Creek. Dino held up his own drink. "Welcome to Los Angeles."

"Glad to be here."

Dino nodded toward the back of the house where the master suite was located. "I distinctly remember you saying something about spending time with Holly."

"I did. Twelve hours, give or take."

"The North Korea thing?"

"The North Korea thing."

"I applaud your speed at finding a replacement."

"Monica's not a replacement. We happened to hit it off."

"Conveniently, right after your previous arrangement fell apart."

"Not *right* after. There was a day and a half in between."

"That makes it all better."

"That reminds me."

"What reminds you?"

Stone ignored him and went to the house phone. He was just finishing up his call to arrange a car for Monica when she reentered the living room.

"There should be a golf cart out front," Stone said.

"I think I'll need something more robust than that to get to Echo Park."

"The sass is strong with this one," Dino said. "I like her."

"If you two are through," Stone said. "The golf cart will take you to where a vehicle better suited for your needs will be waiting."

She smiled and gave him a quick kiss. "I appreciate it."

"How long will you be gone?"

"Not sure, but I should be back in time for dinner. I hope you don't get too bored without me."

"I'll soldier on."

"And I'll make sure he doesn't get into too much trouble," Dino said.

"Has that worked in the past?" she asked.

"Not as often as I would hope."

"Good luck, then. Work calls, so I'm off." She and Stone kissed again, and she headed outside.

"What kind of business is she in?" Dino asked.

"Insurance investigator, though currently unemployed."

"I feel like there's a critical piece of information missing."

"Perceptive as ever."

Stone called Peter and found out both he and Ben Bacchetti were free for lunch. Stone and Dino met them at the Centurion Pictures cantina, where their sons had already claimed a table on the exterior patio. Billy Barnett was with them.

The boys rose and hugged their fathers. Then Billy shook their hands.

"I hope you don't mind that I tagged along," Billy said.

"That was my doing," Peter said. "He and I were meeting when you called."

"I don't mind at all," Stone said. "Always happy to see you, Billy."

They ordered and their meals arrived soon after.

To Billy, Peter said, "You should tell my dad what happened."

"Nothing serious, I hope," Stone said.

"A bit serious," Billy conceded. "I purchased a painting at auction that was to be delivered yesterday. The delivery van was ambushed and robbed before it arrived."

"Was anyone injured?"

Billy shook his head. "According to the two men in the vehicle, the thieves used a knockout spray that rendered them unconscious."

"That sounds familiar," Stone said.

Billy nodded. "I was thinking the same thing."

"You're talking about the spray the Russians used on Carly in New York," Dino said.

"Do you think the thieves were with the mob?" Ben asked.

"No way to know," Stone said, "but I doubt the Russians have a monopoly on the stuff."

"Billy, you said things could have been a lot worse," Peter said.

"True. The robbers stopped the van by forcing it down a road blocked by a fire."

"Fire?" Stone said, Monica's investigation immediately coming to mind.

"A guy in a uniform sprayed them before they could turn the van around, stole the painting, and left. Luckily, I got there before the fire spread too far. I called nine-one-one and got the delivery guys out of there."

"Do the police have any idea who did it?" Dino asked.

"None. I've asked Mike Freeman to look into it, too."

"That's a good idea," Stone said. "I'm sure the painting will turn up soon."

"I hope you're right. I bought it for you."

"For me?"

"It's one of your mother's. I was going to give it to you at the party Saturday night."

"Billy, I don't know what to say."

"Nothing to say until I get it back."

"Which picture was it?"

"*Summer at Sheep Meadow.*"

Stone stilled for a moment. The painting was one of several his mother had painted of Central Park, but that wasn't the reason for his reaction. In the picture was a family on a picnic. *His* family. The three of them had featured in a handful of her paintings, and while he loved everything she'd created, those were the pieces he cherished the most.

"I've been looking for that one for a long time."

"So I've heard. I also heard the boy is you."

"It is. I hadn't realized the painting was up for sale."

"You're not the only one who has people keeping an eye out for her work."

CHAPTER 26

Monica found Tristan Williams's place off Echo Park Avenue, on the eastern slope of a narrow valley. The house itself sat at the midpoint of the slope, accessed by a steep set of concrete stairs.

When her first knock went unanswered, she thought no one was home, but when she knocked again, she heard movement inside.

The guy who opened the door was either half asleep or high or both. His eyes drooped, and his long, disheveled hair stuck out from his head like a halo. He stared at her without saying anything.

"I'm looking for Tristan Williams," Monica said.

"Who?"

"Tristan Williams. I was told he lives here."

His eyes scrunched together momentarily, then he nodded. "Right. Tristan. Yeah, he lives here."

"Is he home?"

"No idea." He turned around and yelled Tristan's name. When there was no response, he shrugged. "He must be out."

"Is he at work?"

"Might be."

"Do you know where that is?"

"Not a clue."

"Do you know the name of the company he works for?"

"Sorry, this is my girlfriend's place. She and Tristan are room-mates."

"Can I talk to her?"

"She's not here, either."

"I see. Okay, then, sorry to have bothered you."

"It's cool." He shut the door.

Monica considered leaving a note, but Tristan had already made it clear he wasn't interested in talking to her. Seeing him face-to-face might be the only chance she had to find out what he knew.

She decided to check out the area where Stone's contact said Tristan's phone had last pinged. It took her forty minutes to drive to Melrose Avenue and another ten to find an open parking space.

The block was mostly filled with clothing shops. She ducked into each and asked if Tristan Williams worked there, but no one knew him.

She headed down Melrose, extending her search. A few blocks from where she started, she stopped and stared. Across the street was the Los Angeles location for Duchamp Galleries. That seemed too much of a coincidence to be mere chance. She crossed over and went inside.

A handful of customers browsed the artwork, while three gallery employees hovered nearby. At the back was a desk where a fourth employee sat, leafing through a magazine. There were no customers near him.

He looked up as she approached. He was impeccably dressed and appeared to be in his late twenties. His gaze seemed to be assessing her, like he was trying to determine if she could afford to shop there.

"Good afternoon. How may I help you?"

"I'm looking for someone."

"Oh?" he said, his tone turning dismissive.

"Do you have someone who works here named Tristan Williams?"

He blinked. "I'm Tristan."

She smiled and held out her hand. "I can't believe I found you. I'm Monica."

He hesitated before taking her hand.

"We talked yesterday." She laid her business card on the desk.

He looked at her, seemingly having no idea what she was talking about. Then he picked up the card, sucked in a surprised breath, and whispered, "You can't be here."

"I just need a few minutes of your time."

"I have nothing to say to you."

"Please. It's important."

He held her card out to her. "I'm sorry. Take this and leave."

"What time do you get off work?" she asked, not taking the card.

"It doesn't matter. I told you I'm not talking to you."

"I'll be at the bar at the Hollywood Roosevelt Hotel from eight until ten. I'd appreciate it if you could join me."

"Not going to happen."

"I understand, but if you change your mind, remember the Roosevelt, eight until ten." Monica turned and walked out, leaving her business card behind.

Dalton was starting to wish he'd stayed at the Verdugo Royale Hotel instead of tagging along with Simon to his gallery. They'd been there for over three hours already. Simon had been busying himself on a computer in a back office the whole time, doing God knew what.

Dalton had occupied the only other chair in the room, filling the time by answering a few work e-mails and playing Candy Crush on his phone. But there was only so long he could stare at his screen.

Deciding he could use some fresh air, he pushed himself out of his chair and said, "I'll be back. Don't go anywhere without me."

The only sign Simon gave that he'd heard him was a low grunt.

Outside the office was a larger space that made up the rest of the employees-only area of the gallery. It was broken into three sections: a break area, a storage area for artwork, and a workstation, where at that moment a gallery employee was packing something into a box.

"Any good places to eat around here?" Dalton asked.

It took the woman a moment to realize Dalton was talking to her. "Oh, um, there's a couple coffee shops that have food, I think. If you go down the block and around the corner, there's a NORMS."

"What's NORMS?"

"A diner."

That would do. "Which way?"

"Go out the front door and turn right. At the next corner go right again."

"Thanks."

A pair of walls separated the employees-only area from the showroom. They overlapped so that there was a passageway between them, instead of a door between the two parts of the store. Which meant when Dalton left the employees-only area, he wasn't immediately visible.

That turned out to be a very good thing, because while he was still hidden, he heard a familiar woman's voice. He paused, trying to figure out who it was.

That sounds like—

He shook his head. No way. It couldn't be her. To be sure, he eased forward and peeked around the dividing wall, then cursed to himself.

He'd been right. It was Monica Reyes.

She was talking with one of the store employees, who was holding out a business card to her. She didn't appear interested in taking it, however.

She said something else. Dalton didn't catch it all, but he was pretty sure the last two words were "until ten." Then she started to turn toward him.

He jerked out of sight and pressed himself against the wall. He heard her steps heading toward the exit, then the sound of the door opening.

To be safe, he waited a full minute before peeking into the showroom again. She was gone.

He looked at the employee she'd talked to. The guy was seated now, but was staring toward the front of the store, his expression agitated.

"Dammit," Dalton whispered. Fucking Monica Reyes.

Whatever she'd been doing here, it couldn't be good. Then another thought hit him. What if the guy said something to Simon?

Dammit. Dammit. Dammit.

As much as he'd been hoping otherwise, she was a complication that wasn't going away, and if he didn't head her off at the pass, he'd be screwed.

He returned to Simon's office.

"We might have a problem."

Simon stopped typing and looked at Dalton. "What kind of problem?"

"You remember that employee I fired who was poking into areas she shouldn't have?"

"I don't recall you saying anything about anyone poking around where she shouldn't. I do recall you mentioning that you had to fire an employee that was a pain in your ass."

"That's the one."

Simon studied him silently before saying, "Are you saying she knows about us?"

"Nah. She just thinks there's someone stealing paintings and covering them up as accidents."

Simon gawked. "She's been looking into the work we've taken?"

"I mean, yeah, but—but not anymore. That's why I fired her. She's harmless now."

Simon narrowed his eyes. Dalton may have fired her, but

from the way he was stammering, it would be obvious to anyone that she was anything but harmless. "You're bringing her up now because . . . ?"

"I saw her in the gallery, talking to one of your employees."

"You're kidding me, right?"

"I wish."

"Which one?"

"Which one what?"

"Which *employee* was she talking to?"

"Oh, the skinny guy with the perfect haircut. He was sitting at the desk."

"Tristan?"

"How would I know his name?"

"Did you hear what they said?"

"A word or two, but nothing that made any sense."

Simon took a deep breath. "So, let me make sure I've got this right. One of your employees was looking into pieces that my people have obtained, and now she's come into *my* gallery." He cocked his head. "Hold on. Was she aware of the anonymous tip?"

"She might have been."

Simon groaned and looked at the ceiling.

"But I told you I fired her," Dalton said quickly. "We don't need to worry about her."

"You also started this conversation by saying we might have a problem. So, do we or don't we?"

Dalton had no answer for that.

Simon stood. "Show me who she talked to. I want to be sure." They went into the showroom.

Dalton pointed the guy out and whispered, "That's him."

Simon clucked his tongue against the roof of his mouth

several times, then motioned for Dalton to follow him back into the employee area.

"Are you going to talk to him?" Dalton asked.

"Not yet."

"He might be the guy who sent in the tip."

"He's not. That person has already been taken care of."

"Really? How?"

"*That* is none of your business."

"Right, okay. But what are we going to do about Monica?"

"That's her name?"

"Yeah. Monica Reyes."

"*You* are going to tell me everything you know about her, then you're going to take a walk, while Phillip and I figure out how to clean up your mess."

CHAPTER 27

After lunch, Stone and Dino met with Ben in his office to go over the agenda for the board meeting, so it was nearing four p.m. by the time they returned to the Arrington.

They found Monica in Stone's private pool, floating on a raft.

She shaded her eyes and smiled. "I was wondering when you were coming back."

"We would have returned sooner if I'd known you were waiting. Can I interest anyone in a vodka gimlet?" Stone had made a pitcher before leaving for the studio that should be perfectly chilled by now.

"That sounds divine," Monica said.

"What she said," Dino replied.

"Coming right up."

By the time Stone made it back with the drinks, Monica had

left her raft and was sitting at the nearby umbrella-shaded table with Dino.

"Any luck with Tristan?" Stone asked.

"He wasn't home, so I went to the last place your friend said his phone had pinged. You're never going to believe where I found him."

"In an art gallery?"

She looked at him, surprised. "How did you know?"

"It seemed a logical leap."

"I'll have to give you that one." Her disappointment turned into a devilish sneer. "But I bet you can't guess the name of the gallery."

"Duchamp Gallery." It was the first gallery name that came to mind, only because it was the last one he'd visited.

She crossed her arms. "I'm never playing this game with you again."

"You mean I'm right?"

"You are, but don't you dare try to rub it in."

Dino looked back and forth between them. "I feel like I'm missing a crucial piece of information."

"Monica and I met at the Duchamp Gallery in Santa Fe. If memory serves, she was there to meet a contact for her investigation."

"That's correct," she said.

"The art theft ring you were telling me about?" Dino said.

Monica nodded.

"What happened to your contact there?" Dino asked.

"Remember that fatal car crash I asked you to look into?" Stone said.

"Yeah."

"That's what happened to him."

"Now I'm starting to get it."

"What did they say when you talked to them?" Monica asked.

"That they didn't suspect foul play. But maybe I should suggest they take a closer look."

"Not a bad idea," Stone said.

"Did he work at the Santa Fe gallery?"

"No idea," Monica said. "He only said he'd contact me at the opening night of the exhibit. I assumed he would have been just another guest, but given where Tristan works, maybe I was wrong."

"I'll check that, too," Dino said.

"What happened when you found Tristan?" Stone asked.

"As soon as he realized who I was, he told me to leave."

"Not happy to see you, no doubt."

"More like terrified, I think. It was like he couldn't get me out the door fast enough. I did try to make an alternative meetup." She explained about telling Tristan she would wait for him at the Hollywood Roosevelt Hotel that evening.

"Did he agree?"

"No, but I made sure he knew I'd be there, if he changes his mind. Hopefully, he'll show."

"Would you mind some company?"

"He might get scared off if I'm not alone."

"I can sit nearby. He'll never know we're together."

She considered it for a moment, then nodded. "Actually, that's a great idea."

"Dino, you've never been to the Roosevelt, have you?"

"I haven't."

"You want to join us?"

"Let me check my social calendar." He took a sip of his gimlet. "You're in luck. My evening is free."

"It's settled, then."

"Thank you both," Monica said. She took a sip of her gimlet. "That was my afternoon. What kind of trouble did you two get up to while I was away?"

"We had lunch with our sons, at Centurion Pictures."

"I bet she'd be interested in what Billy told us," Dino said.

"Billy who?" Monica asked.

"Billy Barnett, Peter's producer," Stone said. "He joined us for lunch, too."

"And what did he tell you?"

"He recently purchased a painting by my mother. It was to be delivered yesterday, but the delivery van was intercepted en route, and the painting stolen."

"That's horrible. But that's not the MO of the people I've been investigating."

"I haven't told you the pertinent part yet."

"Please, go on."

"The thieves redirected the van onto a road that was blocked off by a wall of fire."

"Fire?" That had her attention.

"When the van stopped, the robbers sprayed them with a knockout gas, took the painting, and left. The fire had begun to spread to the surrounding brush by the time Billy found them. If the fire department hadn't reacted so quickly, dozens of homes could have been destroyed."

"You said Billy Barnett is the owner of the painting?"

"Correct."

She thought for a few moments. "I don't think he's insured by Vitale."

"You know all Vitale's customers?" Dino asked.

"The ones with expensive art pieces, I do. I'll ask around and see what I can find out. Thanks for the tip."

"Leaving early?"

Tristan jerked in surprise, then glanced over at Mr. Duchamp's ever-present bodyguard, Phillip.

"My shift ended at seven, so I'm actually late." It was 7:45.

"I see. My mistake. Heading home then?"

Tristan nodded.

"Have a nice night."

"Thanks."

Tristan exited the gallery through the rear door that led into the small parking lot behind the building.

As he climbed into his Prius, his gaze flicked back to the gallery, half expecting to see Phillip standing outside, watching him. But the bodyguard wasn't there.

Quit overthinking, he told himself.

Even if Mr. Duchamp had seen Monica Reyes come into the gallery, there was no way he would have known who she was. And Mr. Duchamp had not been in the main gallery when she visited. Tristan was sure about that.

He pulled onto the street and headed east toward his place in Echo Park, anxiety burning a hole in his stomach.

"Dammit, Joshua."

What had he been thinking, giving the woman Tristan's number?

It's not like Tristan had firsthand knowledge of anything.

Tristan had met Joshua more than a year ago, when Joshua had come to the shop to pick up something. He hadn't worked for any of the galleries but did what he'd called special projects for Mr. Duchamp.

They'd struck up a friendship, and over time, Joshua told Tristan about Mr. Duchamp's illegal activities. He said his job was to deliver stolen artwork to buyers.

The stories had been riveting, but the truth was, Tristan had never fully believed him. That is, not until Joshua died and something he'd said began playing on repeat in Tristan's head. "If I turn up dead someday, it'll be because Mr. D doesn't want me around."

Tristan had laughed then, like it was some kind of joke, but he wasn't laughing now.

"Shit."

He swerved into the left-turn lane.

He'd stop by the Hollywood Roosevelt Hotel and tell the woman enough to ease his mind, then never talk to her again.

He could do that much for his dead friend.

Stone, Monica, and Dino dined at Koi on La Cienega, then made their way to the Roosevelt, where a pair of valets opened the doors.

"Do me a favor," Stone said to the one who took his keys. "Keep it close." He slipped the man a hundred-dollar bill.

"No problem, sir."

Stone joined Dino and Monica on the sidewalk.

"What time do you have?" she asked.

Stone checked his watch. "Ten to eight."

"I doubt he'll be here yet."

"If he comes at all," Dino said.

"I'll go in first," she said. "Wish me luck."

"It'll be fine," Stone said.

She crossed her fingers, then walked into the hotel.

They gave her a five-minute head start, then went inside.

"Wow," Dino said as they stepped into the chandelier-lit lobby. "Not bad. Reminds me of old Hollywood."

"This *is* old Hollywood. The first Academy Awards were held here."

"In this room?"

"In one of the ballrooms, I believe."

"I guess that makes more sense. Be strange if someone was trying to check in while Clark Gable was getting an Oscar."

"Your deductive reasoning never fails to amaze me."

They made their way to the bar, took the table two away from Monica's, and signaled for the waiter.

Phillip watched Tristan through the spy hole in the gallery's rear door. As soon as the Prius pulled out of the lot, Phillip jogged outside. After seeing which way Tristan turned on Melrose, he hopped into the town car and took up pursuit.

Tristan headed east, but instead of continuing to his home in Echo Park, he stopped in Hollywood and parked down a side street near Grauman's Chinese Theatre.

Phillip drove past him and found an empty spot half a block down. Watching through the rear window, he saw Tristan exit his car and start walking toward Hollywood Boulevard. He hopped out and followed.

Tristan was a half block from the boulevard when he turned into a parking lot, vanishing from sight. Phillip quickened his pace and caught a brief glimpse of Tristan right before he disappeared again, this time through the entrance of the Hollywood Roosevelt Hotel.

Phillip could wait until the kid reemerged, but he needed to find out what Tristan was up to.

He entered the hotel and paused long enough to scan the lobby and determine Tristan wasn't present. If he'd gone to one of the rooms, then Phillip wasn't going to find him, but that wasn't the only place Tristan could be.

Phillip approached one of the hotel employees. "Does this place have a bar?"

CHAPTER 28

———◦———

The moment Tristan stepped into the bar's entrance, he almost turned around and left. The only thing that stopped him was that Monica had already spotted him and was waving him over to her table.

He swore under his breath and joined her.

"Thank you for coming. Please, have a seat."

"I—I can only give you five minutes. That's it."

"I'll take it."

He reluctantly sat.

"Something to drink?" she asked. "My treat?"

"Um, thank you. Wine."

"Any preference?"

He shook his head.

She asked the waiter to bring him a glass of chardonnay.

"How long have you worked at Duchamp Gallery?"

"Why is that important?"

"It isn't. I'm just asking."

"Oh. Sorry. Uh, almost two years."

"Do you enjoy it?"

"It's okay, I guess. I like meeting the artists and talking to them about their work."

"What about your job don't you like?"

Tristan was saved from answering by the return of the waiter with his wine. "Thanks," he said, then gulped down half in one go.

"Are you all right?" Monica asked.

"I'm fine. Why?"

She looked pointedly at his glass.

"I—I was thirsty."

She nodded as if that was an acceptable answer, then her expression softened. "I should have said this first. I'm sorry for your loss."

"My loss?"

"Joshua Paskota. I assume he was your friend."

"He was."

"I was supposed to talk to him in Santa Fe, but I didn't get the chance before the accident."

Tristan huffed. "Accident. Right."

"You know something about it?"

He hadn't realized he'd said that out loud. He shook his head. "No, nothing."

"You know, he gave me your number because he thought you could help me."

"He actually told you that?"

She pulled a piece of paper out of her purse and showed it to him. It was a note that included Tristan's name and number. Tristan recognized Joshua's handwriting.

"When you called me, you said this was about an art theft?"

"Several actually. I believe they are being carried out by the same group. Anything you may know would be a great help."

He downed the rest of his wine and glanced toward the bar's entrance to gather his thoughts.

At first, he didn't notice the man sitting on a chair outside the bar, but then the man shifted his position, drawing Tristan's attention.

It was Phillip.

"Why don't you start at the beginning?" Monica said. "When was the first time—"

Tristan shot to his feet. "I'm sorry. I shouldn't have come."

He scanned for an alternate way out, but there was none. Head down, he walked briskly to the exit, then hurried out of the hotel.

As soon as he was outside, he broke into a run and didn't glance back until he reached his car.

But before he could open the door, Phillip clamped down on his shoulder and whirled him around. Tristan would have opened his mouth to scream, but Phillip's fist smashed into his face before a sound could leave his lips.

Monica watched Tristan all but sprint from the bar, then she turned to Stone and Dino. "What happened?"

"I've seen that look before," Dino said. "He was spooked."

"Was it something I said?"

"Everything you said spooked him," Stone said. "But I don't think that's why he left."

"Neither do I," Dino said.

"What then?" she asked.

Stone tapped Dino on the arm and stood. "How about we find out?"

"I'm coming, too," Monica said.

After dropping money on their tables, they exited the bar. Tristan was nowhere in sight.

"You check the exit onto Hollywood Boulevard," Stone said to Dino. "We'll take the parking lot."

They parted ways in the lobby.

When Stone and Monica reached the passenger drop-off area, Stone caught the attention of a valet. "Did a guy just come through here? Late twenties, thin, a few inches shorter than me."

"Yeah. He ran that way." The valet nodded toward the street.

"He wasn't parked here?"

"If he was, he left without his car."

Stone gave him a ten. "Thanks."

Before he and Monica could take a step, the valet said, "There was a guy chasing him, too."

"What guy?"

"A big one. Wore a suit and moved great for his size. Didn't see his face, though."

"Which way did they go when they reached the street?"

"To the right, away from the boulevard."

Stone and Monica raced from the parking lot and turned down the sidewalk. Parked cars filled nearly every available spot for as far as they could see, but the sidewalks were empty.

At the end of the block, they stopped. Stone scanned both ways down the intersecting road but saw no sign of either Tristan or the other man.

Stone's phone vibrated. It was Dino.

"I'm betting you didn't find him," Stone said.

"Did you?"

"No, but the valet told us he came this way. He also said Tristan was chased out of the parking lot by what he called a big man."

"And do we know who this man is?"

"We do not."

"I see two cameras from where I'm standing. I'll bet you there's some in the parking lot. May I suggest a visit with hotel security?"

"Excellent idea."

"I'm sorry," the nighttime security manager said. "Without a warrant, I can't allow anyone to view the footage."

"Even if a person might be in danger?" Stone asked.

"In danger how?"

"He was chased from your parking lot by someone. When we looked for them, they were both gone. Keep in mind, we were no more than a minute behind them."

"A minute is a long time."

"It is. Which is why we are concerned. A lot could have happened to our friend in that time."

She grimaced, unsure what to do.

"If something does happen to him," Stone said, "the police will find out his attacker chased him from here and will wonder why you didn't report it."

Her discomfort grew but she still didn't relent.

"As a member of law enforcement, I can confirm what my friend has said," Dino chimed in.

"You're LAPD?" she asked.

"New York City."

"He's the commissioner," Stone said. "That means he's the top cop."

"But not here," she said.

"That's correct," Dino said. "But I know the top cop here. Would you like me to call him?"

"Oh, for heaven's sake," Monica said. "A man is in trouble. Please, just let us look at your video."

The woman sighed. "Follow me."

She took them to a room where another security guard sat behind a desk, looking at several monitors.

"I need you to show us the main parking lot cam from about ten minutes ago," the head of security said.

"You mean when those two guys ran away?" he asked.

"You saw that?"

"Sure. I flagged it in case they were running out on a bill."

"Show it to us."

He tapped a few keys and the video popped up on the center screen. Tristan raced out of the lot first, and then the big man followed. The angle only provided views of their backs, however.

"Do you have another camera that could have caught their faces?" Stone asked.

"Sure," the man said. "I marked those, too."

The first clip he brought up was of Tristan sitting in the bar with Monica.

"And the other guy?" Stone asked.

The next clip showed the big man sitting in a chair outside the bar.

"Anyone recognize him?" Dino asked.

"Not me," Stone said.

"Me, either," Monica said.

"Is there any chance you can take a still of him and send it to us?" Stone asked.

"No problem," the guard at the controls said.

"Wait a minute," his boss protested. "We can't just—"

Monica leaned forward and took a photo of the screen. She showed the image to Stone and Dino.

"There. Nobody has to send anything."

CHAPTER 29

Once again attired as a sheriff's officer, Benji pounded on the door to the house containing their newest target. "Anyone home?"

Nothing happened.

"I think they're gone," Devin said. He was in a uniform, too. "What about the light?"

A light that had been shining in a second-story window had suddenly gone out twenty minutes earlier.

"Probably on a timer."

Benji frowned, unsure.

This was the problem with doing a rush job: no time to prep. By the time they'd arrived on-site yesterday, it had been one a.m. and the house had been dark. So they were winging it instead of taking their usual few days to discover any patterns.

Benji had even called Simon that morning to beg for extra time, but his brother had insisted, "You will get it tonight and come back. There's another job I need you for." He hung up without letting Benji say anything else.

The house sat on ten acres of scattered groves of ponderosa pines and meadows of long brown grass. From the front stoop, Benji could see the glow of flames in the meadow from the fire Sticks had set off. It seemed larger than it should have been at this point, and he was getting nervous they might not have as much time as planned.

"Screw it," Benji said as he stepped aside. "Open it."

Devin swung a handheld battering ram into the door. The second the door swung open, the shrill of an alarm filled the air. It didn't matter. By the time anyone showed up they'd be gone, and the house would be burning.

"I got this floor, you take upstairs," Benji said.

He made a mad dash through the ground floor, searching for the Matilda Stone painting that was supposed to be there. It was the second Stone in a row they were snatching, which seemed kind of odd. But who was Benji to question his brother's whims?

He found the painting in the library and was about to let Devin know over their walkie app when Devin's voice came over his earbud. "We have a problem."

"What kind of problem?"

"Who the fuck are you?" The voice that came over the radio was not Devin's.

Someone else was in the house.

"Shit," Benji hissed.

He retrieved his pistol and ran up to the second level.

Devin was standing in the doorway to the master bedroom, while a few feet inside stood a man in his fifties or sixties. He was tall and wore only a pair of red-and-black-checked boxers, which left his significant paunch on full display.

"I said, who the fuck are you?" he slurred. His hair was disheveled, and he was weaving slightly.

"We're with the sheriff's department," Devin said. "There's a fire heading toward your house. We're here to evacuate you."

"Fire? Nobody told me about any fire."

He started walking toward a window and within two steps tripped over his own feet. When he tried to right himself, he ended up backpedaling into a dresser and toppling onto the floor.

He lay there, unmoving.

"Is he dead?" Devin asked.

"I hope not," Benji said. No one had suffered more than a few scrapes and bruises in connection with any of their previous heists. "Check him."

Devin knelt next to the body, put a hand on the man's neck, then gave Benji a thumbs-up. "Still alive."

Benji grimaced. While that was a good sign, they still had a problem. "Help me get him downstairs."

"We're taking him with us?"

"We can't leave him here."

"Why not?"

"The fire?"

Devin's eyes widened. "Oh, shit, right. The fire."

They propped him up between them and moved him into the hallway.

"Jeez, he's even heavier than he looks," Devin complained.

"Just keep moving."

They had to switch tactics at the stairs, Devin taking the guy's feet and going down first, Benji grabbing him under the arms.

They had just reached the ground floor and laid the guy on the carpet, so they could readjust, when Sticks threw the front door open and hurried in.

"What's the holdup? Fire's almost here."

Benji twisted around. "What do you mean it's almost here?"

"A fire's gonna do what a fire's gonna do." Sticks noticed the unconscious man. "Who's he?"

"Don't worry about him," Benji said. "Worry about getting your devices set up in here."

"I'm not sure we're gonna need them."

"We're not taking any chances."

Sticks glanced at the open front door, then grimaced. "Fine."

"Devin, with me," Benji said.

Benji and Devin collected the painting, then returned to the foyer to find Sticks standing exactly where he'd been before.

"I told you to get everything set," Benji said.

"I did."

Benji nodded at the man on the floor. "Then help Devin carry him to the car."

"No way. You're not paying me to carry bodies."

"He's not dead."

"I don't care."

"Fine. Then take this." He held out the Matilda Stone.

"You don't pay me to—"

"Just take it, dammit!" Benji shoved the painting into Sticks's chest.

Sticks grumbled but took it and headed outside.

Benji and Devin picked up the man and exited the house.

"Oh, my God!" Devin said, his gaze locked on the meadow behind the home.

Benji looked over his shoulder and sucked in a breath. The blaze couldn't have been more than twenty yards behind the house and moving fast in their direction.

"Move it," Benji said.

They piled into their fake sheriff's car, Devin in back with their extra passenger, and Benji sped away as fast as possible.

Half a mile later, they left the guy from the house next to several dumpsters behind a closed restaurant, then made a beeline for the freeway, to put as many miles between them and the scene of the crime as possible.

It wasn't until they'd been driving for a couple of hours that Benji realized he'd forgotten to call 911 to report the fire.

CHAPTER 30

———◎———

"Wake up."

Dalton parted his eyelids, then slammed them closed again. Someone had turned the light on in his room. Confused, he rolled onto his back and eased his eyes open.

"Simon? What the hell?"

"Get dressed. We have somewhere to go."

Dalton sat up. "How did you get in here?" While he was staying at the same hotel as Simon, he had not given the art dealer a key to his room.

"Quit dawdling and get up."

Still half asleep, Dalton swung his legs off the bed, grabbed his phone off the nightstand, and checked the time. It was barely five a.m. "Where are we going at this time in the morning?"

"To find out how much your friend Monica Reyes knows."

"Monica? What are you talking about?"

Simon headed for the door. "I'll be in the lobby. If you're not there in ten minutes, I'll leave without you."

Dalton threw on some clothes and rushed into the lobby with two minutes to spare.

He had assumed Simon had come with his driver, but it was Simon himself who got behind the wheel.

"Can you tell me where we're going?" Dalton asked as they drove over the hill into the San Fernando Valley.

"You'll see soon enough."

Simon was equally unhelpful when Dalton asked what he'd meant about Monica, and he finally gave up trying to get anything out of him.

Thirty minutes later, they were in the northeast end of the San Fernando Valley, traveling on a windy road into the foothills of the San Gabriel Mountains. The houses along the road were far apart from each other, often out of sight of their neighbors.

Dalton was starting to think they were heading to the top of the mountain when Simon pulled into a driveway and stopped. Planted in the front yard was a FOR SALE sign that looked as if it had been there for years, which made sense, given that the house appeared just as neglected.

"What are we doing here?"

"Getting our answers."

Simon climbed out. Dalton hesitated a moment, then did the same.

The front door of the house swung open before they reached it, Phillip on the other side.

"Is he ready?" Simon asked.

Phillip nodded. "Primed and waiting."

"Lead on."

They passed through a dingy living room into a dark hallway, the whole place stinking of mold and rot, then stopped at a closed door at the very end.

"In here," Phillip said.

He opened the door and stood to the side so that Simon and Dalton could enter first.

The space was lit by a single, bright light focused on a man tied to a chair in the middle of the room. He was slouched forward, his face hidden. The only sign of life was the rise and fall of his torso as he breathed.

Simon walked over, grabbed the man's hair, and shoved him into a sitting position. The man's face was bloodied and bruised, but there was something familiar about him to Dalton.

He was still trying to figure it out when Simon slapped the man's face, and the man's eyes opened.

Simon grinned. "Hello, Tristan."

Realization hit Dalton. "That's the guy from your gallery."

"The very same," Simon said. "Thank you for pointing him out to us."

Dalton felt his throat constrict. Whatever he'd thought joining an art theft ring would involve, it hadn't been something like this.

"You're looking a little peaked," Simon said. "Are you feeling all right?"

"I . . . it's just . . . can't you just talk to him."

"I am going to talk to him."

"I mean without . . ." He waved a hand at Tristan.

"Does a little violence make you feel uneasy?"

"I . . ."

"Sometimes a heavy hand is needed. You're a partner now,

remember? If you can't take it, we can cancel our agreement and go back to a per job fee."

Dalton almost said yes, but the thought of giving up all that cash was enough to stop him. "No. I was a little surprised, that's all. It's my first time. Sorry."

"May I continue?"

"Of course. Sorry."

Simon turned back to Tristan. "I understand you've been giving away my secrets."

"No. I didn't . . . say anything." He spoke as if he had to push each word out.

"Phillip saw you with the woman."

"I only went there . . . to tell her I didn't . . . know anything . . . because . . . because I don't."

Tristan's head started to droop. Simon grabbed his ear and pulled it back up, causing the kid to yelp in pain.

"I'm telling the truth. I didn't . . . I didn't . . . I—"

His eyes fluttered and his whole body fell forward, the rope the only thing keeping him from tumbling to the floor.

"Tristan," Simon said.

When he didn't respond, Simon pushed him up so that he flopped against the back of the chair.

"Tristan." Simon slapped his face. "Tristan." He did it again, but Tristan remained unconscious. Simon looked at Phillip, who stood near the door. "Did he tell you anything of use?"

"He gave me the same story he gave you."

"Do you believe him?"

"He wasn't with her very long, so he couldn't have said much."

"That's not what I asked you."

Phillip shrugged. "Yeah, I believe."

"I do, too." Simon stood.

"What are you going to do with him?" Dalton asked.

"First off, he's fired," Simon said.

Phillip snorted.

"You're going to let him go, though, right?" Dalton asked.

Simon looked at him with pity. "Do you think that would be a good idea?"

Dalton tried to swallow, but his mouth was too dry. "Probably not."

"Then you have your answer." He glanced at Phillip. "It's time to deal with that other matter."

"Understood."

"What other matter?" Dalton asked.

Phillip's pistol smacked into the back of Dalton's head, dropping him to the floor.

He groaned as someone toed his ribs.

"Do you think you're the only dirty insurance executive out there?" Simon asked. "Let me answer that for you. You are not. The only thing you are is a nuisance. And I'm afraid I can't abide nuisances."

A boot slammed into Dalton's head.

As darkness began to close in, Dalton heard Phillip say, "The woman's still going to be a problem."

"Not for long," Simon replied.

"You have a plan?"

"I do. One that our two friends here can help with."

Whatever that plan was, Dalton didn't remain conscious long enough to hear it.

CHAPTER 31

———◦———

Monica woke Stone in the most delicious way, after which he returned the favor. One thing led to another and by the time they made it downstairs, it was nearly ten a.m.

They found Dino poolside, sipping on a glass of freshly squeezed orange juice, and his wife, Viv, lying on a nearby lounge, clad in a black bikini.

When Dino saw them, he looked at his watch. "Viv, you owe me a twenty." To Stone and Monica, he stage-whispered, "I said you wouldn't be down until ten. She said nine."

"Put it on my tab," Viv said.

"Viv, let me introduce you to Monica Reyes," Stone said. "Monica, this is Dino's wife, Vivian Bacchetti."

"A pleasure to meet you," Viv said. "And please call me Viv. Dino tells me you've been keeping Stone in line."

"It's a burden, but someone has to do it," Monica said.

Viv grinned. "We're going to get along just fine."

"I think we're in trouble," Dino said to Stone.

"You're just now figuring that out?" Stone said.

"I blame jet lag."

To Viv, Stone said, "When did you get in?"

"Around three a.m."

"You must be exhausted," Monica said.

"I slept most of the flight, so I'm not too tired yet."

"Have you two eaten?" Stone asked.

"Two hours ago," Dino said.

"Then I guess it's just you and me," Stone said to Monica. "What would you like?"

"What are my choices?"

"Room service can whip up pretty much anything you might want."

"I keep forgetting we're in the middle of a hotel."

"Think of it as a fancy resort," Dino said.

"It *is* a fancy resort."

"See? You've already adapted."

"Breakfast?" Stone reminded her.

"Right. Eggs Benedict?"

"One of my favorites. Anything else?"

"Some strawberries, if they have any."

"Done."

Stone called in their order, and they joined Dino at the table. Monica checked her phone, then frowned and set it down.

"Still no word?" Stone asked.

"No." She had sent Tristan several texts since the premature end to their meeting the previous evening, but he had yet to respond. "The gallery opens at eleven. I'll call him there."

"Tell him you're planning on coming by again. I have a feeling he'll agree to an alternate location to keep you from showing up."

"That's devious. I like it."

"Unfortunately, in my line of work not all the people I come in contact with are on the up-and-up."

"I thought you'd have a better clientele than that."

"Not my clients. More the people with whom my clients have issues."

"Ah, so you *are* a bastion of truth and justice."

"I try my best."

To Monica, Dino said, "It's not my nature to poke my nose in something without being invited—"

"Since when?" Stone and Viv said in unison.

Ignoring them, Dino continued where he left off. "But remember, Stone *is* a lawyer, which makes him a professional liar."

"Don't listen to him," Stone said. "He's law enforcement and making lawyers out as less than truthful is a stereotype his ilk likes to perpetuate."

"Says the former police detective, who I recall on several occasions saying something similar."

"The key word there is *former.*"

"Careful, Monica," Viv said. "If you wind them up too much, they'll be like this all day."

Breakfast soon arrived. Monica checked her phone several more times as she ate, but still no word from Tristan. By the time she and Stone finished their meals, it was twenty to eleven.

"Someone has to be at the gallery by now, don't you think?" she said.

"Seems reasonable," Stone said.

She made the call.

After two rings, a female voice answered, "Duchamp Gallery, Los Angeles. How may I help you?"

"I'm looking for Tristan Williams."

For a moment, Monica thought they'd been disconnected, then the woman said, "I'm sorry. Tristan Williams doesn't work here any longer."

"I saw him there yesterday. He didn't mention anything about leaving."

"Perhaps I could assist you?"

"Did he get a new job or give any reason why he left?"

"I don't know any more details than what I've already told you, and even if I did, I wouldn't give them out to someone over the phone."

"If I came down there, would you be able to—"

"Ma'am, as I'm sure you're aware, all employment information is a matter of personal privacy. Is there something else I can help you with?"

"No. Thank you for your time."

"Have a good day," the woman said and hung up.

Monica stared at her phone, brow furrowed.

"I take it from what you were saying that Tristan is no longer an employee of the gallery?" Stone said.

"That's what she said," Monica said.

"Do you know if he quit or was fired?" Viv asked.

"She didn't give a reason," Monica said. "But last night, when I asked how long he'd worked there, he didn't act like he'd lost his job."

"What about the man who chased him last night?" Stone said. "Maybe he caught Tristan and did a number on him."

"Do you think so?" Monica asked, concerned.

"I have no idea, but it's another possibility. Though I don't know why he'd quit or be fired because of that."

"Could be as simple as he was skimming from the register and they finally found out."

"For the most part, transactions at galleries would either be by credit card, bank transfer, or check."

"Please tell me you've heard of credit-card skimmers."

"Right. I hadn't thought of that."

"I can think of one other reason," Stone said. "What if he told someone about his conversation with you, and they weren't happy."

"But why fire him for that? He didn't tell me anything."

"Perhaps they thought he did."

"However he lost his job, he probably hasn't responded because he's not in the mood to talk to anyone," Viv said.

"How about this?" Stone said. "Let's give him a few more hours. If he hasn't gotten back to you by then, you and I will drive out to his house."

"That's a great idea," Monica said, her tension easing. "Thank you."

"In the meantime, how about we take a drive along the beach? It'll take your mind off all this."

"I'd love that."

"Viv, Dino, you are welcome to join us. I was thinking we could have lunch in Malibu."

"Sounds great to me," Dino said. "But I defer to my beautiful bride."

"We'd be delighted."

———————

"When I was in high school, my friends and I would drive to Malibu to look for movie stars," Monica said, as they passed the city limits sign.

"You grew up in Los Angeles?" Viv asked.

"Just north of it, in Ventura County."

"Did you ever see any?" Dino asked.

"Only once. We were at a stoplight and Martin Sheen pulled up next to us. I waved to him, and he smiled and waved back. And then the light turned green and that was it."

"You won't be able to miss them at the party on Saturday."

"Party?"

"Billy Barnett is throwing a post–board meeting party at his house. Didn't Stone invite you yet?"

"As a matter of fact, no."

All eyes turned to Stone.

"Monica, would you like to join me at Billy Barnett's party on Saturday?"

"Are you only asking because you're being pressured into it?"

"I'm asking because I planned to do just that but hadn't gotten around to it yet."

She smirked. "In either case, my answer would be yes."

"Great," Dino said. "I'll introduce you to my daughter-in-law."

"Who's your daughter-in-law?"

"Tessa Tweed."

Monica turned and looked into the back where he and Viv sat. "You're not pulling my leg, are you?"

"He is not," Stone said.

"In that case, I would be thrilled to meet your daughter-in-law." She faced forward. "I *will* need to do some clothes shopping first, though."

A few miles on, Stone said, "Does anyone mind if we make a stop before we eat?"

"I'm still full from breakfast," Monica said.

"Okay by me," Dino said.

Viv nodded her agreement.

Stone turned into a private seaside neighborhood where many celebrities had homes.

As he pulled up to the guarded gate, Monica whispered, "Do you know someone who lives here?"

"Not yet," Stone said.

He identified himself to the guard, and they drove into the colony. They passed several large homes before Stone turned into a driveway and parked.

"This is gorgeous," Monica said, looking at the house. "Whose house is this?"

"At the moment, mine."

They all climbed out and he led them inside.

"Oh, my," Monica said as they entered the living room.

The all-glass back wall overlooked the beach and the ocean beyond.

"Like it?" Stone asked.

"It's spectacular. Are you planning on moving here?"

"Not a chance. I enjoy visiting California, but my home is in New York, and always will be."

She looked around. "There's no furniture. Don't you ever stay here?"

"My house at the Arrington is more than enough for me."

"You're going to let this place sit empty then?"

"That, I'm afraid, is a state secret."

Her eyes narrowed. "Has anyone ever told you that you can be exasperating sometimes?"

"We have. Multiple times," Dino chimed in.

"I've never said that," Viv disagreed.

"You don't hang around him enough."

"You want me to hang around him more?"

"Viv, I would welcome spending more time with you," Stone said.

"On second thought," Dino said, "you spend more than enough time in his presence already."

"I thought as much," Viv said.

They spent some time outside, admiring the view, then Stone gave them a tour of the house.

Once they were back in the car, Monica checked her phone and let out a breath of surprise.

"You miss a call?" Stone asked.

"No, a text from Tristan. He asked if I could meet him this evening at eight at Shutters on the Beach in Santa Monica. Do you know it?"

"It was my go-to hotel before the Arrington was built." He glanced at Dino and Viv in the back seat. "Do you two have plans tonight?"

"Nothing specific," Viv said.

"I think we should go, too. Between the three of us, we should be able to make sure what happened last night doesn't happen again. Viv, Dino can fill you in on the details." To Monica, he said, "Work for you?"

"Very much. Thank you."

She replied to Tristan's text, telling him they were on.

An hour and a half later, after they were sated and headed back to the Arrington, Stone's phone lit up with a call from Mike Freeman.

"Hi, Mike. What's up?"

"Are you still in Santa Fe?" Mike asked, his voice coming over the car's speakers.

"L.A., I flew in yesterday."

"Perfect. So am I. Herb just arrived in town and would like to meet with both of us. Since we're all in the same place, let's do it at Strategic Services' L.A. office."

"Sounds good. I should be able to get there by four p.m."

"Works for me. I'll let Herb know."

Mike hung up.

"Do you mind if I tag along with you?" Viv said. "There are a few things I need to deal with at the office."

"Fine by me."

"If she's going, I'm going, too," Dino said.

Stone glanced at Monica. "How about you? Want to join us?"

"If it wouldn't be too much trouble, could you drop me off at the hotel? I'd like to go over my notes again."

"No trouble at all," Stone said.

"If you have time, get a massage," Viv said. "They'll bring the table to the house and set it up by the pool."

"That sounds exactly like what I need."

"If you want," Stone said, "I can call it in now and they'll be there when you arrive."

"Perhaps you're not as exasperating as I thought."

CHAPTER 32

———◦———

Stone dropped off Monica at the Arrington, then he, Dino, and Viv continued to Strategic Services' L.A. offices.

The company's West Coast presence had expanded considerably over the last few years. To accommodate this, they had moved into a new, larger location. This was the first time Stone was visiting it.

While not as grand as Strategic Services' main headquarters in New York, the new three-story facility in Koreatown did take up an entire block.

Mike met them in the lobby. After shaking Stone's and Dino's hands, he raised an eyebrow and scowled at Viv. "If I'm not mistaken, you're supposed to be taking a few days off."

"I am."

"Your presence says otherwise."

"Pretend like you don't see me."

"A day off means not coming in."

"When has that ever stopped me?" She grinned, then slipped an arm into Dino's and led him to the stairs.

Mike shook his head. "I'd ban her from all our facilities when she's off, but I doubt that would work."

"What do you do on *your* days off?" Stone asked.

"Days off? What's that?"

They went to a conference room on the third floor that had windows overlooking the rear third of the building, the space open from the ground to the ceiling.

"Our training area," Mike explained.

There were ropes attached to the rafters for climbing, exercise equipment, and a basketball court.

"First floor has locker rooms and showers. It's also where our equipment and firearm storage are located. We've taken a page out of your playbook and have a shooting range in the basement."

"More than one lane, though, I'm guessing."

"Twelve."

"Impressive."

"I'm very happy with how this place has turned out."

The conference room door opened again, and Herb walked in followed by Eliza Dinh, Cory Aldridge, and Ellen Herlin, the experts who had helped him with the Santa Fe assessment.

Greetings were exchanged and then they sat.

"I take it you've made a determination on the site," Stone said.

"There are a few small issues that still need to be answered, but otherwise, we've compiled what I believe to be a comprehensive assessment."

"How about we start with your determination?" Stone said. "We can go over the details after."

"You're taking all the fun out of it. But okay. My recommen-dation is to authorize me to finalize the deal immediately, then sign it as soon as it's ready."

Stone turned to the experts. "You all concur?"

"Absolutely," Eliza said.

The other two nodded.

Monica was in the middle of her massage when her phone rang.

"Sorry," she said to Chet, her masseur. "Can you hand me my phone?"

"No problem."

He grabbed her cell off the lounge chair and handed it to her.

She checked the screen. The caller ID read: PATRICIA EASTLY. Patricia was Monica's friend at Vitale Insurance who had been keeping her apprised of the happenings there since she'd left. Monica had asked her to look into the theft of Billy Barnett's painting.

"I need to take this. Can you give me a minute?"

"Of course." The masseur walked toward the far end of the pool to give her privacy.

"Hi, Patricia," she answered. "What did you find out?"

"You were right. Billy Barnett's not one of our clients. But the auction house that sold the painting to him is. That's not the rea-son I called, though."

"It's not?"

"Another painting burned last night," Patricia said.

"Last night?"

"Yep."

It had barely been two weeks since the last time a similar incident occurred, and if the supposed art ring was real and had also been responsible for what happened to Billy, that was three robberies in fifteen days. In the past, the shortest time between events had been four weeks.

"Where did this happen?"

"Marin County, north of San Francisco."

"Who was the insured?"

"Randall Vernon."

Monica knew they had several clients in that area, but she didn't immediately recall the name.

"Same situation as the others?"

"Yes and no. It *was* another brushfire that burned down the house. The difference is, they've found a body."

"Whose?" To this point, there had been no deaths associated with the suspected thefts.

"Police haven't confirmed the person's ID yet." Patricia lowered her voice to a whisper. "Unofficially, we've been told that a distinctive ring belonging to Mr. Vernon was found on one of the fingers. But you want to hear something even stranger?"

"What?"

Monica's phone vibrated with the arrival of a text, but she ignored it.

"The body wasn't found in the house or anywhere near the property. It was a half mile away. The fire grew out of control before emergency services had been alerted. They weren't able to get to the area where the body was until early this morning, after the flames had moved through. My understanding is that they are still trying to get the fire under control."

"Do the authorities think he was trying to run away?"

"They're not saying, but . . ."

"But what?"

"He was found behind a couple of dumpsters and wasn't wearing any shoes."

"Oh my God."

"If it *is* your thieves, they've just added murder to their list of deeds."

That was exactly what Monica was thinking. "What painting was lost?"

"Hold on . . . Here it is. *Morning on the Avenue* by Matilda Stone."

Another Matilda Stone? There's no way it's a coincidence.

"Are you still there?"

"Sorry," Monica said. "Was there anything else?"

"That wasn't enough?"

"More than enough. Thank you for the info." Monica was about to say goodbye when she thought of another question. "What's Dalton doing about it?"

"Nothing at the moment. He took a couple of days off. His assistant tried to reach him, but you know Dalton. His phone has been off."

"Thanks again, Patricia. Let me know if anything else comes up."

"I will."

When Monica disconnected the call, she noticed the alert on her message app and remembered the vibration from earlier.

She tapped on it and saw that she had another text from Tristan.

Change of plans

Can't do 8 but am free until 5

I'm at the Waving Palm Motel
in Mar Vista room 120
LMK if you can't make it

She knew she shouldn't go alone, but five p.m. was in less than an hour. No way she could wait for Stone to get back then get there in time. Letting this opportunity slip through her hands wasn't an option, though—especially given the news Patricia had told her.

She replied:

Be there in 30

She pulled the towel around her and hopped off the table.

"Sorry," she called to the masseur. "Something's come up, and I need to leave. Thank you. It was great."

"Oh, okay. Well, um—"

By then she'd already rushed back into the house and couldn't hear anything else.

Monica took an Uber to the Waving Palm Motel.

"You sure this is where you wanted to go?" her driver asked when they arrived.

The motel's sign was so faded that it was barely legible, and the bottom edge was bent as if the top of a truck had run into it. The building itself wasn't in any better shape.

"It is. Thank you."

She climbed out.

The motel was L-shaped and two-storied, all the rooms

accessed by exterior doors. In the middle of the parking lot was a fenced-off area, inside of which was a pool that looked as if it had been empty for decades.

She looked inside the office as she passed, but no one was there. Room 120 turned out to be on the ground floor, farthest from the street. Like the other rooms, it had a faded green door and a large window. The curtains were closed, so she couldn't see inside.

She doubled-checked the room number on her phone, to make sure she remembered it right, then took a steadying breath and raised her hand to knock. The moment her knuckles struck the door, it moved inward several inches.

"Tristan?" she said.

She heard not a sound from inside, so she peeked through the gap, but the room was too dark to see much of anything.

"Tristan? It's Monica Reyes."

When that failed to garner a response, she pushed the door open wide enough to stick her head inside.

"Anyone here?"

There were a pair of beds inside. On the one farthest from the door, she could just make out what appeared to be a person lying under the covers.

"Tristan?"

The lump didn't stir.

She found the switch and flipped it on.

The lump was definitely Tristan. She recognized his face, though there seemed to be something wrong with his nose.

She stepped toward the bed. "Are you okay?"

She was still a few steps away when she jerked to a stop.

It wasn't just his nose that was wrong. His eyes were half open and dried blood covered his cheeks and chin.

She hurried to his side and checked his neck for a pulse. His skin was unnaturally cold and there wasn't a beat to be found.

She covered her mouth and backed away.

That's when she saw the feet sticking out of the bathroom.

As much as she wanted to get out of there, the investigator in her wouldn't let her go yet. She crept over for a better look.

The bathroom light was off, making it hard to see the body on the floor. Thankfully, the switch was on the outside. She turned the light on and nearly screamed.

Staring up at her was Dalton Conroy, his eyes as dead as Tristan's.

She backpedaled into the wall and shoved her hand into her pocket to get her phone, only the phone wasn't there. She remembered then that she'd been holding it when she walked in. She whirled around, scanned the room, and spotted it on the floor next to Tristan's bed, where she must have dropped it.

As she unlocked the screen, the buzz she'd been hearing since realizing Tristan was dead began to recede, only to be replaced by the wail of sirens.

She shot a glance toward the front of the room. Red and blue lights reflected off the door and walls.

She focused back on her phone, but instead of calling 911, she called Stone.

From the parking lot, an amplified voice said, "Come out of the room with your hands on your head."

The call connected. "Hi, we were just about to—"

"Stone, I think I'm in trouble."

CHAPTER 33

———◦———

Fifteen minutes earlier, Simon paced the gallery's office, waiting for a call from Phillip.

When his cell finally rang, he snatched it up and said, "Is it set?"

"Mr. Duchamp?" said a voice that did not belong to Phillip.

"Who is this?"

"Nico Savage."

"My apologies, Mr. Savage. I thought you were someone else."

"Mr. Petry would like an update."

"You can tell him the second Matilda Stone will be in my possession within the hour."

"And the third?"

"By Friday, as promised," Simon said, more confident than he felt.

Simon heard muffled voices on the other end, then Savage

came back on and said, "Mr. Petry asked me to express his appreciation for your efforts."

"Pleasing my clients is always a priority. Now, if there's nothing else, I have a rather busy afternoon."

"We understand you're in Los Angeles."

"Well, um, yes." Simon hadn't told them that, but it wasn't like his presence in the city was a secret.

"So, today's delivery will be happening in L.A."

"It will."

"Excellent. Mr. Petry and I arrived a few hours ago and would like to be there when the painting arrives."

"Well . . . that . . . um . . . I don't think—"

"Didn't you just say pleasing your clients is a priority?"

"Yes, of course, but—"

"Mr. Petry insists we be there."

"That was never part of our agreement."

"It is now."

"You can't simply change the terms on the fly."

"One moment."

More muffled voices, then Nico said to Simon, "Mr. Petry says that he understands the inconvenience, but if you refuse, the deal is off, and he expects our deposit to be returned immediately."

Simon wasn't about to refund a half million dollars even if Petry wanted to call the deal off.

But before he could say anything, Nico continued, "And Mr. Petry wants to make sure you understand that if you don't refund the money, he will honor you with a lovely wreath at your funeral."

Simon had resources, but he had no doubt Petry had even

more. "There's no need for threats. I would be happy to have you both join me for the delivery."

"I thought you might. Where shall we meet you?"

"I have a gallery in town."

"On Melrose. Coincidentally, we're parked in front. Would it be all right if we come in now?"

"No," Simon blurted out. "I mean, not through the front. There's a parking lot in back. Pull in there and I'll meet you at the rear door."

As soon as they hung up, Simon called Phillip. "Well?"

"I don't think we need to worry about the Monica Reyes problem anymore."

"When can you get back here?"

"An hour, hour and a half. Why? You need me?"

"Petry and Nico will be here in a minute."

"If I leave right now, I might make it in forty-five."

"That will probably be too late. Wait until they arrest her, then come back."

"Will do."

"Wait here," Benji said to Devin and Sticks.

He climbed out of their car, jogged to the back door of his brother's gallery, and pressed the buzzer.

Within seconds, Simon yanked the door open and peered out. "Finally."

"You want us to bring it inside?"

Simon lowered his voice to a whisper. "Of course I want you to bring it inside. What are you? An idiot?"

Benji signaled Devin and Sticks to fetch the painting.

"The client is here," Simon said, his voice still low. "None of you say anything. Got it?"

"Got it."

"I mean it. Not one word."

"I said I got it."

Simon held his gaze for a moment, then headed away, forcing Benji to catch the door to keep it from closing again.

Devin's right, Benji thought. *Simon really is a prick.*

When Devin and Sticks arrived with the container that held the stolen painting, Benji told them what Simon wanted.

"Whatever," Devin said.

Sticks acted like he hadn't even heard, but he never said that much anyway, so Benji took his silence for a yes. He pushed the door all the way open, and they carried in the painting.

Simon waved Benji and his flunkies over to the sitting area, where he, Petry, and Nico waited. "Hurry up."

They carried the package over and laid it on the coffee table.

Simon tried to pull off the Bubble Wrap, but there was too much tape.

"I got it," Benji said, pulling out a pocketknife.

Simon shot his brother a glare to remind him he wasn't supposed to speak, then snapped, "Be careful!"

Petry snorted. "Like it really matters."

"Excuse me?" Simon asked.

Nico forced a smile. "Mr. Petry is excited to see it, that's all."

That was not what it sounded like to Simon, nor was the sneer on Petry's face helping to sell the excuse.

After Benji finished and stepped out of the way, Simon peeled back the wrapping. For a second, he lost himself in the beauty of the piece until Petry jerked him out of his reverie.

"That's it?"

"Were you expecting something different?"

"I don't know. I guess I thought it would be more impressive."

"More impressive?" If Simon hadn't had doubts about Petry's intentions before, he did now.

Nico whispered in his boss's ear.

Petry rolled his eyes, then said to Simon, "I meant, sure, it's impressive. Love it. Where's the special one?"

"The special one?"

"From the list," Nico clarified

"Right. It's stored elsewhere. We can set up a time to see it later, if you'd like."

Petry nodded at the painting on the coffee table. "It's like this one, right?"

"Well, no. The subjects are completely different."

Nico started to lean toward Petry again, but Petry waved him off. "I know they're different. I just meant— You know what? Never mind."

"So, you don't want to see it?"

Nico smiled. "What Mr. Petry means is he can wait until you have all three."

"Of course." It was actually a relief to Simon. The less time he spent in these men's company, the better.

"You only have forty-eight hours left," Petry said. "You damn well better get the last one in time."

"Have no fear. It will be here by then." Simon could feel Benji's surprised gaze on him, but he kept his attention on his clients.

"When should we come by to pick them up?"

"I can't give you a specific time yet."

Petry looked over at Benji, Devin, and Sticks. "These your guys?"

Sticks snorted. "I'm nobody's guy."

"No disrespect intended. I meant, you're the ones who do the stealing, right?"

Sticks sneered at Simon. "You think he has the balls to do it?"

Petry smiled. "Oh, I like you. Do you do all his dirty work?"

Having heard more than enough, Simon stood. "Mr. Petry, Mr. Savage, thank you for coming. I'll let you know when you can collect your paintings."

He motioned to the door, but Petry remained seated, his attention still on Sticks.

"I'm curious. I gotta think there's a lot of security around these things. How do you get around that?"

Simon shot Benji and the others a warning gaze, then said, "Mr. Petry, how we conduct our business is none of your concern. Please." He motioned toward the back door. "I have many things I need to deal with this afternoon."

Petry's attention stayed on Sticks for another moment, then he stood. "I look forward to our next meeting. We can see ourselves out."

"What the hell was all that?" Simon yelled as soon as Petry and Nico were gone.

"Sorry," Benji said. "Sticks didn't—"

"I told you to say *nothing!*"

While Benji was cowed and kept his mouth shut, the same could not be said for Sticks.

"I don't see what the big deal is."

"Of course you don't, because you don't understand the bigger picture. If I tell you to keep quiet, then you keep quiet."

Sticks made an exaggerated bow. "I'm sorry, boss man."

"That's right. I *am* the boss. Don't forget it."

"Kinda hard to do when you—"

"Sticks," Benji hissed.

Sticks mimed zipping his mouth shut.

Simon shook his head in disgust, then turned and walked toward his office. "Benji, come with me. We need to discuss the next job."

Once Simon and Benji disappeared into Simon's office, Devin plopped down on the break-area couch.

"Might as well take a load off," he said to Sticks. "Who knows how long they'll be in there."

Instead, Sticks headed for the back door.

"Where you going?" Devin asked.

"Out for a smoke."

"That stuff will kill you."

Sticks flipped him off without looking back, then stepped out into the parking lot.

He leaned against the wall and pulled out his cigarettes. As he was knocking one out of the pack, he heard the hum of a car window opening.

"Hey, buddy."

Sticks looked over.

The younger of the two men who'd just met with Simon was smiling at him from inside a black BMW 530i.

"You got a minute?"

"Maybe," Sticks said.

"Easier to talk if you come over here."

Sticks put the unlit cigarette behind his ear and walked over to the car. "What's up?"

"My boss would like to have a word with you." The guy motioned to the back seat. "In private."

Sticks glanced back at the gallery's rear door, then shrugged. "Why not?" He climbed into the back seat.

The older guy, the one who'd done most of the talking earlier, held out a hand. "Winston Petry."

Sticks shook it. "Sticks."

"Nice to meet you, Sticks." Petry motioned to the driver. "That's Nico Savage. He's one of my lawyers."

Sticks and Nico exchanged nods.

"I'm here. What do you want?"

"You seem like a man who could help me out."

"Help you out how?"

"I'm based out of New York. Which, unfortunately, means I don't have a lot of connections out here. Specifically, connections that are not averse to breaking the law. You know what I mean?"

"Yeah. I get you." Sticks didn't mention that he wasn't from L.A., either.

"I knew you would. See, I have a delicate task that I need taken care of, and my gut tells me you could connect me to the right person. If you can, I'll pay you a finder's fee."

"What kind of fee?"

"How does five thousand dollars sound?"

That was more than Sticks earned per job for Simon. But if there was one thing he knew in his world, it was never to take the first offer. "Ten sounds better."

Petry laughed. "You get me the right guy, and you'll have your ten. But this conversation can never get back to Duchamp."

"Like I'd tell him anything."

"Your buddies might."

"Not if they don't know."

Petry sneered. "So, we have a deal?"

"You haven't told me what you want yet. I might not know anyone who can help you."

"The worst possible outcome would be you don't make any money." Petry held out his hand.

Sticks took it and said, "Deal. So, what's the job?"

As Petry explained what he wanted done with the paintings, Sticks couldn't keep a grin from spreading across his face. He didn't give a crap about art. But destruction, that was something to get excited about.

When Petry finished, Sticks said, "Shit, man, that's diabolical. Make sure Simon doesn't find out. I accidentally brushed a finger against one of his precious paintings once, and he freaked. Said I was getting oils all over it. If he knew what you're going to do, he wouldn't give them to you."

"He's not going to find out from me. But even if he knew, what's he going to do?"

"I take it you haven't met Phillip yet."

"Who's Phillip?"

"His muscle. Big as a tank and smart. I avoid him whenever possible."

"Nico?"

"I'll look into it," Nico said.

Petry smiled and returned his attention to Sticks. "Back to getting someone to help me. Does anyone come to mind?"

"Oh, yeah. I know the perfect person."

"See, I knew I could count on you."

"I'll need to know how much you'll pay him."

"What do you think is fair?"

Sticks pretended to consider the question. "He'd probably do it for twenty-five K."

Petry thought for a moment, then nodded. "Done. How do I contact him?"

"You already have."

"What do you mean?"

"You're looking at the perfect guy right here."

CHAPTER 34

Thanks to a call from Dino to his LAPD counterpart, an officer was waiting for Stone and him as they walked into the department's Pacific Division Station, and they were immediately escorted to the lead detective's office. A placard on his desk identified him as Kelvin Eldridge.

"Which of you is Bacchetti?" the detective asked.

"He's Commissioner Bacchetti," Stone said.

Eldridge didn't look particularly pleased to be reminded of Dino's rank. "I don't want there to be any misunderstandings. I couldn't give a rat's ass if you're friends with the chief or the damn president, for that matter. We do things by the book here. So, who you know isn't going to get you any special treatment."

"We aren't asking for special treatment," Stone said.

The detective looked at him over the top of his glasses. "And you are?"

"Stone Barrington."

"Mr. Barrington, the fact that you and *Commissioner* Bacchetti are standing in my office right now says otherwise."

Dino said, "Detective Eldridge, we're not here to cause you any problems. In fact, we're here to help."

"Yeah, I heard our person of interest is a friend of yours."

"Good," Stone said, "that'll save us some time. I'd like to speak with her."

"She's in the interview room, so that's not happening."

"You're saying she's being questioned without a lawyer present?"

"Why? Are you her lawyer?"

"I am."

"Of course you are." He looked past them. "Kwan!"

A female detective named Kwan entered the office. "Yes, sir?"

"Is the Reyes woman still being questioned?"

"No. She asked for her lawyer."

"Did she give you a name?"

"Stone Barrington. I was just about to call him."

Eldridge closed his eyes for a moment. "No need. Detective, meet Stone Barrington."

Kwan looked at Stone, surprised.

"Are you planning on arresting my client, Detective?" Stone asked.

"That'll depend on what we learn when we question her."

"Let me save you the trouble. Even if that conversation happens, you won't be arresting her."

"And you know this why?"

"First, she arrived on the scene a few minutes before the police did. You can talk to her Uber driver to confirm that." Monica had told him as much as she could before the police barged in.

"She could have gone and come back," Eldridge countered.

"Actually, she couldn't have. Before she went to the motel, she was at the Arrington, getting a massage. And before that, she was with the commissioner and me."

"For how long?" Kwan asked.

"With both of us since breakfast. With me since before we both saw Tristan last night, when he was still alive."

"You saw this Tristan guy last night?"

"I saw him, too," Dino said.

"Maybe we should be interviewing you two."

"We'd be happy to oblige, but the conclusion will be the same."

"You'll give sworn statements about all this?" Eldridge asked.

"We will."

Twenty minutes later, Stone was shown into the windowless interview room where Monica had been waiting. She jumped up as he entered and hugged him.

"Oh, thank God!"

"Let's get you out of here."

"I'm free to go?"

"You have a solid alibi. Me."

She kissed him. "Thank you."

"You're welcome. But next time, think twice before heading into a situation like that alone."

"You're right, and I'm sorry. I shouldn't have gone, but I was worried that Tristan would disappear again."

They joined Dino in the hallway and soon were ensconced in

an Arrington Porsche Cayenne. Now that they were away from the prying eyes and ears of the LAPD, Stone said, "Tell me exactly what happened."

She went through the afternoon' events. "When they brought me to the station, I did exactly what you told me, and said that I wanted to talk to my lawyer."

"You didn't tell them anything?"

"Not a word."

"What about at the scene?"

"I was too shocked to say anything."

"That should have been the first sign you weren't the murderer," Dino said.

"Describe what you found there," Stone said.

"I had to flick on a light because it was so dark. That's when I saw Tristan on the bed. I thought he was asleep, but . . ." She closed her eyes and took a deep breath. "When I found Dalton on the bathroom floor, I called you."

"What about wounds? Perhaps from a bullet or a knife?"

She thought for a moment. "Their faces were bruised and had a few cuts. Tristan's nose looked broken. Oh, I remember a large dark spot on Dalton's shirt." She touched the area right below her ribs. "Somewhere around here."

"Was there a lot of blood on the floor?"

"Actually, I don't recall seeing any. But I was pretty freaked out at that point."

"What about on the walls of the bedroom or bathroom?"

"I don't think so."

"If they'd been killed at the motel, there should have been blood all over the place," Dino said.

"You're saying they weren't killed there?"

"I doubt it," Stone said. "I think someone was trying to set you up."

"But why?"

"The same reason anyone gets set up," Dino said. "You're getting in someone's way."

"My investigation."

"Bingo."

"But I'm not any closer to answers than I was a week ago."

"In that time, two potential sources have died. Just because you didn't get the chance to talk to them doesn't mean you're not on the right track."

"I know you're right, but it sure doesn't feel like it. I'm not sure what to do next."

"There is one person we know of who is still alive."

Monica furrowed her brow. "Who?"

"The guy who chased Tristan out of the Roosevelt."

"We don't even know who he is, or where to find him."

"We don't know *yet*."

"Do you have any reason to believe Dalton and Tristan knew each other?" Dino asked.

"I wouldn't have thought so before today, but that seems likely now."

"Is there someone you trust at Vitale who can search Dalton's office? He may have left a clue, perhaps in his calendar or contacts."

"My friend Patricia. Oh, I almost forgot. She called me earlier. There was another fire at a client's house last night. He owned one of your mother's paintings."

"Was it destroyed?"

"We don't know yet, but I suspect not. The fire got out of control and has already burned several hundred acres. I'm not sure they can even get to the house yet. One thing they do know, the owner of the house died in the fire."

She explained the circumstances.

"Was his car found nearby?" Dino asked.

"No. And I can't imagine he would have tried to outrun the fire without shoes."

"If this was another theft," Stone said, "he could have been home when they broke in. They probably dropped him at a spot they thought would be far enough away from the fire."

Dino nodded. "But then the fire didn't behave like they assumed it would."

"Or the fire department didn't get to it as fast as the thieves expected." Stone looked at Monica. "Has anyone ever looked into who called the fires in?"

"Not that I know of," she said.

"There should be recordings of the calls. If we can compare them, I bet we'll hear the same voice, at least a few of the times."

"If that's true," Monica said, "that would be solid evidence I've been right all along." Her optimism soured. "But I'm not in a position where anyone would just hand over the recordings."

"You may not be, but I know someone who is . . ." Stone said, then looked at Dino.

"Are you asking me to abuse my powers?" Dino said.

"Not at all. Monica, which city is home to the largest percentage of fine art collectors insured by your company?"

"That's easy. New York."

Stone turned back to Dino. "It's not abuse of power. It's crime prevention."

"It's a marvel to watch a spin doctor such as yourself at work," Dino said.

"I live to serve."

CHAPTER 35

S imon poured the martini into his glass, then took a seat on the couch in his suite at the Verdugo Royale Hotel. He downed a few aspirins with his first sip. If the combo didn't alleviate the headache he'd had since Petry's surprise visit to the gallery, nothing would.

He was more convinced than ever that hiring Rudy to create the forgeries was the right move. There was no question in Simon's mind that Petry had something monstrous in mind for the Stones. He just couldn't figure out what it was. But unless Petry did something to change his mind, the paintings the asshole would be taking with him would be the forgeries from Rudy Morgan.

He sat up, a smile creeping onto his face. That meant the originals would be staying with him. And what better way to rid himself of his headache than priming the pump for their sale to someone who would appreciate them.

He hunted through his suitcase until he found the business card he'd received in New Mexico and dialed the provided cell number.

"Stone Barrington."

"Mr. Barrington, this is Simon Duchamp. We met at Ivonne Cervantes's opening at my gallery in Santa Fe."

"Yes, Mr. Duchamp. I remember you."

"Please, call me Simon."

"Only if you call me Stone. What can I do for you, Simon?"

"You asked me to call if I heard of any of your mother's work coming up for sale. I don't want to get your hopes up yet, but there is the possibility that some will soon be available."

"Some? How many are we talking about?"

"It's my understanding perhaps as many as three."

"That's marvelous. Who's the seller?"

"I'm afraid that's all I know at the moment. It's more rumor than anything, at this point. But if you are interested, I would be happy to investigate it further."

"I would like that very much."

"Then I will make inquiries and get back to you when I know something more."

"I look forward to hearing from you."

Stone hung up, then stared at his kitchen wall, replaying the conversation in his mind.

"Stone?"

He blinked and turned to find Monica in the doorway.

"You looked lost there for a moment," she said. "Are you okay?"

"I just had an interesting phone call."

"From whom?"

"Simon Duchamp."

Monica looked as surprised as Stone felt. "What did he want?"

"Dino's going to want to hear this, too. Can you take this?" He handed her the bottle of wine he'd come to fetch, then got three wineglasses and they returned to the living room where Dino waited. Viv was still dealing with a situation at work and wouldn't be home until later.

As Stone poured drinks for each of them, Monica said, "So?"

"So what?" Dino asked.

"Simon Duchamp just called Stone."

"What did he want?"

"That's what I'm trying to find out."

"He said there might be three paintings by my mother on the market soon," Stone said.

"Your mother?" Monica said. "You don't think . . ."

"That the pictures he's trying to sell me have been recently stolen?"

Monica nodded.

"If Stone doesn't, I do," Dino said.

"I do, too," Stone said.

Monica frowned. "But if I'm right about the thefts, there are only two missing paintings."

"So far. You might want to tell your friend at Vitale to warn any clients that have one of my mother's pieces of the potential threat."

"Good idea." Monica placed the call, then after several seconds, whispered, "Voicemail. She must be asleep." She left a message explaining the possibility of an upcoming heist.

When she hung up, Stone said, "Is there anyone else you can call?"

"No one who will listen to me."

"So, are we all thinking Simon Duchamp is part of the ring?" Dino said.

"Either that or he's the front they use to sell everything," Stone said.

"Either way, he must know what's going on."

"That he must."

Monica stood, then seemed to think better of it and sat again, frustrated.

"What's wrong?" Stone asked.

"Part of me wants to pay Duchamp a visit right now and find out what he knows. The other part thinks doing so won't accomplish anything because he'll act innocent and claim he has no idea what I'm talking about."

"I'd listen to the second part," Dino said.

"Dino's right," Stone said. "Three people are dead already. If he is involved and we confront him, he may try to add a few more to that total."

"Four people," Dino said. "Don't forget the guy from the fire last night."

Monica blanched. "Then what do we do? Call the police?"

"We could," Stone said. "But all we have now is a suspicion. Law enforcement hasn't even connected all the potential thefts. What we need is something concrete linking Duchamp to at least one of the crimes."

"I'm open to suggestions."

Stone and Dino shared a look, then Stone said, "What we need is the assistance of an expert."

"Do you know any?"

"I do, and he lives here in L.A."

Help arrived at Stone's house one hour later.

"Monica, I'd like you to meet my friend Billy Barnett."

"A pleasure," Billy said, shaking her hand.

"Billy Barnett?" Monica said. "The film producer?"

"One and the same."

"Oh, you're here because your painting was stolen. Has there been any news?"

"Nothing yet."

Monica turned to Stone. "How long until your expert gets here?"

"That would be Billy."

She glanced at each of them. "Please don't take this the wrong way, but how can a movie producer help us?"

"That's an excellent question," Billy said. "What you don't know is that I have a friend who worked in intelligence. If I think he can help, I'll pass on everything to him."

"You're a middleman, then?"

"Exactly."

"I'm not sure if I'm any less confused, but since Stone trusts you, then I do, too."

"Billy, would you like a drink?" Stone said.

"Maybe after you've told me what you need."

"I think that's my cue," Dino said. "If you'll all excuse me, I'm going to call it a night."

Monica looked surprised. "You're not staying?"

Dino feigned a yawn. "Jet lag. Gets me every time."

He headed to the guest room.

"He didn't seem tired before," Monica said.

"Probably because he wasn't," Stone said. "There are some conversations the police commissioner would be better off not hearing."

"I hadn't thought of that."

"You'll get used to it the more you hang around with us."

"The *more* I hang around you? I like the sound of that."

"We all live in New York. You never know who you'll run into."

She raised an eyebrow. "I hope we can do more than run into each other."

"We will," Stone promised. "Much more."

"I hate to break up whatever's going on here," Billy said, "but I believe there was something you wanted to discuss."

Stone brought Billy up to speed.

After, Billy said, "Any ideas on why Duchamp would be stockpiling your mother's paintings?"

"I've been trying to figure that out but haven't come up with anything. Until a few days ago, I didn't even know who he was."

"What about his gallery in New York? I assume he has one there."

"He does," Monica said.

"Have you ever visited it? Maybe purchased something?"

Stone shook his head. "As far as I know, the only purchase I've ever made from him was in Santa Fe, the night I met him."

"No other ties between you? Something to do with Woodman & Weld, perhaps?"

"I can't think of any, but I've left a message for Joan to look into it. I'll let you know if she digs something up."

"I don't suppose that either of you know where Simon is staying."

"Only that he's not at the Arrington." Stone had checked before Billy arrived.

"Okay. I'll talk to my friend. Assume he'll look into it unless you hear differently from me."

They all stood.

"Thanks, Billy," Stone said.

"If either of you think of anything else, let me know. I'll be in touch."

CHAPTER 36

────────◎────────

Teddy drove from the Arrington to his office at Centurion Pictures, as it was more convenient than his home in the Hollywood Hills.

A year earlier, he had personally installed a floor safe, hiding it under the credenza behind his desk. With the touch of a button, the credenza slid out of the way. He tapped in the code and swung the safe's door open.

From inside, he retrieved a laptop that was loaded with the CIA's latest black ops digital tools. He'd obtained them via a back door into the Agency's system that he'd created himself.

One of the apps contained links into restricted record databases throughout the world. Teddy used it to get into the property records for the state of California, where he conducted searches for Simon Duchamp and the Duchamp Gallery. There were no hits for either.

Another link led him to a very handy, aggregate database

that combined hotel booking records from the major chains in the U.S. This proved more fruitful.

Three rooms at the Verdugo Royale Hotel in Beverly Hills were currently booked by Duchamp Gallery. Two standard rooms and a suite. Teddy was sure Simon Duchamp would be in the latter.

He exchanged the laptop for a few items he thought he might need from the safe, then returned his office to its normal state.

At the studio's costume department, he picked up a pair of gray coveralls and black work shoes, and at props, a length of rope, all of which went into a duffel. He then returned to his Porsche and headed out.

His next stop was a parking garage at Cedars-Sinai Medical Center. At this time of night, there were several open spots and almost no one walking around. With the help of the makeup kit he kept in his car and a wig from his safe, he turned himself into a middle-aged everyman, with a face not even a mother would remember. He then donned the coveralls and shoes to complete his transformation. Sporting a new identity, he drove to Beverly Hills and parked a few blocks from the Verdugo Royale Hotel.

Ten minutes later, he was rappelling from a balcony of an unoccupied suite onto the one belonging to Duchamp's room. He landed without a sound, untied himself, and crept to the windows.

Inside, a man sat at a dining table, working on a laptop. He was angled so that Teddy could only see a portion of his face, but it was enough to determine he fit the description of Duchamp.

Teddy pulled out a listening device designed specifically to pick up voices through glass and stuck it to the lower corner of the windowed wall. He then climbed back to the balcony above.

On his way out of the hotel, he hid a relay in a maintenance supply closet. The device would upload to the cloud everything the bugs picked up, allowing Teddy to access the data whenever and wherever he wanted.

One hundred and twenty miles to the south, near the city of Del Mar, Benji and his crew were crouched behind a hedge, preparing to steal the final Matilda Stone for Simon. Tonight, they were dressed as firefighters.

"Are we going to just wait around or what?" Sticks whispered.

Benji grimaced. "You're sure you can control it?"

"Have I ever not been able to?"

Benji almost brought up last night's blaze. It had definitely burned out of control and had even taken the life of the guy they'd dumped at the side of the road—the potential repercussions for which Benji was trying hard not to think about. He knew if he mentioned the fire, though, Sticks would throw the blame right back into his lap. Benji *was* the one who forgot to call 911, after all.

So instead, he said, "Sorry. The schedule just has me on edge."

"I can control it, okay?"

"Okay."

When Simon had pulled Benji into his office to talk about the next job, Benji was already expecting the worst. He'd been there for his brother's conversation with the client, and his eyes had nearly bugged out of his head when he heard that the client was expecting three paintings on Friday. He'd assumed Simon would have given Benji a day to prep, meaning they'd steal the painting on Thursday night. But no, Simon wanted it at the gallery Thursday morning. Which meant they had to get it tonight.

Two thefts in two nights. They had never done that before. Hell, before last night, they had never done two within a week of each other.

The target was also less than appealing. Instead of being surrounded by wilderness, it was in an upscale gated community. Using the brushfire excuse wasn't going to work here. Plus, they had to sneak into the area on foot and would have to leave with the painting the same way. Even a week of preparation wouldn't have been enough to do this one right.

Benji didn't like it, but it wasn't like he could say no.

"Check your devices one more time," Benji said to Sticks.

Sticks rolled his eyes but kept any comments to himself and crept away. He returned ten minutes later and gave Benji a thumbs-up.

Benji tapped Devin on the shoulder and nodded.

Devin headed off on a route that would take him to the street the house was on. Soon, his voice came over Benji's earpiece. "In position."

"Do it," Benji whispered to Sticks.

Sticks smirked and tapped his phone screen.

Within seconds, flames sparked at several points along the back of the house at the north end. Benji waited until he was sure the wall was burning, then turned on his mic. "Devin, you're up."

"Copy," Devin said.

As planned, Devin left his mic on so that Benji heard him pound on the front door until it opened.

"What the hell?" a man's voice said, muffled by the door.

"Your house is on fire," Devin said. "You need to get out."

"What?"

"Is there anyone else in the house?"

"Um, my son's upstairs."

"Is that it?"

"Yes."

"I'll get him, it's safer that way. Please, I insist you move to the street."

"Wait. Are you alone? Where's your truck?"

"Not alone and the truck will be here soon. Now, sir, you need to go now!"

The man moved as instructed, and the conversation was replaced with the sound of movement. Then there was a *click* and Devin said, "Back door unlocked."

Benji and Sticks ran to the French doors at the back of the house. Pulling it open, Benji rushed inside just in time to see Devin disappear up the stairs to grab the son.

"This way," he said to Sticks.

With how quickly this job had been thrown together, Benji half expected the info about the painting being in the formal dining room would be wrong. But sure enough, the Stone hung right where it was supposed to be.

Benji pulled it down, removed it from its frame, and leaned the frame against the wall. Sticks then placed one of his fire starters on the floor against the frame. Since there had been no time to prep any false evidence, the frame alone would have to sell the idea that the painting had burned.

By the time Sticks said "Ready," Benji had the Stone wrapped in a fire blanket.

"Light it up," Benji said.

The device burst into flames that quickly spread onto the wall.

"Let's go," Benji said.

He raced into the living room.

From across the room a deep voice yelled, "What the hell are you doing?"

A middle-aged man stared at Benji from the base of the stairs, one foot on the first riser, as if he had been about to go up, his voice identical to that of the homeowner Devin was supposed to have sent away.

"This house is on fire!" Benji shouted. "You need to get out!"

"What is that under your arm?"

"Sir! You shouldn't be in here. It's too dangerous."

From above came the sound of running feet. A younger clone of the guy came halfway down the stairs, then stopped. Devin was right behind him.

"Dad?" the kid said. "This guy said the house is on fire."

"Let's go, let's go," Devin said.

The father's gaze moved past Benji and Sticks to the dining room entrance. From his angle he could see the empty frame and the flames below it.

He looked back at Benji. "Is that my painting?"

"Let's go!" Benji yelled and began running toward the open French doors.

"You're the people the insurance people called me about to-day, aren't you?"

Benji nearly tripped over his own feet. He looked back. Before he could ask what the guy meant, Sticks grabbed his shoulders and pushed him toward the French doors. "Run, dammit!"

They sprinted out the doors and across the backyard. They

had just reached the hedges when a gunshot sounded behind them.

"Oh, shit!" Sticks exclaimed, then raced past Benji toward the fence around the community.

Benji glanced over his shoulder, looking for Devin, but didn't see him. He told himself it had probably been easier for his friend to escape through the front door, not wanting to consider the alternative.

Sticks scaled the fence first and started to run again.

"Where the hell are you going?" Benji said. "You have to help me."

There was a moment when it looked like Sticks was going to ignore him, but he came back and Benji passed the painting to him before scaling the fence himself. They hurried back to their car.

Devin wasn't there yet. They climbed in, and Benji started the engine, but didn't put it into gear.

"We gotta go!" Sticks said.

"We're waiting for Devin."

"Fuck Devin. If he got out, he would have radioed us by now."

Benji had completely forgotten about the radio. He checked his mic. It was still on. "Devin, you there?"

Silence.

"Devin?"

Still nothing.

"Maybe his radio broke."

"Right, sure." Sticks clearly didn't believe that. "Come on, Benji. Maybe he got caught, maybe he didn't. Whatever happened, we're dead meat if we don't go."

Benji scowled, then started the car, knowing Sticks was right.

Once they were safely on the freeway heading north, he called his brother.

"Did you get it?" Simon said, through the car's speakers.

"We did, but—"

"Then why are you calling me? It's . . . after midnight."

"We might have a problem."

"What kind of problem?"

"Something might have happened to Devin."

"*Might* have?"

"Things went sideways before we left the house. The owner saw us. Sticks and I got away with the painting, but I don't know what happened to Devin. I can't reach him."

"He's probably just—how do you say it?—lying low."

Memory of the gunshot echoed in Benji's mind. "I'm not so sure."

"You got the painting. That's what matters."

"Except the guy we took it from knows it didn't burn."

There was a long pause in which Benji feared his brother realized the severity of the situation. Instead of addressing it directly, though, Simon's tone simply turned low and threatening. "I'll be at the gallery tomorrow morning by nine-thirty. I expect you to be waiting for me."

He hung up.

"Devin was right," Sticks said. "Your brother is an asshole."

Benji sighed. "He is."

"How much longer are you going to work for him?"

"Until he doesn't need us anymore."

"Buddy, there is no 'us' here. After the drop-off, I'm done with him."

"And then what? You're not going to find a job that pays as good as this one."

Sticks snorted. "I already have."

Benji shot him a surprised look. "With who?"

"Why would I tell you?"

Neither said a word for the next few miles.

Then Benji said, "Any room on that new job for me?"

CHAPTER 37

⸻◈⸻

The first thing Teddy did when he woke up Thursday morning was check the recording from the audio tap on Simon's hotel room.

The device was voice activated and had only gone off once, at 12:13 a.m., when Simon received a phone call. Teddy could hear only his side of the conversation, but it was more than enough to confirm Simon was dirty.

"You got the painting," Simon had said on the recording. "That's what matters."

Simon wasn't tangentially connected to the thefts. He was directly involved. He also revealed that the painting was to be delivered to *him* at *his* gallery in just a few hours.

That sounded like an event Teddy should attend, too.

By 8:15, he was parked a few blocks from the gallery. Dressed as an elderly retiree, he shuffled to a spot where he had a view of the gallery's parking lot.

Twenty minutes later, a dark gray BMW 530i pulled into the lot, carrying two passengers. The engine shut off, but the men didn't get out.

Whether they were the art thieves or not, Teddy had a strong feeling they had an interest in the upcoming delivery.

He snapped several pictures.

At the same time Teddy was disguising himself for his stakeout, Simon woke to find a voice message awaiting him from Nico Savage.

"Hi, Simon. Mr. Petry has learned that you'll be receiving the third painting this morning. We want to be there when that happens, so expect us at the gallery at nine."

Simon stared at his phone.

Only five people knew about last night's job: himself, Phillip, Benji, Devin, and Sticks. And of that group, only Simon and his brother knew about the delivery time.

Wait, he thought.

Sticks had been in the car with Benji, so he would have heard everything. He had to be the one who'd told Petry.

The son-of-a-bitch pyro needed to be dealt with, but after Simon took care of the more immediate problem of Petry.

Simon had promised him the paintings tomorrow, not today, so the other two were with Rudy Morgan. Simon had planned on personally taking the third one to the forger this morning.

While he could swing by and pick up the originals on his way to the gallery, he was loath to turn them over to Petry.

Screw it, he decided. He'd give Petry the one Benji was bringing this morning but would make up some excuse as to why the other two wouldn't be available until tomorrow, when he could stick Petry with the forgeries. Saving two out of the three originals was better than saving none.

Knowing it would be easier to deliver this news with Phillip behind him, Simon rang his bodyguard, but was immediately sent to voicemail. That was odd. Phillip always took his calls.

After the beep, Simon left a message for him to be at the gallery by eight-forty-five.

When Simon pulled into the gallery's lot, he was annoyed to find no sign of Phillip, and worse, Nico and Petry were already there. As Simon exited his sedan, Petry and Nico climbed out of their vehicle.

Simon forced on a smile. "Good morning. I hope you haven't been waiting long."

"Morning," Nico said.

Petry only nodded, and neither said anything else.

Simon unlocked the back door and led them inside.

"Would either of you like a coffee?"

"Please," Nico said.

Since Petry was still playing the silent game, Simon took Nico's answer to apply to both. He started up the Keurig and went to his office to send his brother and Phillip identical texts.

Get your ass here now!!

Teddy watched Simon escort the two men from the BMW into the gallery. Neither of Simon's visitors carried anything, reinforcing Teddy's sense that the men weren't the thieves. They might be the buyers, however.

At twenty past nine, a Ford Taurus pulled into the lot. Like the BMW, it had two passengers. Teddy shot pictures of both.

The driver hopped out and went into the gallery for less than a minute before stepping back out and returning to his car.

Instead of getting in, he said something to his buddy in the passenger seat, then circled back to the trunk and opened it. As his friend climbed out, the driver removed a rectangular package from the back.

Now, that *could be a painting,* Teddy thought.

The driver carried the package to the back door, his buddy trailing behind. After they disappeared inside, Teddy waited a few moments to make sure they didn't come straight back out, then walked into the parking lot and attached tracking bugs to all three vehicles.

Simon motioned to the package in Benji's hands. "Mr. Petry, I'm honored to present you with your final painting, a day ahead of schedule. Would you like me to unwrap it?"

Petry shrugged. "Sure. Why not?"

Benji put the Stone on an easel, and Simon removed the paper and Bubble Wrap.

"As you can see, it's a spectacular piece."

Petry shrugged. "Yeah, it's great."

Ignoring the man's indifference, Simon said, "Since delivery wasn't supposed to be until tomorrow, I had stored the other two at my secure off-site location. I'm not sure how quickly I—"

"We won't be taking any of them with us."

"I'm sorry?"

"Mr. Martin will be accepting delivery for us."

"Mr. Martin? I'm afraid I don't know who that is."

"That seems unlikely." Petry's gaze shifted to where Benji and Sticks were standing.

Simon turned his head to follow it.

Sticks grinned and said, "That's me."

Simon whipped his gaze back to Petry. "You want *him* to pick them up for you?"

"That's what I said."

"Sticks—I mean, Mr. Martin—works for me, not you."

"The fuck I do," Sticks said.

"It's my understanding that Mr. Martin is a freelancer who has just completed a job for you," Petry said matter-of-factly. "Now he'll be doing a job for me."

"What kind of job?"

"That's none of your concern."

Simon couldn't believe what he was hearing. "Do you . . . Do you realize . . . You know what he does, don't you?"

"I'm aware of Mr. Martin's special skills. Why do you think I hired him?"

It all clicked into place. "Y-y-you're going to burn the paintings?"

"Did I say that?"

"Why would you do that? They're irreplaceable. They're—"

"Don't you worry. I'm planning on getting my full money's worth out of them."

"By burning them?"

"By using them as a message."

Simon clasped his hands together to keep them from shaking. He had feared Petry's intentions, but having them confirmed was too much. He could not just stand there and do nothing.

"I'm sorry, Mr. Petry, but our deal is off." He gestured to the exit. "Please leave."

Petry chuckled but didn't get up. "Nico?"

"Transfers complete."

"See, Simon. You've already been paid. The paintings are mine."

"What? No. I—I—I'll transfer it right back to you."

"Not going to happen."

The back door swung open. Simon whirled around, hoping Phillip had finally arrived, but it was only one of his employees.

"I'm sorry, Jessica, but I'm in the middle of a meeting. Could you come back in fifteen minutes?"

"Um . . ."

"Here." He hurried over and handed her twenty bucks. "Grab a coffee on me."

He ushered her out the door and scanned the lot for Phillip's car, but it wasn't there.

"Looking for your muscle?" Petry asked.

Simon closed the door. "My what?"

Petry looked at Sticks again. "Mr. Martin, what was his name?"

"Phillip," Sticks said.

"What about Phillip?" Simon asked.

"I'm not a man you want to cross," Petry said. "I figured with him around, you might try to do just that. All I did was remove a potential obstacle."

"What does that mean?"

"Beats me. I leave those details to others. The important thing for you to know is that our deal is done. All you have to do is to turn everything over to Mr. Martin tomorrow." He paused, then added, "Unless you'd like an up-close and personal look at those details I don't know about."

Simon blanched.

"So, we're cool?" Nico asked.

Simon had no choice but to nod.

"Mr. Martin, any requests?" Petry said.

"I want 'em boxed up all together. And none of that cardboard shit. Make it out of wood." He grinned at Petry. "Make things easier when the time comes."

"Sounds good to me. Good by you, Simon?"

Another reluctant nod.

"Great." Petry stood. "Nico, I feel like some pancakes."

"I know just the place."

As soon as the two men left, Simon leveled a glare at Sticks. "I don't want to see your face ever again."

"It's not like I enjoy looking at you, either, asshole," Sticks said. "But we still have business to finish. I'll pick them up tomorrow afternoon. Don't forget about the box."

"I have no intention of doing anything for—"

"Or I can call Mr. Petry right now. Doubt they've left the parking lot yet." He pulled out his phone.

"Wait." The delay would give Rudy enough time to finish all three forgeries, meaning Simon could hand them over instead of the originals. "What time in the afternoon?"

"Now, that's the right attitude. I'll call you later and let you know." Sticks glanced at Benji. "You comin'?"

"Uh, yeah. Right behind you."

Sticks flashed Simon a toothy grin. "Forgot to tell you. Benji works for me now."

They walked out the door, leaving Simon staring after them.

CHAPTER 38

———————◎———————

S tone finished his last lap and climbed out of the pool.

"Please tell me this means we can order breakfast now," Monica said.

When he'd come down for a swim, he'd been alone. Now, Monica was sitting at the poolside table with Viv and Dino. Viv was typing on a laptop while Dino was working his way through the *New York Times*.

Stone grabbed his towel off the nearby lounge and started drying off. "You didn't have to wait for me."

Dino folded down the paper. "That's what I told her."

"Nonsense," Monica said. "I wasn't going to eat without you."

"Looks like she's not tired of you yet," Dino said.

"I don't plan on there being a *yet*," she said.

"None of them ever do."

Stone walked over to Monica and kissed her. "Don't listen to Dino. He doesn't understand romance."

"I understand it fine. Viv, tell them."

Viv looked up. "Tell them what?"

"That I know all about romance."

Her eyes narrowed. "Not sure you want me to answer that question."

"On second thought, I believe someone said something about breakfast?" Dino said.

Viv closed her computer. "None for me, thank you. I need to get to the office. I was there until almost midnight working out logistics with our team in Jakarta, and there's still more to do."

"I thought you were taking a few days off," Stone said.

"This *is* her taking a few days off," Dino said. "Look, the sun's already up and she's only now talking about going to work."

Viv stood and kissed Dino on the cheek. "Try to stay out of trouble today."

"I take it Dino mentioned our travails yesterday," Stone said.

"In detail."

"I also told you I wasn't the one found at the scene of a murder yesterday."

"Today's a new day, so you never know."

"Again, don't look at me," Dino said, gesturing at Monica.

"In fairness, that was the first time that's happened to me, too," Monica said.

"You came close in New Mexico," Stone said.

"Not the same thing."

"If you say so."

"See you all later." Viv headed into the house.

"Before I forget," Dino said. "Ben sent over some documents he said we should look through before the first board meeting tomorrow. I left your set on the dining table."

Monica's phone began vibrating. She checked the screen, then said, "It's my friend Patricia. Excuse me for a minute."

She got up and took the call out of earshot. When she returned, she said, "They messed up."

"Who messed up?" Stone asked.

"My art thieves. They went after another painting last night, this time in Del Mar. And before you ask, yes, it was another one of your mother's."

"Were they caught?"

"Not exactly. Two of them escaped with the painting. The other was shot by the homeowner."

"Please tell us it wasn't fatal and the police were able to question him?"

"I wish I could. The house was on fire when the homeowner caught them in the act. He shot the one guy and tried to follow the other two. By the time he got back to the house, the fire had spread, and he couldn't get inside to pull the guy out."

"I'm guessing it's too soon for the police to have IDed the body," Dino said.

She nodded. "The good thing is, since the owner saw the other two run off with the painting, the higher-ups at Vitale are starting to wonder if the other fires might have been distractions as well. My friend showed them the reports I'd been giving to Dalton. Turns out he hadn't passed any of them on."

"Maybe they'll give you your job back."

"I don't want my job back. If I return, I want Dalton's."

"Tell them that," Stone said.

"I will."

They ordered food, and it arrived with an unexpected visitor.

"Morning, Billy," Stone said. "If I'd known you were coming by, I would have ordered something for you, too."

Billy waved him off. "Ate before I left the house this morning."

Dino motioned to an empty seat. "Take a load off."

Billy did so. "Where's Viv?"

"One guess," Dino said.

"Ah. At least one of your family actually works for their salary."

"Not true," Stone said. "Ben and Tessa also work for theirs."

"I sit corrected," Billy said.

"I'll have you know I earn every penny I make," Dino said.

"Whatever helps you sleep at night."

"I take it this visit means your contact has learned something," Stone said.

Billy nodded. "Last night, my friend happened to overhear Simon Duchamp on a phone call, during which he arranged for the delivery of a painting this morning."

"A *stolen* painting?" Monica asked.

"He didn't come right out and say that, but that's what it sounded like. He also said that the painting had been obtained last night, and that there was some sort of problem with the job."

"Monica, I think you should tell Billy what your friend told you," Stone said.

She did so.

"Do you know the dimensions of the stolen painting?"

"I can find out." She sent Patricia a text and received an immediate reply. "She says it's two and a half feet by three and a half."

"Something like this?" Billy turned his phone so everyone

could see the screen. On it was a photo of a sedan in a parking lot. One man was climbing out of the front passenger seat, while a second was next to the open trunk, holding a rectangular package.

"Looks like the right size to me," Stone said. "Do we know who the men are?"

"Not yet, but my friend's convinced one of them is the person Simon had talked to on the phone."

"Two people here and two people missing from the crime scene in Del Mar," Monica said.

"That's what I was thinking," Stone said.

"Does anyone recognize them?" Billy asked.

"I don't."

Monica studied the picture a few seconds longer, then shook her head. "Sorry, no."

"Apparently there were two other people present this morning, beside those two and Duchamp. It's possible they're the buyers." Billy flipped through his photos until he came to the best one of the men from the BMW, then showed it to the others.

"I've never seen them," Monica said.

Stone gestured to the phone. "May I?"

Billy handed it to him.

Stone pinched the image to magnify the men's faces. "I'll be damned."

"You know them?" Monica asked.

"Not this one." Stone pointed at the younger man, then moved his finger to the older one. "But him I do."

"Who is he?"

"Winston Petry."

"That name sounds familiar," Dino said.

"It should. He was the defendant in the lawsuit that Herb won for my client."

"Wait, now that rings a bell. Was he the guy that confronted you in front of the Seagram's building?"

"The very same."

"Let me see that."

Stone passed Dino the phone.

Dino checked out the picture. "He looks like an asshole."

"He is," Stone said.

"Is he an art collector?" Monica asked.

Stone shrugged. "I have no personal knowledge of it, but if he is, my guess would be that his tastes run more toward *Dogs Playing Poker* than my mother's work."

"Then why was he there?"

"Revenge would be my guess."

"For losing a lawsuit?"

"A thirty-two-million-dollar lawsuit."

"Oof."

"But Petry's anger doesn't stem solely from losing the suit. Our paths have crossed before."

"What happened then?"

"He lost his business and was a hair's breadth away from federal prison time."

"Because of you?"

"Because of me."

"So he's twice burned."

"I'm sure he sees it that way."

"Then you think he hired Simon to steal your mother's paintings to . . . what? Keep you from obtaining them yourself?"

"I'm sure that's part of it. But something tells me that wouldn't be enough for him."

"Then what?"

"I'm not sure, but whatever it is, it can't be good."

"You don't think he'd harm them, do you?"

"I feel certain he'd have no problem doing that."

"That's what I'm thinking, too," Billy said.

"Because he broke the law, and you called him on it?" Monica said. "Talk about petty."

"You haven't known Stone long enough yet, my dear," Dino said. "He's a revenge magnet."

"This has happened before?".

"Variations on a theme," Stone said.

"The good news is that it appears your life isn't in danger this time," Dino said.

"Yet," Billy said.

Monica's eyes widened. "Someone has tried to kill you?"

Dino shook his head. "Not one person. Many."

"How many?"

"We stopped counting a few years ago."

"Dino, you're scaring her," Stone said. "It's not as bad as he's making it out."

"Have you ever been shot at?" she asked.

"Well, yes."

"More than once?"

"Also, yes."

"How many times?"

"At the risk of repeating myself, we stopped counting a few years ago," Dino said.

"Would Petry try to kill you?"

"I have no doubt he'd like nothing better than to see me take my last breath. But until that happens, I'm sure he'll be content with hurting me in other ways."

"Like possibly doing something to your mother's paintings?"

"It's no secret how important they are to me. It's one of the places he could hurt me the most."

She stared at Stone. "Exactly what kind of law do you practice?"

"Only the good kind," he said.

"Excuse me for butting in," Billy said. "But I need to know how you'd like to proceed."

"We should go to the police," Monica said.

"Okay," Stone said, "let's say we do. With what we have right now, we could probably convince them to open an investigation into Simon Duchamp. And they might even turn up enough evidence to arrest him and shut down his operation."

"Call me crazy, but isn't that what we want?" she asked.

"It is, but it's not *all* we want."

She chewed on her lip, thinking, then said, "You're worried that Petry will get away?"

"I am, but again not my largest concern."

"That would be your mother's paintings," Dino said.

Stone nodded. "If Simon begins receiving attention from the police, Petry might act sooner than he's currently planning."

"And we still don't know when that is or what he's going to do," Monica said.

"Correct. *But* we might be able to find out. Do that, and we can put them all in prison and save my mother's paintings in the process."

"You make it sound so easy," Dino said.

Monica turned to him, confused. "Isn't this one of those conversations you shouldn't be here for?"

"In the future, if anyone asks, I was inside taking a nap," Dino said.

Stone rubbed his chin. "I think I know of a way to learn what Simon's been up to without tipping off that we're onto him. As far as Petry goes, though, it would probably be best if he thinks I don't know he's in town. Billy, do you think your friend can deal with finding out his plan?"

"I'll ask, but I'm sure he can."

"What about me?" Monica asked.

"Assuming Simon was involved in setting you up and knows who you are, you can't be anywhere near him."

"Do you have any reason to believe Petry knows about Monica?" Billy asked.

"That doesn't seem like the kind of business Simon would share with a client, so I doubt it."

To Monica, Billy said, "I'll let my friend know you're available if he needs help."

"Thank you."

CHAPTER 39

S tone and Dino arrived at Duchamp Gallery at noon and approached one of the gallery employees.

"Welcome, gentlemen. My name is Mindy. How can I help you?"

"Is Mr. Duchamp in?" Stone asked. "I have something I'd like to discuss with him."

"He was here earlier. Let me check if he's still around. Can I give him your name?"

"Stone Barrington."

"One moment, Mr. Barrington."

She disappeared behind a wall at the back of the room and returned a minute later.

"You're in luck. He's in his office and asked me to bring you back."

She led them through a gap between offset walls and into the back room of the gallery.

As they neared the office door, Stone said, "Would it be okay if my friend waited out here?"

"That shouldn't be a problem." The woman gestured toward a couple of couches in the corner and said to Dino, "You can have a seat over there, if you'd like, and feel free to make yourself a coffee."

"Thanks," Dino said, and veered off.

The woman knocked on the door, then opened it. "Mr. Barrington is here."

She moved out of the way and Stone entered.

Simon jumped up and came around his desk, smiling broadly. "Stone, what a pleasure to see you again." He thrust out a hand.

Stone shook it. "Good to see you, Simon."

The art dealer returned to his seat and gestured to the guest chair. "I had no idea you were in Los Angeles."

"Here for a business meeting."

As Stone sat, he noticed a package wrapped in brown paper leaning against the wall behind Simon that looked exactly like the one in the photo Teddy had showed them.

"Of course, of course. A busy man such as yourself, you must constantly be on the move. May I ask, how did you know I was here?"

"I didn't. I was in the neighborhood, saw your gallery sign, and took a chance."

"I'm so glad you did. Did you enjoy the Cervantes exhibit in Santa Fe?"

"So much so that I bought one of her pieces."

"Is that right? I didn't realize. Which one?"

"*Escape.*"

Simon put a hand on his heart. "One of my favorites. You have a very good eye."

"I just know what I like."

"That's the approach more collectors should take. I don't mean to rush you, but I am a bit busy today. May I assume you're here to discuss your mother's paintings?"

"I am."

"I see. Unfortunately, I don't have much I can tell you at the moment, but I do anticipate news by tomorrow or possibly Saturday."

"The good kind?"

"If I say anything more, you might get your hopes up."

"Not even a hint?"

"Well, maybe a hint." Simon leaned forward and lowered his voice. "I'm hearing that the paintings may be available *very* soon."

"How soon is very?"

"You can't hold me to this."

"Of course not."

"It's possible they could be in your possession before the end of the weekend."

"That's fabulous news. How many are we talking about?"

Simon smiled excitedly. "Three."

Stone had to force himself not to look at the package behind the art dealer. "Titles?"

Duchamp wagged his palm in the air. "I've said too much already."

"I understand."

"The minute I know more, I will contact you."

"I'll be in meetings for the next two days, so if you need me during that time, text me, and I'll slip out and call you back."

"Very good." Simon hesitated, then said, "There *is* one matter we need to discuss."

"Price?"

Simon smiled and shook his head. "You of all people are aware of the value of your mother's work. I won't even attempt to gouge you."

"Glad to hear it. Then what do we need to discuss?"

"Any sale has to remain between the two of us."

"I don't follow."

"The sellers are experiencing financial issues and have no choice but to sell to raise funds. If anyone they deal with finds out, that could cause problems for them."

"You mean no publicizing the sale."

"Precisely."

"What I spend my money on is my business and no one else's."

"I'm so glad you understand."

"Is there anything else I should know?"

"I believe that's it."

They stood.

"Thank you for taking time to see me," Stone said.

"It was my pleasure. Here, let me see you out."

Stone waved him off. "Don't bother. I remember the way." He opened the door, then looked back as if he'd just thought of something. "You can't give me even a hint of which paintings they are?"

Simon mimed zipping his mouth closed.

"Thought I'd give it a shot. I'll let you get back to work."

Stone met up with Dino in the back room, and they returned

to their SUV, neither saying a word until they were on their way to the Centurion lot.

"Anything?" Stone asked.

Dino shook his head. "No sign of them." He'd spent the time hunting the back area for the stolen paintings.

"It would have been nice if he'd made this easy for us."

"Since when does anyone make things easy for us? How did your conversation go?"

Stone recounted what he and Simon had talked about.

"So, he's offering you the exact number of your mother's paintings that are confirmed as missing. What a coincidence."

"It is, indeed."

"What I don't get is: If he's been stealing them *for* Petry, why is he selling them to you?"

"If you come up with an answer, let me know."

Prior to Barrington's unexpected visit, Simon had been staring at his computer, wondering how everything had become so twisted. He had been running this ring for years without a hiccup, and now everything was hanging by a thread. Bad enough that even his brother had betrayed him. But the conversation with the lawyer had knocked him out of his funk, and he was finally able to see things clearly.

It was time for Simon to get out of the art business, of every kind.

Years ago, he'd socked away a substantial stack of cash in a Cayman Islands bank. With that and the million he'd just received from Petry, he would have more than enough to live comfortably a good long while.

His plan formed quickly. He'd give the forgeries to Sticks, sell the originals to Barrington to add to his nest egg, then he'd sneak out of the country on a false passport he kept for emergencies. He just needed to make it through the next thirty-six hours, then Simon Duchamp would never be seen again.

He shot to his feet. There was work to do.

Rudy Morgan's studio was located downtown, in an old factory that had been refurbished and divided into townhomes.

Simon had to press the doorbell three times before Rudy's voice came through the intercom. "I'm busy. What do you want?"

"It's Simon. I have the final painting for you."

The door buzzed.

He located Rudy in the man's basement-level studio, sitting in front of a pair of easels.

"Where should I put this?" Simon asked, holding up the painting from Del Mar.

Rudy nodded toward a wall without looking away from what he was doing. Simon deposited the painting, then joined the forger.

On one easel was the Matilda Stone original stolen in Marin County, and on the other was a near identical painting, missing only a few details.

"That's better than I expected," Simon said.

Rudy scowled. "It's crap, but I guess that's what you get when you don't give me any time."

"It'll be fine. The client won't notice."

"Are you blind? The brushstrokes are wrong. And look at this." He pointed at a tree on the original and then the same spot on his fake. "I can't get the color right."

Simon leaned in for a closer look. He could see what Rudy was talking about, but he knew Petry would never notice.

"It's more than good enough for the time you've had."

Rudy snorted, then started painting again.

"The other one?" Simon asked.

Rudy yawned and nodded toward the corner. "Over there."

"May I?"

"Knock yourself out."

Summer at Sheep Meadow leaned against the wall, next to its original. If anything, it looked even better than the one Rudy was working on.

"When will you get to the one I just brought?"

"When I finish this one, which"—Rudy paused to yawn again—"is getting further and further away the longer you bother me."

"They'll all be ready tomorrow morning, though?"

"You said noon."

"Fine, fine, noon."

Rudy tried to stifle a third yawn but failed. "They'll be ready."

"I need them boxed, too."

"You never said anything about boxing them."

"I'm saying it now. All in one. But don't make it too big. You and I will need to carry it out of here."

"Anything else, your lordship?"

"That's all for now."

"Fuck you very much, Simon."

"I'll see you tomorrow. Oh, and if you do happen to get them done early, let me know."

"Get out!"

———

Pain shot through Phillip's skull as he lifted his head and opened his eyes.

He was in a dingy, dimly lit room, tied to a chair. He tried to pull free from his restraints, but his arms barely moved.

The last thing he remembered was being rear-ended while heading to the hotel for the night. He'd gotten out to give the other driver a piece of his mind when someone had come up behind him and plunged a needle into his arm and everything went dark.

From the way his body ached, whoever had kidnapped him had been having fun working him over. They'd realize their mistake when he returned the favor.

He heard voices and the room's only door opening. Someone flicked on the overhead light, forcing him to shut his eyes against the glare.

When he pried open his lids again, he could see at least a half dozen people in the room, snickering and glaring at him. Based on the choice of tattoos climbing up their necks and arms, they could have been models for an Aryan brotherhood recruitment poster.

"He's awake," one of them yelled into the other room.

Another one approached Phillip and tapped his cheek. "How you feeling, big guy?"

Phillip stared at him unimpressed and said nothing.

"You think you're tough?" The guy slapped him harder. "You ain't tough. If you were, you wouldn't be the one tied to the chair, now would ya?" He pinched Phillip's cheek and laughed.

Two more men entered. One had the same rough-edged look

as the others, though he was older and carried himself as if he were in charge. The other Phillip knew—Nico Savage, Petry's pet lawyer.

Nico leaned down so that he was eye to eye with Phillip. "Really sorry about this. It's not personal. You were in the way. That's all."

Phillip spit in his face.

Nico stood and casually wiped off his cheek. "I like you. In different circumstances, we could have done great things together, but my hands are tied." He turned to the guy he'd come in with. "Let me know when it's done."

As soon as he left, the beating commenced. Fists and clubs and boots pummeled Phillip from all sides, until someone tilted his face upward.

He sneered.

The guy let Phillip's head drop back down. "Shit. He ain't dead yet."

Boots approach the chair, then fingers slipped under Phillip's chin and gently raised his face again. It was the older guy who'd come in with Nico.

He chuckled. "You're something else, aren't you?"

"You want us to give it another go?" someone behind him asked.

The boss shook his head. "We've been here too long already."

"What should we do with him?"

"Bring him along. If he wants to be a punching bag, we'll let him be a punching bag."

"You heard the boss. Jared, do your thing."

A few moments later, a needle pierced Phillip's arm again.

CHAPTER 40

S tone and Dino were meeting with Constance Mueller, Centurion Pictures' CFO, when Teddy called.

"When you finish up with Connie," Teddy said, "I thought we could go for a drive."

"Hold on." Stone put a hand over the receiver. "How much longer do you think we'll be here?"

"Ten minutes at most," Constance said.

"Ten minutes and we're yours," he told Teddy.

Teddy was waiting for them when they stepped out of the administration building, a duffel bag in one hand. "Unless you're okay with Dino sitting on your lap, we'd better take your car."

Stone tossed him the key fob. "You drive."

Soon they were heading east, toward downtown.

"First stop, Taylor Foods Packinghouse," Teddy said.

"First stop?" Stone asked.

"I've had a busy day."

"How so?"

"I put trackers on Duchamp's and Petry's cars, and on the one used by the potential art thieves. After meeting with Duchamp, Petry went to Du-par's Restaurant, then the Four Seasons, where I confirmed he's staying. The vehicle remained there for fifteen minutes, then headed north, all the way to Simi Valley. That's northwest of San Fernando Valley. The car remained there for approximately a half hour and then headed back to the hotel."

"What was Petry doing all the way out there?" Stone asked.

"I don't know if it was Petry or not, but hopefully we'll find out."

"That's where this packinghouse is?"

"No. Simi Valley is our second stop. The packinghouse is in downtown L.A. It was converted into townhouses years ago. At lunchtime, your friend Simon Duchamp went there."

"Lunchtime? I met with him around noon."

"I know. I saw you."

Stone raised an eyebrow.

Billy told them about Simon leaving soon after they had, with a package that looked exactly like the one brought to him earlier. Billy had followed him to a townhouse at the packinghouse owned by someone named Rudy Morgan.

"Who's he?" Dino asked.

"That's what we're going to find out," Teddy said.

"You said you put trackers on all three cars," Stone said. "Where did the last one go?"

"It made a stop at a Home Depot, then went to a motel in North Hollywood. It hasn't moved since."

They soon arrived at Taylor Foods Packinghouse. Stone and

Dino went to Rudy Morgan's front door and waited for Teddy's signal.

When the text came, Stone rang the doorbell, but no one responded. He pushed it again, and still no one came.

"Maybe Rudy's not home," Dino suggested.

Stone called Teddy. "Either he's out or he's avoiding visitors."

"Got it. You guys hang tight. I'm going in."

Stone hung up, and he and Dino took a walk down the block, so they didn't look so suspicious. They were almost to the corner when Teddy sent a text.

Front door. Knock once.

They returned and after Stone knocked, Teddy let them in, a finger to his lips.

They followed him down a set of stairs to a dimly lit lower level that appeared to be a single open space. The sounds of deep breathing drew Stone's attention to a sofa against a wall upon which a person lay, dead asleep.

Teddy led them to a pair of easels deeper in the room and turned on his phone's flashlight.

On each easel was a version of Stone's mother's painting entitled *Twilight on the Water*, which featured a view of the Williamsburg Bridge from the East River Park. If it weren't for the fact that one still glistened from fresh paint, the two paintings would have been near identical. Stone had lived with his mother's work his entire life, though, and it didn't take new paint for it to be obvious to him which was the original and which a fake.

Teddy guided them to the side of the room, where *Summer at Sheep Meadow* leaned against the wall with a look-alike painting. The fake was even better than that of *Twilight*, but even though the forgery had been aged to match the original, Stone could also tell them apart right away.

This painting was special, a snapshot of his life, and for a moment, he was taken back to that carefree day and the picnic he'd had with his parents. While that might have choked him up when he was younger, now it brought a smile to his face.

He forced himself to look away. There would be time to study it later. He held up three fingers, silently asking Billy if the last missing painting was here.

Teddy took them to a table. On it was a paper-and-Bubble-Wrapped package that matched the one Stone had seen in Simon's office. Stone peeled back a loose corner for a peek.

Inside was the third piece, *Morning on the Avenue.*

They returned upstairs and found a place far from the stairs, where they could talk.

"What do you want to do next?" Teddy asked Stone.

"Is it too simple to just walk out with the paintings now and get on our way?" Dino asked.

"That depends on our goal," Teddy said. "If we just grab and go, you might be able to still snag Simon, but what if Rudy calls and warns him before the police get to him?"

"He could get away," Stone said.

Teddy nodded. "Another option is to call the cops and wait for them here. Then we'll get the forger and likely Simon and his people."

"But not Petry," Stone said.

"Probably not."

"I want to take them all down."

Teddy smiled. "I was hoping you'd say that."

CHAPTER 41

It took a single slap to wake Rudy. He gasped and looked around, then tensed at the sight of Stone, Dino, and Teddy sitting on chairs next to the couch.

"Have a good nap?" Stone asked.

The forger tried to get to his feet but was quickly thwarted by the duct tape binding his wrists and ankles.

"Who are you? What are you doing in my place?"

"My friends and I have been debating what we should do with you."

"What do you mean 'do with' me?"

"We *could* call the police and show them around your studio. That would be awkward for you. How are you going to explain why there are at least three stolen paintings here? That alone will get you a nice chunk of prison time."

"T-t-they're not mine."

"Which, I believe, is the definition of stolen," Dino said.

"I didn't steal them, I swear."

"Possession of stolen items is still a crime."

"And then there are the forgeries . . ." Stone said.

Rudy started hyperventilating. "But—bu—but—"

"You're very good, by the way. You've only had them for a couple days at most, and while they might not be perfect copies, they're close."

"Um, thank you?"

"You're welcome. Now, where was I?"

"You were going through his choices," Dino said.

"Ah, that's right. You *could* decide to cooperate with us, and by that I mean do everything we tell you to do. If you do that, when this is over, we'll put in a good word for you with the DA."

"That should knock a few years off your sentence."

Rudy stared at them, waiting for more. When it was clear nothing else was coming, he said, "Is there an option that doesn't involve me going to jail?"

"You *could* try to run, I guess, but you won't get far." Stone turned his head toward the stairs. "Lewis!"

The basement lights came on and revealed five unsmiling Strategic Services security officers standing near the stairs.

"Rudy, let me introduce you to my friend Lewis. He's in charge of your minders."

A man on one end stepped forward, nodded his head, and stepped back.

"My *minders?*"

"The day shift, anyway. Another crew will relieve them later."

Rudy looked from the Strategic Services crew to Teddy and

Dino and then to Stone. The realization of how truly screwed he was was written all over his face.

"W-what do you need me to do?"

Their visit with Rudy had taken longer than anticipated, so Stone, Dino, and Teddy didn't reach Simi Valley until almost five p.m.

The location where Petry's car had stopped turned out to be a defunct car wash on the east side of town. The place was encircled by a chain-link fence that looked like it had been there for a few years.

They parked at the curb and climbed out.

"I don't think they came here to get their car cleaned," Dino said.

"What was your first clue?" Stone asked.

"Could be they parked here and walked somewhere else," Teddy suggested.

Across the street was an eight-foot-high cinder-block wall behind which stood a housing development. The closest road into the neighborhood was two long blocks away. If that had been their destination, any sane driver would have parked closer to it.

"Someone could have picked them up and they drove away in another vehicle," Stone said. "If so, maybe they got caught on a security camera."

Teddy looked around. "I don't see any here. Let's have a look around."

The fence enclosed the building but not the entire lot, allowing them to circle the structure.

"Take a look at this," Stone said.

They were on the side opposite from the street, hidden from the view of passing traffic. There was a break in the chain link held closed by several short lengths of wire, like stitches. Unlike the surrounding fence, the wires weren't weathered, so they couldn't have been in place for long.

"I'll be right back," Teddy said.

He went back to the car, then returned soon after with his duffel bag. From inside, he gave Stone and Dino each a pair of rubber gloves.

"Just in case we don't want anyone to know we were here."

He then used a pair of pliers to untwist the wires and open a gap large enough for them to get through.

"After you," he said to Stone.

The lock on the nearest door into the building had been busted long ago. It led into what had been the shop and waiting area, its walls now covered in graffiti, its floor littered with broken shelves and trash.

"Maybe whoever came here is a fan of street art," Stone suggested.

"Not sure if any of this qualifies as art," Dino said.

"Beauty is in the eye of the beholder."

"If there's beauty here, I'm not beholding it."

"Always the critic."

Teddy disappeared through a door at the other end of the room, then called out, "Found something!"

As Stone and Dino stepped into what had likely once been an office, they were hit with the familiar metallic odor of blood.

Stone expected to see a body, but the smell was coming from several dark smears that arced around a chair in the middle of the room.

Teddy picked up one of four short lengths of rope that lay on the floor, then touched one of the chair's arms. He held up a gloved finger. On it were a few tan strands. "Rope fibers. Someone was tied to the chair."

"Whoever it was, he isn't having a great day," Stone said.

"If his friends who brought him here haven't killed him already," Dino said.

"I would also consider that a bad day."

"Fair point."

"The question is, does this have anything to do with Petry or not?" Stone said.

"No way to know for sure," Dino said. "But the blood's not completely dry, so I'd say there's a good chance his car was parked outside when whatever happened here happened."

"Agreed," Teddy said.

A search for other clues turned up nothing.

"Did you happen to bring a throwaway phone with you?" Stone asked Teddy. Even if this was unrelated to Petry, he wanted to tip off the police to what had gone down here.

"Do I look like an amateur?" Teddy asked, then pulled a cell out of his bag and tossed it to Stone.

CHAPTER 42

A t eight p.m., Stone, Monica, and Dino met Viv at Spago
in Beverly Hills.

Viv ran a finger down the menu. "None of you will
look at me funny if I order one of everything, will you?"

"That depends on who's paying," Dino said.

"Stone and I have a bit of business to talk about, so I think we
can put this on the Strategic Services tab," she said.

"In that case, order as much as you want."

She patted his hand. "Always the supportive husband."

"No time to eat today?" Stone asked.

"Not a second. Dealing with Jakarta took up the first half of
the day, and you the second."

"The aforementioned business we need to discuss, I pre-
sume."

"One and the same."

A waiter appeared and took their order.

Once they were alone again, Stone asked, "Can I assume you've been able to arrange everything?"

"I wouldn't be here if I hadn't yet. Surveillance teams are in place, and my people have bolstered our normal security at both the Arrington and the Centurion lot." Strategic Services oversaw security at both facilities.

"And you, my dear, how was your day?" Stone asked Monica.

"Nerve-racking," she said. "I spent most of it at the pool, waiting to hear from you."

"How horrible."

"Well, I was able to finish the massage I'd left in the middle of before."

"Always a silver lining."

Their food arrived, and after the waiters had gone, Monica said, "Quit stalling. I want to hear what you found out."

Stone and Dino filled Monica and Viv in on their afternoon adventures as they ate.

"Who do you think the blood at the car wash belongs to?" Monica asked.

"Not a clue," Dino said.

"We can't even be sure whatever went down there had anything to do with Petry," Stone said. "Though I for one think it does."

"I for two," Dino said.

"Count me in that camp," Monica said.

"Ditto," Viv said.

After they finished eating, Stone excused himself to use the bathroom. He was washing his hands when Dino came in.

"You shouldn't go out there yet."

"Why not?"

"Viv got a call from her team, telling her Petry just pulled up to the valet out front. He's in the bar now."

"By himself?"

"No, that Savage guy is with him."

"Maybe I should buy him a drink. Get him talking. He might show his hand."

"I suggested that. But Viv and Monica argued that now might not be a good time to agitate him. They came up with a plan that doesn't involve us. And before you ask, you're not going to like it."

"Ready?" Viv whispered.

Monica grinned. "Hell, yes."

They strolled into the bar acting like two good friends at the beginning of a night out and walked over to a pair of empty stools next to Nico Savage.

"Are these taken?" Monica asked.

"Nope," Nico said.

"Actually, they are," Petry jumped in. "We've been saving them for you."

Monica put on a flirty grin. "Have you now?"

"We have."

The women sat.

"What are you drinking?" Petry asked.

"Pinot for me," Monica said.

"Me, too," Viv said.

Petry caught the bartender's attention and ordered the wine, which was poured and delivered posthaste.

He turned back to Monica and Viv, the hint of a suggestive smirk on his lips. "What brings you two ladies out tonight?"

Viv held up her left hand and wiggled her ring finger. The wedding band that had been there minutes before was now in her clutch. It its place was a band of untanned skin. "Officially divorced as of this afternoon."

Petry raised his glass. "A toast to your freedom."

"Thank you."

They all clinked glasses and drank.

"We need to do something about the seating," Petry said. "Nico, why don't you switch places with . . . ?"

"I'm Monica, and my newly unshackled friend is Viv."

Once Monica and Nico had traded seats, Petry said, "I'm Winston, but you can call me Win."

"Because you're a winner?"

He smirked. "I would never say that about myself. That's Nico's job."

Nico raised his glass. "Guilty as charged."

"Does that mean you work for Win?" Viv asked.

"I do. I'm his lawyer."

Monica smiled and let her arm brush against Petry's. "You must be pretty important to have your own lawyer."

"More important than you can imagine," Nico said.

"Is that so?" she asked. "What do you do, Win?"

"I wouldn't want to bore you."

"I don't see how you could possibly do that."

"Well, if you insist." He launched into a highly flattering and very boring description of his business.

"Are you based in L.A.?"

"New York City."

"Here on business?"

"You could say that."

"I've always wanted to live in New York," Viv said. "It seems so exciting."

"Now that you're a free woman, you should come check it out," Nico said. "I'd be happy to show you around."

"Would you? I'd like that."

Nico handed her a business card. "Let me know when you're coming to town. I'll pick you up at the airport."

"My, aren't you chivalrous?"

"How about you?" Monica said to Petry. "Are you going to show me around when I fly out there?"

"Honey, not only would I pick you up at the airport, I'll also get you a suite at the Four Seasons."

"Sign me up."

He put an arm around her, and she let herself be pulled against him. "Nothing but the best for a beautiful woman like you."

She playfully batted him and eased away. "Charmer."

The flirting continued for a few more minutes before Viv said, "What was it you said you did? Something about helping other companies?"

"I help them reach their full potential."

"That was it! My financial adviser says I should always be on the lookout for good investment opportunities. Are you out here for an up-and-coming company? And if so, should I buy some of their stock?"

Both men stilled.

"Did I say something wrong?"

"Not at all," Petry said. "It's just . . ."

"It's just that we can't talk about deals in progress," Nico finished for him.

"I bet it's one of those insider trading kinds of things, isn't it?" Monica said.

"Something like that," Petry said.

A member of the restaurant staff approached them. "Is one of you Mr. Savage?"

Nico raised a finger. "That's me."

"Your table's ready."

"Would you ladies like to join us?" Petry said to Monica.

"We'd love to, but we only stopped in for a drink. We're meeting friends in Santa Monica. If we'd known we were going to run into you, we'd have made different plans."

"You still could."

"Tempting, but—" Monica put a hand next to her mouth and stage-whispered, "It's a bachelorette party."

"Maybe we should come with *you*."

Monica laughed. "Wouldn't that be fun? But I'm afraid girls only."

"How about tomorrow night?" Petry suggested.

"Eh, boss," Nico said. "We should probably keep tomorrow night open in case there's any issues with setting up for . . ."

Petry looked annoyed but said, "Right."

"I'm free Saturday night," Monica said. "How about you, Viv?"

"Free as a bird." She waggled her empty ring finger again.

Petry grimaced. "Can't Saturday. I'm attending an event."

"That sounds interesting. What kind of event?" Monica asked.

"A Hollywood party in the hills."

"I've always wanted to go to a Hollywood party."

"I'd love to take you, sweetheart, but I'm going to be there more as an observer than a participant. If you're free Sunday, I can promise you a night you'll never forget."

"How can a girl say no to that?" Monica gave him a fake number.

CHAPTER 43

As soon as Stone, Dino, Monica, and Viv were all back in the Cayenne and headed to the Arrington, Dino asked, "So?"

Monica smirked. "If Viv ever gets tired of you, she's not going to have a problem finding a replacement."

"Tell me something I don't know."

"Don't worry, honey," Viv said. "I'll give you plenty of warning before that happens."

"That's supposed to make me feel better?"

"The fragile male ego," Viv said to Monica. "Nothing to be done about it."

"If it's not too much trouble," Stone said, "I'd like to know if you learned anything from Petry."

Monica huffed. "I'm a trained investigator and Viv is COO of a global security organization. What do you think?"

"Do you mind sharing what you learned with the class?"

"Let's see. Where should we start?"

"How about with how full of himself he is?" Viv said.

"Already well aware of that," Stone said.

"Maybe we should start with how he's planning on attending a party Saturday night?" Monica said.

"A *Hollywood* party, I believe he called it," Viv added.

"He did. Which just happens to be the same night as Billy's party."

"Quite a coincidence."

"It is, isn't it?" Monica tapped her cheek in thought. "There was something else Petry said. What was it?"

"That he's going more as an observer than a participant."

"That was it. That seems odd."

"Very odd."

"You two sound pretty proud of yourselves," Stone said.

Viv grinned. "We do, don't we?"

"Yes, we do," Monica agreed.

"Are you done patting yourselves on the back?"

Monica shrugged. "For now, I guess."

"Then, Viv, I think you should extend the extra security to cover Billy's house."

"I'll do that. Maybe I should also have some of my people dressed as partygoers on Saturday night as well."

"That's a great idea."

Stone's phone rang. On the screen was the name Simon Duchamp.

"Everyone stay quiet," Stone said, then answered. "Hello?"

"Stone, it's Simon. I apologize for calling so late, but do you have a moment? If this is a bad time . . ."

"Not at all. What can I do for you?"

"I have excellent news. The owner has agreed to sell you all three."

Stone exchanged a glance with Monica. "That *is* excellent news. What is he asking?"

"Given your relationship to the artist, he is willing to part with them for eight hundred thousand apiece, which I'm sure you realize is less than he would get if he let them go to auction."

"That's quite generous. Can you tell me which ones they are now?"

"I can. *Twilight on the Water, Morning on the Avenue,* and *Summer at Sheep Meadow.*"

Stone shared a look with Monica.

"There are a few conditions, however," Simon said.

"I'm listening."

"In addition to the prohibition on publicity we already discussed, he would like the sale completed by midnight Saturday."

"Saturday's a bit tough for me. I'll be in a board meeting most of the day and then at an event that evening."

"I'm sorry, Stone, but I've been told the deadline is non-negotiable."

"What about tomorrow?"

Simon was silent for a few seconds. "I'm afraid that won't work, either. The paintings won't be here until Saturday morning."

"Let me see if I can make some time in my schedule. Give me a few minutes, and I'll get back to you."

"I'll await your call."

As soon as Stone hung up, Monica said, "Someone's anxious."

"But not anxious enough to part with the paintings before Petry's had the fakes for a day."

"Simon probably wants the originals at hand, just in case Petry realizes he's been stiffed," Dino said.

"But why the midnight deadline?" Viv asked.

"Only one answer I can think of," Stone said. "He wants to cut and run."

They discussed options, then Stone called Simon back.

"You have a solution, I hope?" Simon said.

"I do, as long as you don't mind meeting late."

"What time do you have in mind?"

"How about eleven p.m., Saturday, at your gallery? I should be able to break free from my event by then."

"I think that will work. And payment?"

"Once the paintings are authenticated, I'll make the transfer."

"Authenticated?" Simon sounded surprised, but then seemed to realize his mistake. "Of course, that's perfectly reasonable. Whoever you bring in will have to agree to keep the transaction confidential."

"Lucky for both of us, I don't need to bring anyone as I'm the foremost authority on my mother's work."

CHAPTER 44

———◦———

Early the next morning, Monica exited her bathroom and eyed Stone as he pulled on the jacket of his dark gray Armani suit.

"My, you do clean up nice. Just one little thing." She walked over and adjusted his blue-patterned tie. "That's better."

"Thank you, dear." He motioned to the door. "Shall we?"

Viv was already in the back of an Arrington golf cart when they stepped outside. They joined her and the driver took them to the front of the hotel, where an Audi A6 sedan with a driver awaited them.

"Good morning," Teddy Fay said from the driver's seat after they'd climbed in. He'd changed his appearance to that of a fit, middle-aged man, with dark brown hair going gray.

"You must be Billy's friend," Monica said.

"Call me John."

"I'm Monica."

"Pleasure," Teddy said.

She narrowed her eyes, studying him. "You and Billy wouldn't happen to be related, would you?"

"Not that I'm aware of. Why?"

"Something about your eyes." She sat back. "Sorry. Hazard of working with fine art. I tend to pick out details that others don't."

"Maybe you and Billy should take DNA tests," Stone suggested. "You might be long-lost brothers."

"I'll suggest it to him."

They made it downtown before the morning rush hour kicked into high gear, and were at Rudy's door a few minutes before six a.m.

The door was opened by a member of the Strategic Services security team. As Stone and the others entered, they could hear hammering coming from deeper inside the townhouse.

"I take it he's awake," Stone said.

The woman nodded. "He hasn't slept since you spoke to him yesterday."

"That doesn't sound like painting."

"He's building a box to hold the pictures."

Downstairs, they found Rudy crouched at the open end of a large crate, examining the inside. Leaning against the wall beyond him were three paintings.

"Rudy?" Stone said.

The man jumped at the sound of his name and whirled around. "You're . . . you're back."

"As we said we would be."

"What's with the women?"

"The *ladies* could be the difference between you serving a five- or twenty-year sentence."

"They aren't cops, are they?"

"Not anymore," Viv said.

Rudy swallowed hard.

Monica's brow furrowed. "Hold on."

She walked past Rudy to the canvases leaning against the wall and brushed the tip of a finger against one of them.

Rushing over, Rudy yelled, "Careful!"

He pushed her away and leaned in for a closer look. The spot she'd touched now sported a tiny smudge.

"Dammit."

He went over to one of his worktables, grabbed a few items, and returned to the damaged painting, then set to work fixing it.

"What tipped you off these were the fakes?" Stone asked Monica.

"I've been studying up on your mother's work, and I knew something was off."

"And here I thought I was the only one who could tell that quickly."

"Is that another way of saying I continue to impress you?"

"One could interpret it that way."

Rudy took a step back and studied his patch job, then faced the others. "Please, do not touch any of the paintings."

"If they can be ruined so easily, no one's going to believe they're real," Monica said.

"The other two are fine. This one will be dry enough by pickup time. Well, except for that spot, thank you very much."

"The box is for them?" Stone asked.

Rudy nodded once.

"Simon's still coming at noon?"

"As far as I know."

"Where are the originals?" Monica asked.

While Teddy hung back and examined the box, Rudy led Stone, Monica, and Viv to the other end of the studio, where dozens of canvases were stacked like books on a shelf. The Matilda Stones were hidden among them.

Monica sighed. "These are the real ones." She glanced at Stone, her eyes sparkling. "She was an amazing talent."

"She was."

"I'm sure she would be very happy that you found these."

"Thank you." Stone looked at Rudy. "Do you know yet if Simon's taking these with him when he picks up the fakes?"

"The *reproductions*," Rudy corrected him. "I do and he's not. He texted me last evening that he wants me to hold on to them until tomorrow."

"I believe we told you to let us know if he contacted you again."

"You try creating one of these overnight and tell me how much free time you have."

Teddy caught Stone's eye and tapped his watch. If Stone was going to get to the Centurion lot on time, they needed to leave soon.

"Here's how it's going to go, Rudy," Stone said. "I'm leaving, but my friends Monica and Viv are going to stay for a while, and you're going to tell them everything you know."

"Not just about these," Monica said, indicating Stone's mother's paintings. "About everything you've been involved with, from your first forgery until now."

"Are you trying to get me killed?"

"Would you rather spend the rest of your life in jail?"

Rudy looked unsure as to what would be the worse fate, but after a few seconds, he groaned. "Like I have a choice."

"Good call," Stone said.

As he and Teddy headed for the stairs, Monica pulled out her phone.

"You don't mind if I record our conversation, do you?"

Rudy groaned again.

Simon had not slept well.

First, Sticks had woken him with a call at midnight to tell him he'd be at the gallery at two p.m. It took an hour before Simon relaxed enough to doze off again. But then his dreams became one long parade of all the ways his plan could fail.

It was almost a relief when dawn came.

Before he even climbed out of bed, he called his bankers in New York and instructed them to transfer all the money in his personal account and the bulk in his business account to his Cayman Islands bank account. He left enough in the gallery's account to keep it from dipping into the red until the middle of next week. By then, he'd be living under the first of several new names, designed to eliminate any chance he would ever be found.

He didn't know yet where he would settle, but he did know his first stop would be Argentina, as it was one of a handful of countries without an extradition treaty with the U.S.

Not willing to risk being yanked off a commercial flight, he'd spent far more than he would have liked on a charter jet, set to leave at one a.m. Sunday.

After showering and dressing, he spent the next few hours checking in with his East Coast galleries, which had already opened. He didn't particularly care how they were doing, but he needed to keep up the pretense that all was normal.

At eleven-thirty, he picked up a rental cargo van and drove to Rudy's place.

A dark-haired woman with tanned skin opened the door and smiled. "You must be Simon."

"And you are?"

"I'm Rudy's girlfriend. Come in. He's expecting you."

There was something vaguely familiar about her, but he couldn't place it. Maybe he had seen her with Rudy in the past. Whatever the case, he didn't have time to worry about it. He stepped inside. "Where is he?"

"Downstairs."

The woman didn't follow him, for which he was glad. He'd much rather keep the business between him and Rudy.

The forger scowled as Simon entered the studio. "You're early."

"Are you done?"

"Yeah."

"Then what does it matter?"

"Whatever."

"I didn't know you had a girlfriend."

Something passed through Rudy's eyes too quickly for Simon to decipher.

Rudy picked up a piece of wood that would fit over the open end of the box that sat in the middle of the room. "And I don't know anything about your personal life, either. So, what does it matter?"

"Do you trust her?"

"That's a stupid question." Rudy gestured to the box. "You want me to close it, or do you need to see the paintings first?"

"That's them?"

"Why in the hell would I ask you that question if it wasn't?"

"Yes, I would like to see them first, please."

Rudy swept a hand toward the box and stepped away. "Be my guest."

Simon slipped the first painting out enough to see it and frowned. "I guess this is the best I could expect from you given the time restraints."

"Gee, thanks."

Simon pushed the painting back into the box, then repeated the process with the other two. Even a halfway competent expert would be able to tell they were forgeries, especially the last, but there was nothing to be done about it. But it really didn't matter. No expert would ever see them.

He stepped back from the box. "*Now* you can close it."

Ruby nailed the cover in place, then the two of them carried it upstairs.

When the girlfriend saw them, she jumped off the couch and said, "I'll get the door, honey."

"Thanks, uh, sweetheart," Rudy said.

Outside, there was a couple engrossed in conversation in front of the neighboring townhouse. They hadn't been there when Simon arrived, but neither seemed to take any notice of him or Rudy.

Simon and the forger slipped the container in the back door of the van and secured it to the wall with some rope.

As Simon was climbing into the driver's seat, Rudy said, "Next time find someone else."

Simon flashed a smile. "You're in luck, Rudy. There's not going to be a next time." He shut the door, started the engine, and drove off.

Monica walked over to Rudy as the van turned out of sight. Viv, who had been one half of the couple talking on the sidewalk, joined them.

"Did you hear what he said right before he left?" Viv asked.

Monica, Rudy's faux girlfriend, nodded. "I think Stone's theory about him going on the run is right." She turned to Rudy. "Nice job on the acting."

"Oh, um, thanks, I guess."

"Maybe prison will have a drama club."

Rudy blanched.

CHAPTER 45

After dropping Stone off at the Centurion lot, Teddy drove to the Duchamp Gallery and used his well-honed skills to break in and disable the alarm.

Thanks to the audio bug in Simon's suite, he'd learned that something was happening at the gallery at two. The obvious assumption being that it would be the time Petry picked up the forgeries.

Teddy spent ten minutes installing microcameras in the gallery's back room, Simon's office, and the showroom. Then, on his way back to the Audi, he placed four more cameras around the parking lot.

Once he'd checked that all the feeds were working, he drove to his house and transformed into Billy Barnett.

Thirty minutes later, he was on the Centurion lot, where he spent the rest of the morning huddled with his assistant, Stacy, going over preparations for tomorrow night's party.

"... and in May of next year, we have three planned releases: *Face to Face*, directed by Lawrence Johns; *Smiling Eyes*, directed by Liesel Zhao; and *Codes of My Father*, directed by Zonnie Turman. There's a chance that—"

The conference room door opened, cutting off Centurion Pictures' VP of production.

Billy stepped in. "Sorry to interrupt. Ben, could I have a moment?"

Ben Bacchetti nodded and said to the room, "We'll take a quick break."

After he and Billy left the room, Dino leaned into Stone. "Twenty bucks says it's about us."

"No bet."

Less than a minute later, Ben and Billy returned.

"There's something that needs my attention," Ben said. "Nothing serious, but it'll take more than a few minutes. If there are no objections, let's reconvene in one hour."

There were no objections.

Billy caught Stone's attention and looked to the door. Stone and Dino followed Billy out and into an office one floor down, where three chairs faced an open laptop.

Once the door was locked and they were all seated, Billy tapped a few keys on the laptop. A grid appeared on the screen showing a dozen different camera feeds.

"I thought you might be interested in watching the handoff of the forgeries."

"You thought right," Stone said.

Billy clicked on a feed covering the back room of Simon's

gallery, and the picture increased to a quarter of the screen, while the others shrank to fill the remaining space.

In the center of the room was the box Rudy had made for the forgeries. Simon was pacing a groove in the floor beyond it.

"Looks like it's time." Billy exchanged the enlarged interior feed with one from the parking lot.

A small cube truck had just pulled into the lot. It performed a three-point turn and backed toward the gallery's rear door. When it stopped, two men got out.

"That's not Petry," Stone said.

"Not his lawyer, either," Dino said.

Billy increased the magnification. "Those are the two who delivered the original yesterday."

"I thought they worked for Simon," Stone said.

The scrawnier of the two reached the gallery's door first and pounded on it.

Billy switched back to the interior view in time to see Simon briefly close his eyes before walking to the exit.

Dino grunted. "I can't tell if he's happy they're there or wishes they hadn't come."

As soon as the door opened, the scrawny one stepped inside. "Hello, asshole."

Simon did not respond.

The guy jutted his chin at the box. "That it?"

"Yes. Just take it and get out of here."

"You're acting like you want to get rid of us. That ain't very nice."

"I don't need to be nice."

The guy laughed. "You don't even know how to be nice. Maybe if you did, your brother and I wouldn't have left you."

"Sticks," the man who presumably was Simon's brother said. "Let's get it and go."

Sticks held Simon's gaze for a few more seconds, then chuckled. "Sure. No sense staying someplace we ain't wanted."

Simon's glare turned ice cold as it fell on his brother, but neither said a word.

Sticks circled the box, rapping on the wood several times. "Nice and dry. This will work perfect."

The microphone barely picked up the brother as he whispered, "We should make sure they're inside."

Sticks shot a look at Simon. "Good point. Maybe big bro is pulling a fast one."

"Go ahead," Simon said. "Check."

"We need a crowbar or hammer," the brother said.

Simon didn't move.

Sticks pointed at Simon. "Hey, jerkwad! You heard him."

Simon frowned, then jutted his chin at the worktable. "Toolbox is over there."

The brother retrieved a hammer and opened one end of the box.

Sticks looked inside, then pulled one of the canvases out a few inches, scoffed at it, and pushed it back in. "The things people call art. Garbage, if you ask me."

He motioned for his partner to put the cover back on.

A few feet away, Simon visibly relaxed, though the other two didn't seem to notice.

"Give me that," Sticks said.

Simon's brother, who had just finished closing the box, handed him the hammer.

Sticks examined it, then cocked his arm back like he was

going to throw the hammer at Simon. Simon brought his arms up to protect his head and ducked.

Sticks laughed, the hammer still in his hand. "You should see your face." He tossed the hammer at the worktable, and it landed with a loud *bang*. "Let's roll."

The second the men were gone and the door closed, Simon sagged against the wall.

"Wait." Stone turned to Billy. "Does the truck have a tracker?"

"Don't need one."

"You have someone following it?" Dino asked.

"Don't need that, either."

Billy brought up a map on the computer, upon which a red dot was moving away from the gallery location.

"While Rudy was showing you where he'd hid your mother's originals, I planted a tracker in the box. Unless they rip the thing apart, they'll never find it."

"If it sounded like I doubted you, I apologize," Stone said. "And I will never do so again."

CHAPTER 46

———◦———

On Saturday morning, Stone lay in bed, attempting to read through the agenda for the final day of board meetings. The problem was his mind had other ideas and kept trying to poke holes in the plan to take down Petry.

Beside him, Monica groaned and nuzzled against him. She tilted her head back, peeking at him through half-closed eyes. "Hi."

"Hello, yourself. Did I wake you?"

Her hand traveled down his stomach, her lips following close behind. "Does it matter?"

He tossed the papers on the nightstand. "Not in the slightest."

A half hour later, they lay in each other's arms, worries of the coming day temporarily banished from Stone's thoughts.

"I believe that's what's referred to as an excellent start to the morning," Stone said. "Here's hoping it's a harbinger for the day ahead."

Monica propped herself up on an elbow. "Tell you what. If everything goes as planned, tomorrow I'll treat you to a repeat performance."

"And if it doesn't?"

She grinned. "Then you'll treat me."

"Deal."

They sealed it with a kiss.

"What time is it?" she asked.

"Five-thirty."

"Too early to get out of bed and too late to go back to sleep. Whatever will we do to fill the time?"

"Perhaps I should practice for tomorrow, in case things go awry."

She lay back on her pillow. "What an excellent idea."

Practice went so well that if this were any other day, they would have never left the bed.

Reluctantly, they showered and dressed, then joined Dino and Viv for breakfast.

"Everyone ready for the big day?" Viv asked.

"As ready as we can be," Stone said.

"Are you carrying?" Dino asked.

"I doubt the board meeting will get heated enough that I'll need a weapon."

"Maybe not, but the party will be a different story."

"I'm already concerned enough about tonight. I don't need to add a gun to my worries."

"What could possibly go wrong?" Dino said.

"Do you want a list? Or . . . ?"

"Now you've both gone and jinxed us," Monica said. "We might as well go back to the room and crawl into bed."

"I hadn't realized that was an option. I'm game if you are."

"Don't tempt me."

"It was your idea."

"That's not an excuse."

"I'm serious about the gun," Dino said.

Stone sighed. "Yes, Mother."

After they finished eating, a golf cart took them to the hotel entrance, where two of the Arrington's vehicles awaited them.

Stone kissed Monica. "See you back here at five."

"If you hear anything more from Billy, let me know."

"I will."

Dino and Viv shared their own goodbye, then the women headed to Strategic Services' L.A. headquarters in one Cayenne and the men to the board meeting in the other.

Teddy was also up early.

The first thing he did was check the locations of the trackers. Petry's vehicle was at the Four Seasons, and Sticks's cube truck was in the same secure parking structure in North Hollywood it had been in since the previous afternoon. Simon's car had also not moved from where it had been when Teddy had gone to sleep. Not at the Verdugo Royale Hotel where Simon had been staying, but at the LAX Hilton, where he had gone yesterday evening.

After turning himself into Billy Barnett, he ventured outside, where he met with the head of the Strategic Services overnight security team. She reported no incidents.

He was about to head back inside when headlights lit up the gate to his property.

The supervisor cocked her head, listening to her earpiece, then said, "Mr. Barnett, Stacy Lange is here."

"Great, let her in."

The gate rolled open and Billy's personal assistant drove up to the house. She climbed out of her car holding a tray with two cups of coffee. She held one out to Billy. "For you."

"Thanks," he said, taking his cup. "You ready to whip everything into shape?"

"You won't even recognize this place in a few hours. Trust me, this is going to be your best party yet."

"You know your way around the house. Help yourself to anything you need."

"Are you leaving? The sun's not even up yet."

"Busy day."

"Don't tell me Ben's making you go to the board meeting."

"No, I've been able to avoid that particular circle of hell."

She grimaced. "Then what could you be doing that I don't know about?"

"I'll let you in on a little secret. There're a lot of things I do you don't know about."

"My life would be a lot easier if that wasn't true."

"Are you sure about that?"

The deep rumble of a motor drew their attention to the gate, where a delivery truck had stopped.

"That'll be the tents," Stacy said.

"I leave everything in your capable hands."

He went inside, grabbed a pair of duffel bags he'd prepped the night before, and took them to his garage.

Today was not the day to be driving around in his easily identifiable Porsche Roadster. The same was true for his new Audi

A6. Anonymity was the theme of the day, which was why he'd borrowed one of the studio's production sedans—a five-year-old silver Ford Taurus.

He gave the guard at the gate a wave as he drove by and headed down the hill into the city.

Simon was packed and driving away from the Hilton by seven a.m., his gaze flitting to his rearview mirror every few seconds to check for tails.

He had switched hotels yesterday, booking his room under the assumed identity he would use to leave the country, to avoid Petry showing up and demanding the original Matilda Stones.

He had hoped that would allow him to get a sound night of sleep, but instead he had tossed and turned, barely getting more rest than he had the previous night.

He had only two things left to do before he could put this whole mess behind him. The first, pick up the originals from Rudy, and the second, hand them off to Barrington. Neither of which would occur until that evening, which meant he needed to lie low until then.

He cursed himself for not insisting the lawyer meet him earlier, but he'd shot himself in the foot by giving an "end of Saturday" deadline. Hindsight, and all that.

He called Rudy.

"Yeah?"

"It's Simon. I'll pick up the paintings from you at nine-thirty tonight."

"Give me a second."

The line was muted for nearly a minute.

When he came back on, Rudy said, "Nine-thirty's not going to work for me."

"Excuse me? I'm paying you *good* money."

"I delivered what you paid me for. What you *didn't* pay me for was to be a storage facility."

"That's not—" Simon stopped himself. Getting into an argument wouldn't solve anything; he also didn't want the paintings in his possession any longer than necessary. "What is the latest time I can come by?"

"Hold on."

The line was muted again.

What the hell was Rudy doing? Consulting a paper calendar or something?

Rudy returned and said, "Seven."

"Seven? You can't do any later?" Simon didn't bother hiding his annoyance.

"You know, you're kind of a son of a bitch. I'm starting to think I'm busy all day."

Simon took a deep breath. "My apologies. I have a lot going on, so I'm a bit stressed."

"And that's my problem how?"

In as contrite a tone as he could manage, Simon said, "Seven p.m. will be fine."

A new call lit up his phone. His eyes widened when he saw the caller ID. It was Phillip.

"I need to go. See you tonight." Simon punched the button to switch calls. "Phillip? Where the hell have you been?"

CHAPTER 47

Twenty-five minutes earlier in a house still under construction, sixty miles north, the rope securing Phillip's left hand finally gave way. He caught it before it flopped onto the floor, then glanced at the guy sleeping in a chair next to the room's only door. The man didn't stir.

While it had taken most of the night to cut through the one rope, it only took a minute to remove the ones around his other hand and his ankles.

He stretched to get the blood flowing and rose to his feet. He hurt everywhere, but he could deal with that later.

He silently moved to the sleeping man and snapped the guy's neck so quickly, the guard hadn't had time to wake.

A search of the body turned up a seven-inch knife and a Smith & Wesson .45-caliber pistol.

He listened at the door but heard nothing, so he eased it open and slipped through.

Seven minutes later, he stood in front of the door to the master bedroom. Scattered throughout the house behind him were the lifeless bodies of the assholes who'd kidnapped him. The only one missing was their boss. And Nico and Petry, of course. But he didn't expect them to be here.

Phillip shoved the door open, startling the naked couple lying on a mattress in the middle of the room.

"What the fuck?" the boss said. Then he realized who it was and dove toward a pistol on the floor.

Phillip pulled the Smith & Wesson's trigger and the concrete just in front of the boss's fingers shattered into dozens of shards.

The man jerked back.

Phillip gestured to the pistol on the floor. "Ma'am, kick that over to me, will you."

The woman looked at the boss.

"Don't you dare," he said.

"I wouldn't worry about what he says if I were you," Phillip said.

The woman hesitated for only a moment before getting up.

The boss tried to lunge for her, so Phillip shot him in the shoulder, knocking him back.

The woman circled around the boss and scooted the gun to Phillip.

"Thanks. You might want to use the bathroom."

"I— It's not hooked up yet."

"Please."

"Oh. Um, sure."

She hurried into the bathroom and closed the door.

Face roiling in pain, the boss yelled, "Jared! Mick! Get your asses in here!"

"Sorry, but they won't be coming," Phillip said.

The man's eyes widened. "Wait. You can just go. I'll—"

Phillip put a bullet through the center of the man's forehead. "Damn right I can just go."

He opened the bathroom door.

The woman shrieked.

"Relax, lady. I'm not going to hurt you. I just have a couple questions."

"Questions?"

"First, do you know where they put my phone?"

"Uh, I think there were a couple in the kitchen."

"Cool. Last question, where are we?"

"What?"

"Our location. I wasn't exactly conscious when they brought me here."

"Right. Uh, this is Palmdale."

"Is that part of L.A.?"

She shook her head. "It's in the desert, about an hour north."

"Thank you. You've been a big help. Probably best if you stay in here for a while. Can you do that for me?"

She nodded.

He smiled. "You have a nice day."

An hour later, Simon picked up Phillip outside a 7-Eleven, a mile from the house where he'd been held.

"You look like shit. What happened?"

"Drive," Phillip said, his gaze fixed straight ahead.

Simon didn't like the tone in Phillip's voice but, given that the man's face was a mass of cuts and bruises, he decided not to call him on it.

Twenty minutes passed in silence before Phillip finally said, "Did you close the deal with Petry?"

"Yes."

"He has the paintings?"

"He has the forgeries. Or Sticks might still have them. I'm not sure."

Phillip looked at him for the first time, the dried blood on his forehead crinkling as he furrowed his brow.

"I guess there's a few things I need to catch you up on."

When they reached L.A., Phillip had Simon drop him off in a quiet neighborhood in the Valley.

Before Phillip closed the door, Simon said, "I'll pick you up at six so we can be downtown for the meeting at Rudy's."

Phillip stared at him, his face blank. "No."

"No?"

"I have other things to deal with."

"But—"

"Goodbye, Simon." Phillip shut the door and walked off.

CHAPTER 48

When the board meeting broke for lunch, Stone and Dino took over Ben's office and initiated a conference call with Monica, Teddy, and Viv.

"So, where are we?" Stone asked.

"Simon's all lined up," Viv said, then played them a recording of Rudy's call with the art dealer.

"Billy, how are things on your end?"

"Petry's vehicle is still at the Four Seasons. I hacked into the hotel's CCTV system to see if he sneaked out, but he hasn't left his room since arriving last night. I've got eyes on the garage where the cube truck is. No sign of Sticks or his buddy yet. Simon, on the other hand, has been very busy. A couple hours ago he drove out to Palmdale. That's in the Mojave Desert, about an hour from downtown."

"What was he doing out there?"

"Whatever it was, it didn't take him long. He stopped at a strip mall parking lot for a minute, then turned around and headed back here."

"And where is he now?"

"Driving around the Valley. I think he's killing time."

"More like he's afraid Petry found out about the fakes and is staying on the move, so he won't be found," Dino said.

"Viv, anything from your people at the party?" Stone asked.

"No sign of trouble yet. I've added a team who will be stationed around the surrounding area."

After they covered a few more items, Stone said, "I think that's it. See everyone in a few hours." He hung up and called the studio's transportation department.

"This is Stone Barrington."

"Good afternoon, Mr. Barrington. The car and driver you requested should be outside the admin building now."

"That's what I wanted to know. Thank you." He disconnected the call.

Dino jumped to his feet. "I guess that's my cue."

"You could act a little heartbroken about missing the end of the board meeting."

Dino put a hand on his chest. "It's with a heavy heart that I must miss more mind-numbing hours of talking. Is that better?"

"Don't count on getting a part in any of Peter's movies."

"You just don't recognize true talent."

"Keep telling yourself that."

Dino gave him an exaggerated bow, then left for a trip to the LAPD headquarters downtown, where he had an appointment to meet with the top brass of L.A.'s police and fire departments.

———

Winston Petry was having a wonderful day. He'd slept in until ten, had room service brunch at eleven, and an in-room massage at noon.

After he finished the latter, he called Sticks.

"Afternoon, Mr. Petry."

"How are you today, Sticks?"

"I'm feeling pretty damn good. And yourself?"

"Same. I'm counting on you to make sure I stay that way."

"Guaranteed. Have you decided when you want me to start the show?"

"We'll play that by ear. I want to make sure the intended recipient of my message is paying attention."

"Works for me."

"Promise me you'll make sure the paintings are displayed in a way that he won't miss what they are."

"Don't sweat it. I got it covered."

"If this goes off without a hitch, I'll find more work for you."

"No if about it."

Petry smiled. It truly was a wonderful day.

Two and a half hours later, Teddy, as Billy Barnett, was on the phone with Stacy discussing party preparations when he spotted Sticks and Benji on the street, walking toward the parking garage.

"Sorry, Stacy. I need to run."

"When are you coming back? There are a few things I want you to check out before the guests arrive."

"Not sure yet, but I trust your judgment."

"Don't blame me if you don't like something."

"Have I ever blamed you for anything?"

"No, but there's always a first time."

"Bye-bye, Stacy."

When Sticks and Benji disappeared inside the garage, Teddy opened the tracker app. The dot representing the box began moving, and soon after the truck exited onto the street. He started his car and followed from several car lengths back.

At Laurel Canyon Boulevard, the truck turned and headed up the Valley side of the Hollywood Hills.

Teddy called Viv. "Looks like Sticks is on the way to my place."

"I'll alert the troops."

"Observe but do not engage."

"I'll remind them."

A few streets from Teddy's house, an incognito Strategic Services team in a Jeep Wrangler fell in behind Teddy. When the truck turned onto the street prior to Teddy's, he let the Jeep follow them and he continued toward home.

He did have a party to get ready for, after all.

CHAPTER 49

———◎———

Simon parked in front of Rudy's townhouse ten minutes before seven. The idea of holding off until the top of the hour didn't even cross his mind. He'd waited long enough.

Rudy's girlfriend answered again, and once more he had the sense he'd seen her somewhere other than at Rudy's.

"Oh, hey, you're back. He's in his studio."

Simon mumbled his thanks and headed downstairs.

Rudy was at the far end of the room, looking through several paintings piled against the wall. He didn't look up as Simon entered the room.

"I'm here for the paintings," Simon said.

Rudy looked over his shoulder, then motioned to a small group of paintings covered by a drop cloth, leaning against a wall. "Have at it."

Simon strode over. "I could use your help carrying them."

"I'm busy."

Simon glared at him, then huffed and shook his head. He retrieved the painting at the front of the stack—*Summer at Sheep Meadow*—turned toward the stairs, and immediately stopped in his tracks.

Standing between him and the way out were Stone Barrington, Rudy's girlfriend, and a man who looked familiar.

"Stone, what are you doing here?" He tried to sound casual but failed miserably.

"You first."

"Me? Well, you see . . . these . . . these are the paintings you're buying. My friend Rudy was kind enough to store them for me. You can take them with you now and save me the trip back to the gallery."

"Thank you, Simon. I'll do that. After which I'll be returning them to the people you stole them from. Well, except the one you're holding. That one *is* actually mine."

"Stole? Why, I would never. How—how could you even think such a thing?"

"Allow me to introduce you to my friend Monica Reyes." He smiled at the woman Simon had thought was Rudy's girlfriend. "You've probably heard her name before. She was a fraud investigator at Vitale Insurance, working for your late friend Dalton Conroy. You remember him. He's the one you had killed along with Tristan Williams."

The blood drained from Simon's face. "K-k-killed? That's pr-pr-preposterous!"

"Don't forget Joshua Paskota," Monica said.

"That's right," Stone said. "And Joshua Paskota in Santa Fe."

"Joshua died in an accident."

"That was the preliminary determination. But at the urging

of my good friend Dino Bacchetti, commissioner of police for New York City"—Stone indicated the man next to Monica—"the Santa Fe Police Department has taken a closer look. Dino, you want to tell Simon about the conversation you had with Detective Eldridge on our way over here?"

"Happy to," Dino said.

Simon realized where he recognized the man from. He had never met him before, but he *had* seen him multiple times on the news.

"Turns out it wasn't an accident at all, but sabotage. When the detectives realized that, they went back and looked at CCTV video and found video of a man tampering with Joshua's car just prior to the accident. They even uncovered his name. Hold on a second . . ." Dino consulted a notepad. "Phillip. Phillip Pierce. That's the same Phillip Pierce who works for you."

"You're also tied to the death of Randall Vernon," Stone said.

"Who?" Simon asked. He didn't know anyone by that name.

"He was the owner of the home your people hit the other night. He died in the fire. That's four homicides on top of the thefts."

"I don't know where you're getting your information, but I didn't have anything to do with any of it!"

"Just like you have nothing to do with the stolen painting in your hands?"

"Or the ones leaning against the wall behind you," Dino said.

"Or the one supposedly destroyed in a house fire on Martha's Vineyard, or the one from a sunken boat in Lake Michigan," Monica said. "If you'd like, I could go on."

"How . . . ?" Simon hadn't meant to say that, but he couldn't stop himself.

"You're not quite as clever as you thought you were."

"Rudy," Stone said, "if you don't mind, please take my painting from Simon."

Simon barely registered Rudy relieving him of his burden.

This couldn't be happening. A few more hours and he'd have been on a jet heading south. He was so close. There must be a way out of this. Maybe if he made a run for it, he could get by them.

"I wouldn't do that if I were you," Stone said, as if reading Simon's mind. "Besides, we have some friends who are very interested in talking to you."

Dino called up the stairs, "Come on down."

Several police officers, some in uniforms and some in suits, descended the stairs.

Simon stared at them, mouth slack, as any hope that he could escape went up in smoke.

One of the uniformed officers cuffed Simon's hands behind his back, while a detective read him his rights.

"I didn't do anything. It was . . . it was my brother and his friends. They stole everything! They're the thieves!"

"We look forward to hearing everything you have to say, Mr. Duchamp," a detective said.

Four of the officers escorted him up the stairs.

"One down," Dino said.

"Two, if you count our helpful forger," Monica said.

Across the room, Rudy was in the process of being put into his own pair of handcuffs and receiving his recitation of rights.

"I think we should classify him as a bonus," Stone said.

"I'm fine with that."

The information Monica had wrung from Rudy on the forgeries he'd created for many more customers beyond just Simon was going to rock the art world.

Stone glanced at his watch. "Look at the time. I think we have a party to attend."

"Will there be more prizes?" Monica teased.

"Now who's trying to jinx us?"

CHAPTER 50

———◎———

Billy Barnett smiled warmly as the first of his guests arrived. "Charlie! So glad you could make it. And, Janice, nice to see you again."

"We wouldn't miss it for the world," Charlie said. He'd been a film producer for more than forty years, and his wife, Janice, was an award-winning production designer.

Behind them came a group of veteran actors, each of whom Billy greeted by name. It wasn't long before the trickle of guests became a steady stream.

As Billy was saying hello to Logan Chase, an actor in Peter's last film, one of the agents from Strategic Services signaled that he wanted a word.

"Grab yourself a drink," Billy told Logan. "I'll catch up to you later."

Billy made his way over to the agent.

"Our two friends are on the east slope and watching the party through binoculars."

"No sign of anyone else?"

"Not yet."

"Thank you." Billy returned his attention to a group of new arrivals. "Gretchen, you look stunning as always."

At the same time guests started arriving at Billy's party, Petry and Nico were finishing up dinner at Crustacean in Beverly Hills.

Petry dabbed his mouth with his napkin. "Call him."

Nico punched Sticks's number.

"Yeah?" Sticks answered.

"Mr. Petry would like to know if everything is ready."

"All set."

"And Barrington?"

"Not here yet."

"All right. As soon as you see him, let us know."

Nico hung up and relayed the information to his boss.

"I suppose we have time for dessert then," Petry said and signaled the waiter.

Stone, Monica, and Dino swung by the Arrington to change and pick up Viv. By the time they arrived at Billy's, it was nearly nine.

Billy shook hands with the men and kissed the cheeks of the women.

"This place is breathtaking," Monica said, taking in the exterior of Billy's house.

"I quite like it."

She looked toward the open-air tents where the party was in full swing. "Wait, is that . . . ?"

Billy glanced over his shoulder. "Victoria Salazar? It is."

"I have all of her music!"

"I'll make sure to introduce you to her."

"I'm not sure I'm ready for that."

"You've already helped take down a notorious art thief to-night," Stone said. "Anything else you do will be child's play."

"If you say so."

"I take it everything went well with Simon," Billy said.

Stone nodded. "Like clockwork. What's the situation here?"

"Sticks and his buddy are on the slope to my left, probably looking at us right now. Their truck is parked on a nearby street."

"And Petry?"

"Last I heard, he was dining at Crustacean. Viv has a team watching him, so we'll know when he moves. Which, given that you're here now, will probably be any minute. In the meantime, grab a drink and introduce Monica to a few movie stars."

"Yes, please," Monica said.

Nico snatched up his phone and read the text that had just ar-rived.

"Barrington's at the party."

"Pay the bill."

After Nico took care of the check, they retrieved their sedan from the valet and headed toward the hills, neither man noticing the black Acura SUV that pulled onto the road several car lengths behind them.

And neither those in the sedan nor the men in the SUV no-ticed the motorcycle that joined the back end of the chase.

CHAPTER 51

That afternoon, Phillip broke into a house not far from where Simon had dropped him off. He washed away the dirt and blood, patched himself up, and donned some clothes he found that fit him well enough. The one thing the place didn't have was a vehicle he could steal.

He checked several more homes in the area and finally found something that was even better than a car. The Yamaha Supersport motorcycle allowed him to zip through traffic and reach the Four Seasons Hotel in plenty of time to see Petry and his son-of-a-bitch lawyer leave for dinner.

Phillip's plan was simple: make the two men pay for ordering his death.

He was surprised, but not particularly shocked, that when the two men left Crustacean, an SUV began following them. Obviously, Phillip wasn't the only one interested in the pair.

The unofficial motorcade made its way into West Hollywood

and then into the hills. When they reached the crest, they turned onto Mulholland Drive and traveled west for several minutes before veering onto a side street.

At an intersection a quarter mile on, Petry and Nico turned right, while the SUV unexpectedly turned left.

Phillip checked his mirrors, in case another car had taken up the chase, but the road behind him was empty. He glanced at the sky, wondering if there might be a drone keeping an eye on Petry. If there was, he didn't see it.

The SUV was intriguing, but Petry was his prey, so Phillip went right.

Less than fifty yards in, the road curved and Petry's sedan moved out of sight. Immediately, brake lights spilled onto the road.

Phillip pulled onto the shoulder and cut his engine. He could hear the sedan idling just around the curve along with what sounded like voices.

He propped the motorcycle on its stand and sneaked through the brush until he could see Petry's vehicle. Someone was leaning against the driver's window on the other side.

When the man stood, Phillip huffed in amusement.

It was Sticks.

Simon had told him of the arsonist's defection and that he was doing something "unsavory" for Petry with the paintings. Given Sticks's presence, Phillip figured whatever that was must be about to go down.

Sticks pointed ahead and said loudly enough for Phillip to hear, "You'll be fine there."

After the sedan parked, Petry and Nico joined Sticks and headed into the woods on the other side of the road.

Phillip moved the Yamaha to a less visible spot, then followed the trio on foot.

"Where?" Petry asked.

Sticks handed him the binoculars. "Standing by the table on the far right. You can't miss him."

Petry swept the binoculars across the crowd until he found Barrington. He was talking to the movie star Tessa Tweed.

Petry started to sneer, then froze. Standing so close to the lawyer that they appeared to be at the party together was the woman he'd met at the bar Thursday night.

He couldn't remember her name. Something starting with an *M*, he thought. If she had such bad taste that she'd go out with Barrington, then there was no way Petry would waste his time on her.

"Are we doing this or not?" Sticks asked.

Petry lowered the binoculars. "We're doing it. Right now."

"Have any of you read Peter's latest script?" Tessa Tweed asked.

"Finished it during the board meeting," Dino said.

"You were supposed to be listening during the board meeting," Stone said.

"I *was* listening."

"And reading?"

"And reading."

"Did you absorb either?"

"The script is great."

"And the meeting?"

"Like I said, the script is great."

"How about you, Stone?" Tessa asked.

"Unlike your father-in-law, I paid attention during the meeting. The script is waiting for me on my nightstand."

Monica raised an eyebrow. "I can think of several better things we can use the bed for other than reading."

"Did I say nightstand? I meant my desk."

"That's better."

Tessa grinned. "I see she already has your number."

"Why, Tessa, whatever do you mean?"

Before she could reply, Billy walked up with Ben.

"I hope you all don't mind if I borrowed my wife for a few moments," Ben said. "There's someone I'd like her to meet."

"Not at all," Stone said.

As soon as Ben and Tessa walked off, Billy said, "Petry and Savage arrived several minutes ago."

"Are they with Sticks?"

Billy nodded.

"Then whatever they have planned is—"

Billy held up a hand and listened to something coming through his radio earpiece. He activated his mic and said, "License number?" He listened again. "Tell them you're clearing a place for them to park and hold them there until I give you the word." He looked at Stone and the others. "There's a truck at the entrance, says they have a gift from another studio, congratulating Centurion on all its success."

"It wouldn't be a cube truck, would it?" Monica said.

"It is, and it's the right license number, too."

"Dino," Stone said.

Dino pulled out his phone to call the police stationed nearby and told them to move in. Before he could punch the number, an engine roared at the front of Billy's property followed by shouts at the gate.

"He's not waiting," Stone said. "Viv, have your people move everyone to the terrace." It was the farthest place from the parking area.

Strategic Services personnel began herding the guests to safety, while Stone and his friends remained behind.

The truck came into view as it careened off the side of a Mercedes. It banged over a curb and raced into the area near the tents. Grass and dirt flew into the air as the driver jammed to a stop.

Triggered by controls in the cab, the back door of the storage cube rolled up, and its front end began rising via hydraulics, like a dump truck.

Pieces of wood began clattering onto the ground, bringing with them the strong odor of lighter fluid. The box Rudy had built fell out next, cracking loudly as it hit the ground. And then the three forgeries slid out of the truck and landed on top of the wood.

"That's it," Benji said over the radio from inside the truck. "I'm out of here."

Down at the party, Petry could see Benji jump out of the cab and run toward the wooded end of the property. He focused back on Barrington. The lawyer was looking at the pile upon which his mother's paintings lay.

"That's right. Nothing you can do now."

"Shit," Sticks said.

Petry lowered the binoculars and looked over. Several police cars were rushing onto Billy Barnett's property, their lights flashing, and right behind them came two fire trucks.

Petry glared at Nico. "How the hell did they get here so fast?"

"I—I—I have no idea."

Sticks pressed a remote, setting off a trio of ignition devices he'd hidden among the wood scraps in the truck, then jumped to his feet.

"It's done."

Without another word, he ran back toward the road.

"We should go," Nico urged.

"No, not until we're sure they catch fire," Petry said.

"If they don't, there's nothing we can do about it, so what does it matter?"

"It matters because I said so."

Petry watched the fire through the binoculars. The flames had started to spread, and the corner of one of the pictures had begun to burn. He smiled and then switched his focus to Barrington.

The lawyer was not looking at the fire anymore. He was staring straight in Petry's direction, as if he knew he was there, and he was smiling.

That wasn't right. He should be screaming, panicked, and trying to rescue his mother's work, but the blaze didn't seem to faze him at all.

Three people ran up to Barrington, each holding something in their hands. At a word from Barrington, they turned so Petry could see what they were carrying. Each held one of the paintings that Petry had bought, the same paintings he could see burning on the fire.

That's when the realization hit him. Duchamp, who had been horrified at Petry's plan, must have teamed up with Barrington to make Petry the fool.

That arty son of a bitch was going to pay for this. "Let's go."

They got up and turned for the path back to their sedan but didn't even make it a step. Standing in their way was the giant frame of a man who was supposed to be dead.

Phillip raised the pistol in his hand. "Going somewhere, gentlemen?"

"Nico," Petry said. "What's he doing here?"

"Uh . . ."

The corner of Phillip's mouth ticked up. "Your fixer isn't so great at fixing things, I guess."

"Hey," Nico said. "There's no need for this to get ugly. I told you, it wasn't personal."

"It felt personal to me."

"Look, we can work something out. Mr. Petry is a very rich man. What will it take so that we can all walk away from here?"

"You think buying me off is going to save you?"

"Everyone has a price. Name yours and I'll make it happen."

Petry watched Phillip's eyes, waiting for them to focus solely on Nico.

The instant they did, Petry shoved his lawyer in the back, sending him sprawling toward Phillip, then he sprinted into the cover of the brush.

Phillip's gun went off. Petry kept running, expecting a bullet to tear into him, but it didn't.

Another shot hit the trunk of a tree as he passed it. He zagged right and moved deeper into the brush, then headed in the direction he thought would take him back to his car.

CHAPTER 52

Stone ducked as a gunshot echoed past Billy's house. He glanced at his friends. No one appeared to have been hit.

Another shot went off.

"It's coming from where Sticks and Petry are set up," Billy said. He listened to something on his radio. "One of Viv's teams is moving in."

"They weren't the ones doing the shooting?" Stone asked.

"No."

Stone glanced at Dino. "LAPD?"

Dino shook his head. "They were hanging back to catch Petry and the others when they returned to the road."

"Then who took the shot and who were they shooting at?" Monica asked.

A Strategic Services security guard hurried over. "The guests are being moved into the house. You all should join them. It's not safe out here."

The radio on his belt squawked to life. "This is team five. We've got a body. Male, approximately forty-five. No pulse." After a short pause, the security officer said, "He has a New York driver's license, says his name is Nicolas Savage."

Viv gestured for her security officer to give her his radio, and he handed it over. "Team five, this is Vivian Bacchetti. No sign of anyone else?"

"No, ma'am. Just the one."

"There are at least two more out there. Proceed with extreme caution."

"Copy."

The fire engine had reached the small blaze, and firefighters were preparing to douse the flames.

"Billy, I need your car," Stone said.

"Where are you going?" Billy asked.

"To find them."

"I'm coming with you," Dino said.

Billy handed Stone the keys to the Audi. "I need to make sure everything here is okay, then I'll catch up to you."

"Here," Viv said, tossing Stone the radio.

Catching it in his right hand, he and Dino ran to Billy's garage.

"Dammit," Sticks muttered.

He had stopped just inside the brush to scan the road. From his angle, he could see several silhouettes crouched behind Petry's car.

More cops, he figured.

That morning, he and Benji had stolen a black BMW 340i and

hidden it by a house that was being remodeled. Keeping under cover, he headed in that direction. He paused again when he reached the driveway, then relaxed upon seeing no sign of the cops.

He jogged to the vehicle and climbed into the driver's seat. As he reached out to start the engine, someone banged against the driver's-side window.

He flinched and glanced over, sure that it was the police.

But it was Petry.

The man yanked on the handle and the door flew open. "Out!"

"What?"

"Get out!"

"The hell I—"

Petry grabbed him by the shirt and tugged him out of the car, then he took the seat. Before Sticks could get back to his feet, the door closed, and the lock engaged.

"Hey!"

The engine started.

"Sorry," Petry said, not sounding sorry at all.

He put the car in gear and sped away.

Stone raced the Audi up the driveway and skidded onto the street.

"Viv said they were set up off the next road," Dino said.

Just as they reached the intersection, a black BMW squealed around the corner onto their road.

It whizzed past, but Stone caught a quick look at the driver. "That's Petry!"

He spun the Audi in a one-eighty and hit the gas.

"You're sure?" Dino asked.

"Positive."

Dino contacted Viv on the radio and reported what was happening.

"I'll let the police know," she said. "Teddy's heading out in his Porsche, so he shouldn't be too far behind you."

"Copy," Dino said.

Stone glanced in the rearview mirror and saw the single light of a motorcycle gaining on them. "We've got company."

"That's not a police bike," Dino said.

The motorcycle came up fast and went around them on the driver's side. The rider wasn't wearing a helmet and didn't even glance at them.

"Isn't that the guy who chased Tristan from the Roosevelt?" Dino said. "The one who works for Simon?"

Stone nodded, having also made the connection. "Phillip Pierce."

"Maybe he's working for Petry, too."

Phillip pulled a gun out from under his jacket and aimed it at the BMW.

"If he is," Stone said, "I don't think he's satisfied with the terms of his employment."

The gun flashed and the BMW swerved slightly but didn't slow.

"Are you armed?" Dino asked.

"Uhh . . ."

"You forgot, didn't you?" Dino said.

"It was a busy day."

"Did we or did we not discuss you carrying tonight?"

"I seem to recall something about that, but I'm not clear on the details."

The radio came to life with Teddy's voice. "I saw a muzzle flash. Are you guys okay?"

"He wasn't shooting at us," Dino replied. "Where are you?"

"Thirty yards behind you."

Stone glanced at the mirror and saw the Porsche's headlights.

"Are you guys armed?"

"Funny, we were just discussing that," Dino said. "I am, but . . ."

"Stone forgot."

"That he did."

"Open the glove compartment," Teddy said. "There's a button just inside, on the left."

Dino found the button and pushed. The top of the compartment lowered. Clipped to it were a SIG Sauer P226 pistol, silencer, and one spare magazine.

He clicked the mic button. "Found it. Very nice. Now he's armed."

A few moments later, the black BMW took a sharp turn onto Mulholland Drive. Phillip shoved his gun back into his jacket before speeding through the turn, almost T-boned by a sedan going in the other direction.

As the Audi reached the intersection, Stone slowed enough to take a quick look at traffic before slamming down on the accelerator and slipping through a slot between cars to rejoin the chase.

Dino contacted Viv again and updated her, as the chase wove around the other vehicles, drawing honks and flashing headlights.

Phillip tried to pull alongside the BMW several times, but each time Petry whipped the wheel toward him, forcing the motorcycle to fall back.

At Laurel Canyon Boulevard, Petry turned south toward West Hollywood, and the motorcycle and the Audi followed. As traffic got worse, Petry veered into the oncoming lanes, forcing vehicles heading up the hill to swerve out of his way.

"Hold on," Stone said, then did the same.

A Tesla missed them by mere inches, but Stone was able to return to the right lane unscathed.

"If you could try not to kill me tonight, I'd appreciate it," Dino said.

"I'll keep that in mind."

When they reached the bottom of the hill, a spotlight lit up the BMW from above. Stone looked at the sky and spotted three helicopters, one the LAPD chopper with the light, and two from local news outlets.

"Smile," Dino said. "I think we're on TV."

Petry flew through the intersection at Santa Monica Boulevard, causing several vehicles to plow into each other in his wake.

He had no idea where he was going. At first, he'd just been trying to get away from the psycho on the motorcycle. But now he had this damn light on him, which meant the cops wouldn't be far behind.

What he needed was an enclosed parking garage where he could ditch the BMW and make a run for it.

When he saw the sign for Melrose Avenue, he felt a dash of hope. Simon's gallery was on that street, and he remembered seeing a big shopping mall with a huge parking garage not too far from it.

He took the turn and immediately regretted it. There was

even more traffic here, and the only way he could keep moving was to weave back and forth across the center line.

Movement in the corner of his eye caused him to jerk his head to the left. The motorcycle was just outside his window, the gun in Phillip's hand pointed at Petry's head. Petry slammed the accelerator to the floor.

The crack of the gun caused him to jerk on the wheel, and his car slammed into the side of a city bus. As he pulled away, he heard a dull *pop*, followed by the *flap-flap-flap* of a shredded tire.

"No, no, no!"

He tried speeding up, but the ruined front tire pulled the car to the right.

He looked ahead for somewhere he could ditch and run. But there was nowhere, not even a—

A sign on a building ahead caught his attention.

DUCHAMP GALLERY L.A.

He wasn't going to make it to the parking garage, but at least he could exact some revenge.

The wheel sparked off the asphalt as he kept the BMW moving. When he came abreast of the gallery, he whipped the car toward it. The few people inside ran out of the way just before Petry crashed through the glass wall across the entrance.

The airbag punched him in the face, so he didn't see the window display fly into a wall or the two easels that somersaulted over the car. But he did feel the impact of the BMW crashing into the back wall and coming to a sudden halt.

He sat there, stunned, as the airbag deflated. For a moment, everything was silent. Then he heard the rumble of a motor.

Petry's eyes went wide at the sight of Phillip pulling up next to him.

He scrambled over the center console to get out on the passenger side, but the door had been damaged and wouldn't move.

He tried to spin around to punch the glass out with his feet, but there wasn't enough room.

Phillip hammered the driver's-side window with the butt of his gun until it fractured. He pushed the glass out of the way and smiled.

"Hello, Mr. Petry."

CHAPTER 53

————◎————

S tone and Dino jumped out of the Audi, ran to the gap in the shattered entrance, then peered inside.

The BMW had smashed against the back wall, collapsing a portion of the divider into the employees-only area beyond. The driver's door hung open, and a few feet from it stood the motorcycle. Neither Petry nor Phillip were present, but Stone could hear muffled voices coming from deeper in the building.

Teddy pulled up in his Porsche and hurried to join them.

"Dino, go around to the parking area in the back," Stone said. "Teddy and I will try to flush them out."

"Try not to get shot," Dino said.

"Top of my to-do list," Stone said.

Stone and Teddy crept carefully into the gallery.

The wall that concealed the entrance to the back room was

teetering but still intact. Stone gestured that he would go in that direction and for Teddy to approach the hole in the wall.

Keeping low, Stone moved to the wall, then checked around the edge. The short passageway was empty. He stepped quickly into it.

"Five million right now if you let me walk away," Petry pleaded. "I can do the transfer right here."

Phillip snorted.

"How—How about ten million?" Petry said. "You can walk away and never have another worry in your life."

Stone chanced a peek into the staff-only area. Petry was cornered against one of the couches with Phillip looming over him, his gun ready at his side.

"Ten?" Phillip said. "Why not twenty?"

"Twenty? Sure, sure. Just let me use my phone and I'll make the transfer."

"What about thirty?"

"Um . . . okay. I—I should be able to do that. You have to understand, some of my money is tied up in—"

Phillip pointed his pistol at Petry's head. Petry yelped and cowered behind his arms.

"How much is your life worth? What about every penny you have?"

"Please don't. I'm sorry for what happened to you. It was Nico's idea. I didn't know until it had already happened."

"I'm not that stupid."

Stone was sure Phillip's patience had just about run out, so he aimed the SIG at him. "Drop the gun, Phillip."

Phillip whipped around, his pistol following his gaze.

"Barrington?" Petry said, confused.

"I said, put the gun down."

"Huh," Phillip said. "So, you're the guy all the fuss has been about."

"I'm the guy. And I'm telling you there's no need for anyone else to die."

"I would think you'd be happy. I am about to do you a favor."

"I'd be happier to see him spend the rest of his life in prison."

Phillip nodded. "I can see how that might be attractive, but it ain't going to happen. *You* put *your* gun down. I don't have any reason to kill you, but if you insist on getting in the way, I will."

From the rift in the wall, Teddy said, "That would be a mistake."

Phillip twisted toward him, surprised. "Who the—"

Before he could say anything else, Petry launched onto Phillip's back. Phillip's finger twitched and the gun went off, kicking up a spray of concrete near Teddy.

Phillip threw an elbow into Petry's face, then grabbed the man's hair, yanked him off, and shoved him to the floor.

Stone squeezed off a shot a second before Phillip pulled his own trigger. Stone's bullet hit Phillip in the chest, spinning him as he fired. Phillip's shot ricocheted off the concrete floor and smacked into the wall near Stone's head.

For a heartbeat, Phillip remained on his feet, then he dropped to the floor with a loud *thud*.

Petry scrambled to his feet and ran to the rear door. But when he pulled it open, he froze.

Dino was standing on the other side. "Leaving so soon, Mr. Petry?"

"And not even with a thank-you for saving his life," Stone

said as he stepped into the room. "Dino, could you please escort our guest back to the couch?"

"With pleasure."

Stone moved over to Phillip and saw that there was no need to check for a pulse. The man was staring dead-eyed at the ceiling, his chest still.

"Where's Teddy?" Dino asked.

Stone looked over to the rip in the wall where Teddy had been, but he wasn't there. "Teddy?"

He hurried to the hole and saw Teddy lying unconscious on the floor surrounded by debris from the crash.

Stone stepped through and kneeled next to him. He had thought Phillip's first shot had hit the wall, not Teddy. Stone didn't see any blood or obvious wounds, however.

He gently shook him. "Teddy?"

Teddy blinked and opened his eyes. "What happened?"

"That's what I was going to ask you."

"Phillip?"

"Dead."

"How many times did you have to shoot him?"

"Once."

"See, I told you that you were getting better. And Petry?"

"Cooling it on the couch with Dino. Now it's your turn."

"The last thing I remember is Phillip's gun going off and the bullet flying past me."

"That's it?"

Teddy shrugged, then winced.

"You're hurt?"

"Back of my head."

Stone helped him into a sitting position, then checked Teddy's head, finding a bump. He looked at the floor near where Teddy had been standing and smirked. "Looks like you slipped."

He pointed at the mark on the floor that Teddy's shoe had made.

"Is that a move the CIA trained you to do, or . . . ?"

Teddy scowled. "If you think about telling anyone, remember that I know forty-seven ways to make your death look natural."

"Noted."

CHAPTER 54

Tuesday morning, Stone opened the door to his house at the Arrington and said, "This way, gentlemen."

Three Arrington bellhops entered, carrying paintings wrapped for transport. Stone led them into the living room and had them place the packages against a wall, side by side. He then thanked them, gave each a tip, and sent them on their way.

He opened each package and checked the contents. After the events of Saturday night, his mother's work had been taken by the LAPD as evidence. Due to their value, it had been decided that each could be returned to its owner. Who, in all cases, was now Stone.

He had purchased one from the estate of the man who had died in Marin County and the other from the previous owner near San Diego. The third was the gift from Teddy.

Upon seeing that each was undamaged, he went out back,

where Monica, Dino, and Viv were sitting by the pool, enjoying mimosas.

"Any problems?" Monica asked.

"Not a one."

He sat on his lounge chair.

"While you were out, I had a call from my counterpart in the LAPD," Dino said. "We are officially free to travel at will."

They'd spent much of the last two days being interviewed by detectives working on the cases against Petry, Simon, Sticks, and Benji. Benji had been captured by Strategic Services personnel before he could escape Billy's property, and Sticks had been maced by one of Billy's neighbors while trying to steal the man's car, then subsequently turned over to the police. Rudy was also in custody, though word was he was being very cooperative.

"I'll call Faith and we can leave this afternoon," Stone said.

"Are you that anxious to get home?" Monica asked.

"Aren't you?"

"Good point."

Monica had several job interviews awaiting her return, including one for Dalton's former job at Vitale Insurance, and another for a similar position at Steele Insurance.

"What time should we be ready?" Viv asked.

"Noon should be fine," Stone said.

Viv stood. "Come on, Dino."

"Where to?"

"Our room."

He checked his watch. "We still have plenty of time to pack."

She raised an eyebrow. "Exactly."

"Oh." He jumped up. "Lead on, my dear."

As they walked off, Stone and Monica shared a look.

"I like your friends," Monica said. "They have excellent ideas."

"They do indeed."

"Shall we?"

"We shall."

They headed into the house.